A fake engagement?

Nelson had really tried to arrange a fake engagement?

That could have worked. The big thing for now was to show a romantic proposal, one that would entice people from out of town to come here.

Mind buzzing again, Mariah asked, "Rachel said no?"

"She had good reasons. I hadn't thought it through."

It was a little smidgen of hope. A possibility. If there was someone else who would agree to a fake proposal with Nelson...

Someone desperate. Someone motivated.

Mariah knew of only one person right now that desperate and motivated. But could she make it work?

"I'll do it."

Nelson's brow creased. "You'll do what?"

"I'll accept your fake proposal. We can get engaged for Valentine's Day."

Dear Reader,

This new series, Cupid's Crossing, was inspired by my Heartwarming editor's wish list. My brain connected a small town and holidays and added in the humor that I find makes everything go better.

Carter's Crossing is a small place a few hours' drive from large cities like New York and Boston. Abigail Carter, matriarch of the Carter family, has the idea of converting the former mill town into a destination for romantic events: proposals, weddings, weekend getaways. This three-book series follows the transformation of the town from Carter's Crossing to Cupid's Crossing.

Abigail reaches out to a former college beau, who sends his granddaughter, Mariah, a wedding planner, to spend a year launching the plan. Mariah decides that staging some events for Valentine's Day would be a great way to kick off the town's new business.

Most of the town is on board, except for Abigail's grandson Nelson, the local vet. Fortunately, Cupid has some tricks up his sleeves, including a Great Dane, some rescue horses, as well as a can't-live-with-them, can't-live-without-them group of friends.

Cupid has his own plans for his namesake town.

Happy reading!

Kim

HEARTWARMING

A Valentine's Proposal

Kim Findlay

HARLEQUIN®
HEARTWARMING™

PLEASE RECYCLE
THIS PRODUCT IS RECYCLABLE
Recycling programs for this product may not exist in your area.

ISBN-13: 978-1-335-17976-0

A Valentine's Proposal

This edition published by arrangement with Harlequin Books S.A.

For questions and comments about the quality of this book, please contact us at CustomerService@Harlequin.com.

Harlequin Enterprises ULC
22 Adelaide St. West, 40th Floor
Toronto, Ontario M5H 4E3, Canada
www.Harlequin.com

Printed in U.S.A.

Kim Findlay is a Canadian who fled the cold to live on a sailboat in the Caribbean and write romance novels. She shares the boat with her husband and the world's cutest spaniel. Bucket list accomplished! Her first Harlequin Heartwarming, *Crossing the Goal Line*, came about from the Heartwarming Blitz, and she's never looked back. Keep up with Kim, including sailing adventures, at kimfindlay.ca.

Books by Kim Findlay

Harlequin Heartwarming

A Hockey Romance

Crossing the Goal Line
Her Family's Defender

Visit the Author Profile page
at Harlequin.com for more titles.

To LeAnne, Amanda, Adrienne and Johanna,
who helped to bring this series to life.

CHAPTER ONE

THE IDEAS WERE pinging nonstop. Fizzing with excitement, Mariah pulled into an empty parking lot, grabbing the tablet beside her and opening up the map app. With the limited parking here in Carter's Crossing, they'd need to set something up with trains, or planes, to get larger parties here, or people without cars from cities like New York or Boston. Where was the closest train station? Airport? How would they convey people from there? Limo? Convertible in the summer? No, that would only be for the big budget events. Maybe a shuttle bus? They'd have to arrange for a van for luggage…

Absorbed in her thoughts, her surroundings faded until a voice near the open car window broke through her concentration.

It had an impatient edge, as if this wasn't the first attempt to reach her.

"Can I help you?"

Mariah's head snapped up, and she shrieked.

The big head, the teeth, the tongue…it took her a moment to place the unexpected image.

A Great Dane, drooling into her car. She backed farther into her seat before the big nose snuffled her ear.

"He's friendly." It was the same voice, and Mariah finally caught sight of the man attached to the dog.

He was at the other end of a leash. Tall, dark hair, wearing blue scrubs for some reason. He was also good-looking, but the smirk on his face canceled out most of the benefit of a strong chin and high cheekbones. The smirk annoyed her. She wasn't afraid of dogs; she'd just been startled.

"I'm sure he is. I'd still rather not wear his saliva."

Okay, maybe her voice was a little…curt, but this was an expensive suit and she already had some drool on her sleeve. Her pulse was racing from the shock.

The dog's head retreated as the man pulled on the leash.

"Back off, Tiny." He pushed the dog behind him and leaned toward her. "We didn't mean to startle you. Just wanted to help you find your way."

Mariah's fists clenched on the map. This man didn't know her. He didn't know her hot buttons, or the number of times she'd been offered unsolicited directions. He probably didn't even realize the assumptions behind that offer. She had literally navigated around the globe, and she could certainly make her way around a town so small it had only one stoplight.

She'd been questioned on that ability a few times too many.

"I'm not lost." She set down the tablet. She wasn't lost. Planning was her forte. She knew exactly where she was and where she was going, and all she'd wanted was a few moments to work out the brainstorm she'd been hit with. This could be her best idea yet, and she wanted the chance to start working it out.

"Just taking the scenic route?" he asked, still smirking.

Oh, to be born with the confidence of those with a Y chromosome. He undoubtedly expected her to admit the map was just too much for her little ole brain and would gladly tell her where to go in that same smug tone… or maybe she was projecting, just a bit. Probably better not to leap to conclusions.

Still, it wouldn't hurt for him to learn to take a hint. If she needed help, she was perfectly capable of asking for it.

So she smiled through gritted teeth and

repeated, "I'm not lost, but I wouldn't mind if you were."

She held the smile as the penny dropped and he lost his smirk.

He backed off, hands in the air, Drooly backing up with him. To his credit, he didn't call her a name, defend his niceness or tell her she was cute when she was sassy.

Maybe she'd gone too far.

"I'm gone. Good luck finding where you're going."

She could do without the sarcasm, too. Yeah, she didn't need to feel sorry for him, or his healthy ego.

He turned to the building at the back of the small parking lot where she'd pulled in. The falling penny this time was for her. He was in scrubs, with a dog, and the sign on the building read Carter's Crossing Animal Hospital.

Okay, first meeting with a local didn't go well. For a moment she considered apologizing.

She checked the time. No, she needed to get going. She didn't have time for him to explain how he hadn't meant anything by it.

Shoving the incident, and the tablet, behind her, she put the car in gear and turned left.

This was an incredible opportunity. She was going to blow the socks off everyone, and then she'd have achieved her dream, all on her own. She was at the helm, and she was kicking butt and taking names.

Fortunately, none of her plans required the assistance of the local vet.

NELSON CARTER WATCHED the car pull out of his parking lot. His empty parking lot.

It was a Sunday afternoon, and the clinic wasn't open. There were no other cars in the lot; just his clinic van. He was here because he'd been called in to help Tiny, the Great Dane.

Great Danes were known to suffer from gastric torsion, as Tiny's owner had read on the internet. Every time Tiny ate something he shouldn't, which he did frequently, Nelson got a call in case Tiny was about to bloat and torque his digestive tract. To date, Tiny's digestive tract was cast iron, but Nelson always responded.

Tiny's owner, Mavis Grisham, was a good friend of his grandmother's, and devoted to her pet, who probably outweighed her by a good thirty pounds. Tiny was a happy, good-natured goof. After checking the dog out thoroughly, he'd taken Tiny for a walk, making sure the guy would survive his first taste of habanero sauce. Nelson was more worried about what would happen when that worked its way through Tiny than he was with what was going to happen while it was still inside the big dog, but he was due for dinner at his grandmother's. Mavis would have to handle that.

He also wondered why Mavis was using habanero sauce but was probably better off not knowing.

Nelson had been about to return Tiny to Mavis when he'd noticed the out-of-state car in the clinic parking lot.

Carter's Crossing was a small town. It wasn't on the way to anywhere else of any consequence, so few people other than locals were likely to drive through. Nelson knew all the locals. He'd grown up in Carter's Crossing. Now that he was back, his practice covered more than just the town. Almost everyone here had an animal, either for business or pleasure. He'd quickly caught up on any new arrivals since he'd left.

In Carter's Crossing there weren't any strangers.

He'd guessed the driver of the out-of-state car was lost, and the map open on her tablet confirmed that she'd gotten confused on the back roads.

His first impression had been good. She

was pretty, with dark, shiny hair, a straight nose; her brow crinkled as she stared at the map like it was her best friend. He'd offered to help, thinking it would be a pleasant interlude to wrap up his day.

She hadn't been nice. Sure, Tiny's face could be startling up close, so the yelp she'd made had been perfectly understandable, but that was no excuse to tell him to get lost. He'd only been trying to help.

He'd learned the hard way not to push ideas or advice on anyone else, so he let her go. She'd find her way, or she'd ask someone else for assistance. As far as he was concerned, she could drive around in circles if she wanted.

In fact, that would be a kind of poetic justice.

He tugged Tiny toward the clinic van. He'd drop the drool monster off to his anxious owner, and then get himself cleaned up for dinner. His grandmother had requested his company because she had something she wished to discuss with him.

His mood improved as he thought of Abigail Carter. She took her position as head of the Carter family, the family for whom the town was named, seriously. It had been a blow to her and to the town when she'd had to close the mill. Since then, she'd been trying to find a way to inject life and money into the local economy.

Nelson had no idea how she'd accomplish that, but if anyone could, it would be his grandmother. He'd carefully avoided any involvement himself. He wasn't going to be that guy anymore, the one who made plans and moved heaven and earth to get them done.

He was happy as things were, handling the care of the animal population of Carter's Crossing and surrounds. He had his horses to fill up his spare time and energy. He had his grandmother for dinners and nagging, and friends to keep him company. He was good.

He wasn't going to hurt anyone again trying to get what he wanted. Even if all he wanted was to give someone directions to wherever they were going.

MARIAH'S JAW DROPPED. The house was beautiful.

Abigail Carter had given her careful directions to find it, and honestly, the town was small. For someone who'd grown up traveling the world on a sailboat, finding the largest house in Carter's Crossing wasn't a challenge. She'd driven all through the town, examining it for potential. The town had charm and beauty in abundance, and she and Abigail could build on that.

She drove through the gates and up the drive before pulling to a stop in front of the immaculately maintained Victorian; its sloping yard carefully manicured. There was a huge wraparound porch decorated with harvest touches. This place was ready for promotional photos as it was, without any additional work. She pictured it with snow and Christmas decorations. It would be gorgeous.

She was creating the publicity materials in her head already. This was the kind of thing that would make Carter's Crossing a romantic destination worth the travel. The excitement was fizzing again.

The front door opened, and a tall, elegant, silver-haired woman came out, smiling in welcome at Mariah as she exited her car. The woman was dressed in wool pants and a silk shirt with a sweater knotted over her shoulders. Her hair was pulled back, and her makeup was perfectly applied. In a town this size, she was a surprise.

Mariah was glad she'd worn her suit.

"You must be Mariah. How lovely to see you."

Even her voice was charming. Mariah had had some doubts about this partnership her grandfather had set up for her, but first impressions were positive.

"Yes, I'm Mariah Van Delton. Thank you so much for inviting me here, Mrs. Carter."

The woman shook her head. "Abigail, please. We're partners in crime now."

Abigail came down the steps and enveloped her in a scented embrace. She then stood back and cocked her head as she examined Mariah.

"How was your drive? Any problems finding your way?"

Mariah thought of the man with the dog and shook her head. "Not at all. You have a lovely town."

"Let me know, before I get myself carried away, am I crazy, or do we have a chance?"

Mariah reined in her own excitement. "I've just got here. There's still a lot to consider." Seeing Abigail's face fall, she added, "But this place has already given me ideas. Big ideas. I just won't tell Grandfather until we've worked the details out."

Abigail's face lit up. "I'm so glad. Now, do come in. Do you have a lot to carry? I can ask Nelson to bring your things in when he gets here, or tomorrow I have the staff to deal with it."

Staff made sense. This house must require

a lot of upkeep. Mariah wasn't sure who Nelson was, but she was perfectly able to carry her own luggage.

"I didn't bring a lot, so I'm quite capable of handling it."

Abigail shot her a look. "Of course you are. I'm undoubtedly capable of mowing this lawn, but I would rather someone else do it. Sometimes accepting help is...strategic."

Mariah paused. At that moment it was all too clear that Abigail had been not just a beautiful woman, but a clever one, as well. Anyone who underestimated her would find themselves in trouble. Mariah made note.

Mariah hadn't brought much with her because she'd had some serious concerns about her grandfather's decree that she should stay with his old college friend. Even if she was confident she could make this plan for Carter's Crossing work, she didn't necessarily want to be sharing a home with someone she'd never met before. But the house was so large that there'd be no problem with a lack of privacy. She already felt sure that she and Abigail could work together. She should have known that her grandfather's friend would be up to this. He hadn't built his business empire by being wrong.

"Let me at least take your briefcase and I'll

show you to your room." Abigail held out a hand.

Mariah passed it over and grabbed the two bags from the trunk. "Thank you again for offering me a place to stay."

Abigail, holding the door open for her, waved that aside.

"This place is much too large for one person. And I'm grateful for your help, and for Gerry sending you."

Gerry? Right, her grandfather. No one had called him anything but Gerald as far as Mariah knew.

"I'm happy to be here, and I'm excited about the project."

Abigail's eyes were sparkling. "Excellent. I expect we can accomplish great things together. I've put you on the second floor, at the other end of the house from me so that we each have our own space. I'm sure we'll soon be heartily sick of each other and need a retreat."

Abigail led her upstairs to a room overlooking the lawn at the back of the house. "I apologize. The room doesn't have an en suite, but there's only the two of us in the house, so the bathroom next door is all yours. Take a few minutes to settle in. I'll be waiting on the porch. I want to enjoy the last of the warm days before the cold keeps us all huddled indoors. We'll eat once Nelson gets here. He shouldn't be long." She glanced at the delicate gold watch on her wrist.

Mariah wasn't sure if Nelson would be serving the meal or eating with them, but she hoped his presence wouldn't interfere with talking to Abigail. The idea she'd been struck with when she drove around Carter's Crossing had inspired her. She'd wanted to blurt it out as soon as she arrived, but this was important. She had to be sure she'd thought it through first.

She weighed the pros and cons in her head again. She had a lot riding on this job. She needed it to be perfect.

THE BEDROOM WAS GORGEOUS. Not a surprise after meeting Abigail. Mariah decided to unpack later. She didn't want to be late for dinner, and she was eager to talk to Abigail.

She found Abigail on the porch, sweater now on to fight the cool of the autumn dusk.

"Come, sit for a minute, Mariah. Did you find the room comfortable?"

Mariah sat on a wicker chair with a plump cushion on its seat.

"The room is beautiful. I'm sure I'll be more than comfortable."

"Thank you, dear. Did you want to start talking shop tonight, or wait till tomorrow? I don't want to press you, at least, not yet. Are you tired from the drive?"

Mariah tamped down her own excitement. "Not at all. I'm ready anytime, but if you'd rather wait..."

"I'm excited about it—oh, but that looks like Nelson coming now."

"Who exactly is Nelson?"

"Nelson is my grandson. He's the only family I have here in Carter's now. He lives in the carriage house, and I insist he comes over for dinner regularly. I tell him it's for his own good, but really, I'm happy to have the company.

"He was called in to work earlier, but he just texted that he was on his way home."

Mariah saw a white van heading toward the house.

"Is Nelson going to be involved in this project?" The information her grandfather had provided her about Abigail Carter had been sparse.

Abigail allowed a small smile and shook her head. "Oh, no, this isn't his kind of thing at all."

The white van turned in the drive. The lettering on the side read Carter's Crossing Animal Hospital.

Mariah's excitement took a nosedive.

"What does Nelson do?" But she knew the answer already.

"He's the town's veterinarian. He was called in this afternoon to take care of Tiny, Mavis Grisham's Great Dane."

Mariah swallowed a sigh. If she was a believer in signs, she'd be worried about now.

NELSON NOTICED THE car parked in front of his grandmother's house as he drove around to the back. It looked familiar. Then he saw the plates.

How had Miss I'm Not Lost ended up here? He'd like to see her explain that, but she'd probably get directions from his grandmother and be on her way before he arrived at the main house. That is, if she'd admit she was lost at all. Maybe she was stopping all over town trying to find her way again. She must be geographically challenged.

Happy he wouldn't have a second meeting with her, he pulled his van into the garage below his apartment in the former carriage house and took a moment to roll the kinks out of his neck. He didn't have time to shower, since Grandmother was big on punctuality, but he had a few minutes to change. She wouldn't let him come to dinner in scrubs. Once in his place, he threw what he was wearing in the laundry and pulled on a cashmere sweater she'd given him last Christmas and some dress pants. Grandmother would never allow jeans or sweats at her dinner table. A quick glance in the mirror assured him he'd pass muster, and he headed over to the house.

He let himself in the back door and sniffed appreciatively at the aromas drifting his way. Coq au vin. His favorite. His grandmother loved the classic French dishes. It had been a few months since he'd enjoyed her coq au vin.

His grandmother insisted he come to dinner a couple of times a week, and he was happy to oblige her. She said he needed to have a civilized meal occasionally. He knew she wanted company. He did, too.

It wasn't just that she was a good cook; he worried about her living here all alone. It was a big place, and he was the only family left in town. She had her staff who came in on weekdays, but evenings and weekends she was still alone.

She'd been left a widow with four kids at a young age, and he admired how she'd handled her family and the family business on her own. He knew she was working on something new, but she hadn't shared the details with him yet. She had a good mind for business, but he hoped her plan didn't involve him. Especially not his personal life.

There was a lot of *grande dame* about his grandmother.

He heard voices coming from the living room and paused. Did she have a guest? She hadn't mentioned it. Normally, it was just the two of them at dinner.

Surely Grandmother hadn't invited the rude stranger to stay. Better Mavis and Tiny.

He made his way to the doorway and stopped in surprise.

"Oh, Nelson. There you are. Nelson, this is Mariah Van Delton. Mariah, this is my grandson, Nelson Carter."

Abigail smiled at him as if she'd just given him a pleasant surprise.

Mariah smiled, as well. It was patently fake. "Oh, we met earlier, though we didn't exchange names."

Nelson had never worried about his grandmother being scammed before, but his Spidey senses were tingling now. Somehow, he knew this woman, with her *I'm not lost* and fake smile, was going to be trouble.

He wouldn't admit that part of that certainty was because she was also much too pretty for his own good.

Abigail raised her eyebrows delicately. "Oh?"

"I offered to give Ms. Van Delton directions." Which, he could acknowledge to himself, might not have been necessary if she was heading to see his grandmother.

But why was she?

"I thought you said you'd found your way without any problems, Mariah?" Grandmother asked, frowning.

Mariah sat a little straighter. Her eyes were flashing. "I did. I merely stopped to make some notes and your grandson *assumed* I was lost."

Nelson narrowed his own gaze. "Not many people stop in at my clinic on a Sunday afternoon to *make notes*."

Abigail was watching them with an amused smile. Very *grande dame*. Nelson quickly changed direction.

"You didn't tell me you were expecting a guest, Grandmother."

"No, I didn't, did I? If we're going to keep each other posted on every little thing, then let me tell you that Mariah is going to be staying here for a while, helping me with a project I have in mind. We'd just started discussing it."

Nelson felt the hair on the back of his neck lift. That look Grandmother had on her face meant trouble. And he already knew Ms. Van Delton was going to be a pain.

Abigail rose to her feet. "Let me bring in dinner, and I can hear more about this new idea of yours, Mariah. It's time we went public, so we can let Nelson in on it."

Mariah insisted on helping and followed Abigail out of the room.

Nelson frowned. He shouldn't be the one feeling left out here. It was his home, his town, and yet he was the last to know what was going on.

Grandmother discussed things with him. At least, the major things. She'd had to shut the mill not long after he'd returned to Carter's Crossing, and he knew how difficult a decision that had been for her.

He couldn't readily imagine Mariah as the savior for the town's economic woes. She didn't look old enough to be the CEO of any well-established business. It was undoubtedly prejudice on his part, mostly as a result of being told to get lost, but he wouldn't trust any business she was touting. His grandmother had been the town leader for so long, she'd come to believe herself a benevolent despot. But sometimes her ideas were a little...unconventional.

He made his way to the dining room, already set for dinner for three, and poured the wine she'd left out. Then he headed for the kitchen. He could help carry in the food.

He didn't make a lot of noise. He'd spent enough time in this house to avoid the squeaky boards by habit. Just before he reached the door, he heard them talking and paused.

The phrase that eavesdroppers never heard any good about themselves wasn't quite accurate. Eavesdroppers didn't hear good, period.

Mariah was speaking, responding to something his grandmother had said.

"In that case, you could say that working for Sherry Anstruthers taught me everything I needed to know about wedding planning, and I've taken those lessons to heart."

After that, all Nelson heard was white noise. He made himself move back to the dining room just as quietly as he'd left, but he was on autopilot.

Sherry Anstruthers was one person he despised, almost as much as he despised himself, or at least the man he'd been three years ago. He could not believe Grandmother had invited anyone connected to that woman to her home.

Maybe she hadn't known that Mariah Van Delton had a connection with Sherry. He sat back in his chair. Right. She hadn't known. She couldn't have. And now she'd send Miss I'm Not Lost packing.

He found his fists clenched so tightly on the chair arms that his knuckles stood out, white against the oak. He relaxed them, with an effort, just as he heard footsteps in the hallway. He stood up when Grandmother and Mariah came back in, bearing hot dishes.

Mariah was here. But not for long.

NELSON HAD JUST swallowed his first mouthful when the hammer hit.

Mariah led off. "Abigail, I think you have a good idea, but you're thinking too small."

No one had ever accused his grandmother of thinking too small. If Mariah was thinking bigger than anything his grandmother could come up with, it was going to be a nightmare. Even if Mariah wasn't going to be staying here, she could do a lot of damage before she left.

He glanced at his grandmother, but she wasn't offended. Her eyes were sparkling as she waited, her fork resting on her plate.

Why wasn't she freezing out this interloper?

"Carter's Crossing would be a beautiful wedding destination, but I don't think we should stop there."

The chicken went down the wrong way in Nelson's throat, and he started choking. Mariah frowned at him, and he'd swear his grandmother was holding back a laugh. It would serve her right if he did choke. He managed to swallow his food, and grabbed his wineglass, needing to soothe his throat so he could talk.

Because no way was Carter's Crossing going to be wedding central. Not if he had anything to do with it.

"Wedding traffic would drive business mostly in the summertime. This is a beautiful four-season location, and we want to take advantage of it. We don't want Carter's Crossing to be a center for weddings."

Nelson's shoulders relaxed. He finally agreed with the woman about something. They didn't want Carter's Crossing to be a center for weddings, especially the kind of weddings that would be connected to people coming from elsewhere. Those wouldn't be the small local weddings the town was used to. The usual, ordinary, happy events. The ones couples planned for themselves, with help from friends and family.

He didn't mind those.

It was the big-production, showstopper weddings that he was opposed to. The ones that required a wedding planner, like Sherry Anstruthers. He'd had personal experience with those, and it had been a nightmare. His nightmare.

He didn't want that for his town, or the people who lived here.

But Mariah didn't finish the sentence the way Nelson would have.

"No, we want Carter's Crossing to be the Center for Romance." She said it that way, like romance had a capital *R* on it. Like Romance was also a big production.

Like it needed a planner.

No way.

Before Nelson could interrupt, his grandmother was asking, "What do you mean?" Nelson had a bad idea he knew what she meant.

Mariah wasn't looking at him anymore. She was focused in on Abigail. "I want Carter's Crossing to be the place people go for romantic getaways. For anniversaries. The place they come to propose, to get married, to fall in love. We find the romance in every season.

Lemonade and boat rides in summer, cider and leaf season in fall, snuggling around the fireplace in winter, drinking hot chocolate…"

Nelson was distracted for a moment, trying to decide what beverage she was serving in spring.

"Oh, that's incredible," Abigail said. "I like that. You're right—if we do this well, it's business for the town year-round."

"And," Mariah added, "we can get started before you have the mill ready."

Nelson finally found his voice. "The mill?"

His grandmother gave him a big smile. A beautiful, elegant, phony smile. She knew. She knew exactly how much he was going to hate this.

"Yes, I'm converting the mill to an event venue."

An event venue? When did his grandmother start talking about things like event venues?

"We'll have a kitchen for catering, and space for indoor and outdoor events."

"Events?" he asked, his voice high and tight.

"Yes, like weddings."

Just kill him now.

CHAPTER TWO

SOMETHING WAS GOING on here. There was a current underscoring this conversation strong enough to tow swimmers out to drown, and Mariah didn't know what it was. But as soon as Abigail said *weddings*, Nelson growled. Honestly, she couldn't think of a more accurate word to describe it.

It gave her pause. The romance destination idea was good. More than good. This town could be perfect; it had lots of big old houses that Abigail swore were set for bed-and-breakfast locations. There were four lovely churches and the town gazebo for wedding and vow-renewal ceremonies, as well as the mill that Abigail was renovating. The small river that wound its way along one side of the town might not be big enough for yachts, but it was pretty, and could handle canoes and kayaks. A couple of nice restaurants, a few more activities for visitors, and this could be stellar.

But if Nelson was opposed, she didn't

know if the plan would go ahead. She had no idea how much influence he wielded over his grandmother or the rest of the people in the town. She had the definite impression he didn't like her.

Well, he hadn't liked her when she told him to get lost. And yes, that was fair. But since they'd served dinner, she'd felt his animosity like a force field around him.

Could he torpedo this whole idea?

There was one way to find out.

Abigail and Nelson were staring at each other like tomcats considering a fight.

"Is this a problem?"

"Yes."

"No."

The answers crashed over each other.

"Nelson," Abigail said. It was the *I'm the parent, you're crossing the line* kind of voice that mothers and fathers had used since Adam and Eve.

"You know..." He was growling again.

"I do. But it's been long enough. I've been trying to find some way to save this town. This is our best opportunity. Can you get past it?"

Mariah wondered if she should have excused herself. But the clash between them had come up so suddenly... She wasn't sure what the issue was, but apparently, it was major. And whatever it was, it was going to have a big effect on her plans for this next year.

Nelson stood. "It's not up to me, is it? You've already made your decision. Just keep me out of it, please. Excuse me, Ms. Van Delton, Grandmother." He turned and left, leaving Abigail and Mariah staring at the doorway where he'd disappeared.

"I'm sorry," Abigail said. "I shouldn't have sprung that on him. You must think we're crazy."

Mariah shook her head. "I'm not the one who's upset here. But I need to ask, are you sure this is a good idea?"

Abigail nodded firmly. "Absolutely. Your idea of a romance destination is wonderful. I'll get the committee on board and you can tell us what we need to do."

Mariah's glance drifted back to the doorway.

"And your grandson?" Mariah wasn't sure Abigail had any other family. She had no desire to find herself in the middle of a family drama.

Abigail sighed. "As you can tell, he has an issue, yes. But it's time he moved on. He won't do anything to stop us."

Mariah was afraid her skepticism must be showing on her face.

Abigail smiled. "I've known Nelson all his life. He'll be fine, once he gets accustomed to the idea. And this shouldn't affect him at all, should it? I don't imagine any of your ideas for romance involve a veterinarian."

Mariah had a quick vision of Nelson, soft lighting, romantic music, and shook her head. No, she wasn't thinking of any romance involving a veterinarian. Definitely not. And not in the way Abigail meant, either. She had limited her vision of romance to people, not animals. She didn't foresee bringing any livestock into the picture.

Though they could—and she slammed the door on any thoughts about indulging people's pet wedding fantasies, Persians in veils or terriers in tuxes. Maybe later.

"Nelson's work won't be affected, so he really has nothing to be upset about. He just needs time."

Mariah had the feeling Abigail was trying to convince herself.

Abigail shook her head. "I should have known better than to make coq au vin. Please, enjoy your meal—I'll take Nelson something later, when he's cooled down a bit.

"Now, what do you need from me to make this work?"

NELSON STALKED ACROSS the driveway to the carriage house. He could *not* believe his grandmother was doing this.

He veered between frustration and anger. He was angry that his grandmother ruined what would have been a spectacular dinner by bringing up the one topic guaranteed to give him heartburn. He was frustrated that she had made such a big plan without talking to him. And he could not believe that Mariah—*Mariah*—was the one still at the dining room table instead of him.

He wished Mariah had been truly lost.

He stormed into his apartment. Yes, being angry with Mariah was something he could get on board with. She'd annoyed him when she turned down his offer of help. Maybe she wasn't lost, but she could have been polite. And here she was, ready to bring the chaos and stress and havoc of elaborate weddings to Carter's Crossing.

He knew *exactly* what that was like. And the people who got hurt as a result.

He didn't want something like that here.

He growled and threw himself in a chair.

If his grandmother was determined, he had about as much chance of changing her mind as he did of stopping the seasons from turning, but he had to try. There had to be another option, some other way to make Carter's Crossing come back to life.

Ways that didn't include Mariah Van Delton.

He just had to think of them before his grandmother got her plan in motion. No problem.

Sometime later there was a knock on his door, and no idea had come. He considered ignoring it, but he knew it was his grandmother, and she had her own key.

He stood and strode over to let her in. He stepped back, arms crossed on his chest, frowning.

She ignored his frown. She was holding a dish, and he didn't need to examine the contents to know she'd brought him some of her coq au vin. But no chicken, no matter how well done, was going to make up for her bombshell.

"I know." She shoved the dish toward him. "But don't cut off your nose to spite your face. You'll want to eat this eventually."

He took the dish from her hands and set it on his kitchen countertop. When he turned, she'd sat herself down in one of his easy chairs.

"You know I didn't drop the news on you this way by accident."

He stiffened. He should have realized, but he'd been too upset to think it through.

"After tomorrow, the news will be spreading all over town. I wanted you to have a heads-up."

He opened his mouth to ask why she hadn't told him herself, when she held up a hand.

"I didn't want to tell you, and have you start an argument. You are a stubborn and determined man, Nelson, and I didn't want you to try to stonewall this. I wasn't going to change my mind, and I did not want the fatigue of endless arguments."

It wasn't much of a stretch to discover where Nelson had learned his determination. He leaned back and crossed his arms again. If his grandmother was going to take over the conversation, he wasn't going to help.

"It's a done deal. Mariah's grandfather is an old friend of your grandfather's and mine, from our college days." A pained look passed over her face. His grandfather had died long before Nelson was born, so he had no memories of him. Grandmother had never married again, so the family assumed it had been a love match, one that she'd never gotten over.

"Gerry Van Delton has a very successful event planning business in New York City. His company handles professional sports events, Hollywood premiers, political fundraisers—all much larger events than anything we could do in Carter's Crossing. When I was trying to think of something we could do here, something to keep the town alive along that line, I reached out to him.

"He thought that a wedding destination was something we could manage and offered his granddaughter as a consultant for a year to get us up and running."

"Why?" Nelson asked. "Why send someone?" It was more assistance than seemed reasonable.

His grandmother stared past him; her lips pursed. "I don't know. We were close, back at school, but I haven't seen him in years. There's more to it. He's not someone to be generous to his own detriment."

She drew her gaze back to him. "I know he had some issues with his own children. He may be wanting to test Mariah in some way. I'm not sure."

Nelson considered. Maybe Mariah couldn't pull this off, and he wouldn't have to worry about it. But she didn't look or act incompetent.

And while he'd be happy not to have big production weddings in Carter's Crossing, he didn't want his grandmother to sink money into an endeavor that wouldn't pay off. Because if she was backing this plan, he knew she'd be putting up cash.

"And, Nelson, it's time."

And that took all those kind thoughts and blew them away.

"I'm fine, Grandmother."

She looked down her nose. It took talent to do that when he was standing, and she was in a chair. "If you were fine, you wouldn't have left the house in a tantrum. Without eating your dinner."

He wanted to argue that he hadn't been in a tantrum, but he had walked out without his favorite meal.

"I don't have to discuss this with you." He didn't.

"Nelson, it's been three years now. You didn't commit a crime. No one died. You were thoughtless, and you hurt someone, but I think you've served your time."

Nelson held back an angry response with effort. He knew what he'd done, and what he hadn't done. That wasn't the point. Or at least, it wasn't the only point.

Getting married was a big deal. It was a major commitment, and one that shouldn't be entered into lightly. Having a big, elaborate party simultaneously added tremendous pressure to an already stressful time. It could result in some terrible decisions. Decisions he'd made.

Made with the help of Sherry Anstruthers.

He couldn't condone that kind of thing. And that was exactly what his grandmother was wanting to rebuild the town on. She couldn't really expect him to support that, could she?

"I heard the two of you in the kitchen." He saw from his grandmother's face that he knew exactly what he was talking about.

"How could you invite someone like that, someone like Sherry Anstruthers, to wreak havoc on Carter's Crossing?"

"Oh, Nelson." She shook her head and sighed. "Mariah is not like that woman."

Nelson snorted. He'd heard the words himself. She was just like that woman. That was what she wanted to be.

"Nelson, people make mistakes. You made a mistake. But it doesn't mean you're a bad person."

Nelson wished he was more sure of that.

"You want proof that Mariah is different? Well, the last wedding she worked on, before coming up here, was Zoey's."

More white noise. Nelson tried to understand what his grandmother was saying.

"Zoey's? My Zoey's?"

She nodded.

His mouth opened, but no words came out.

Zoey was married?

It had been three years. They hadn't kept in touch. But…

But she'd moved on, found someone else and gotten married—with a wedding planner. After…after everything.

Nelson dropped into his seat.

"You didn't know?"

He hated the sympathy in Abigail's voice. He hated that it implied that she worried about him, that he wasn't strong and he wasn't over it.

Maybe he wasn't.

She shook her head at him.

"I guess you do need more time. I didn't realize. I'm sorry that Mariah has upset you. But, Nelson, this is happening. Prepare yourself. It shouldn't affect you so perhaps we just need to agree to disagree on this. I won't ask for your assistance, and you won't take Tiny and come into town stealing all the wedding paraphernalia until your heart grows three sizes, okay?"

She stood up to leave.

"That dog was named Max, and he wasn't a Great Dane."

She opened his door and headed out.

"And I'm not the Grinch!"

MARIAH HUNG UP her suit in the wardrobe in her room. She'd unpacked now and was reconsidering her wardrobe choices. Did everyone in this town dress up all the time?

She shrugged. She'd get her roommate to send her some more of her clothes if she needed.

That gave her a thought, and she went over to her phone. She added a notation to her list: clothing store. If this was going to be a destination, there should be clothes available for emergencies. Not wedding dresses, though if they got far enough along, a wedding dress store would be wonderful; bridal parties could come to shop for dresses and spend time at the spa she'd previously added to her list. But if a guest damaged their outfit, or forgot a tie…

And if people were coming for weekends together, they might like a T-shirt or hoodie with the town's name on it.

In a rare moment of doubt, she wondered if this was going to work.

The place looked like a postcard. Its days of prosperity had left a town of beautiful brick and wooden homes, but many needed attention. Abigail insisted that was being taken care of. And the less attractive homes, the poorer ones, were literally on the other side of the train tracks that used to lead to the old mill.

They needed to include this part of town in the plans somehow.

The churches and the town green were all perfect for their plan. Tomorrow they were supposed to check out the mill and see what needed to be done there to make it the event venue they needed.

There were still things the town required to make this a success, and a year wasn't enough time to get them all done. She had plans for beyond the year. A spa, definitely. And more restaurants. But also, for the wedding part, the support industries like a bakery, a florist, catering, decorating...and for other visitors, activities, things for people to do. Winter was coming, and for that they'd want hikes, cross-country ski trails and other outdoor events. Horses for riding and sleigh rides? Maybe a tour of antiques stores in the area. Were there maple syrup farms around? That would be great in the spring. It was probably too cold for wineries...

She reined in her imagination. This was beyond her brief, so that would be up to other people to realize. Part of the beauty of her idea about making Carter's Crossing a destination for all things romance related was that romantic weekends didn't require the dresses and catering that a wedding did. They didn't need to have the mill finished and ready to go. But it would require more than leaves turning color and a pretty stream.

It would require a lot of community support, and that brought her mind back to Nelson. She'd found him setting up a seat in her head more often than she wanted him to this evening.

Yes, he was attractive. That sweater he'd worn to dinner had been even more flattering than the scrubs had been. He was obviously fit, and the color made his eyes look very blue...but she didn't need to dwell on that. More important, he was not a fan of what she was doing.

Or of hers.

She couldn't help wondering why. His grandmother said it was time to get over it, so something had happened. His wife died? Something went terribly wrong at a wedding? His wedding? His wife died at their own wedding?

She shook her head. Nelson was not her problem, and they should have no issue keeping out of each other's way. She was planning for romance and setting up the support network for romantic events. Overgrown pets like Tiny shouldn't play a part, and she couldn't imagine anything that would take her to the animal clinic.

NELSON WAS ON edge as he made his way into the clinic on Monday morning, running late. He wasn't happy about the plans his grandmother had for Carter's Crossing, he wasn't happy about the woman who was here to help with them and he wasn't happy about the talk he'd had with his grandmother last night.

If any out-of-state cars pulled into his parking lot today, he wouldn't offer assistance unless asked, and even then, the only help he'd give them would be to direct them right out of town.

Okay, that was overkill, but he was unsettled, and hadn't slept well, old dreams popping up out of the depths of his subconscious to poke at him with reminders of just how badly he'd behaved. He didn't need that, he knew, and strived every day to be a different guy.

He wasn't looking forward to the talk he'd be hearing at work today, either. Gossip flew around a small town. Now that Ms. Van Delton had arrived, he expected the news about Romance Central would be everywhere by noon.

His assistant and receptionist were already

at the clinic: Judy would check on any animals they were keeping on-site, and Kailey would prepare their schedules for the day. They were chatting when he came in from the back but stopped as soon as they heard him.

The news had traveled even more quickly than he expected. He didn't want to hear it.

"Morning, Judy, Kailey. Anything I need to know?"

He hoped they knew he meant related to work only.

"The Fletchers were hoping you could come out and see one of their pigs sometime today." Kailey said. Kailey was ten years older than he was and tended to believe she needed to keep him in line. She could keep their clients in line, as well, so he endured the fact that sometimes she thought she was in charge. "You don't have anything booked after two, so I told them you probably could."

Nelson nodded. The Fletchers had a small farm and orchard. It wasn't far from his own property out there, so he could swing by his place when he was done.

"Did you two have a nice weekend?" Nelson didn't want them asking about his grandmother's plans, so he steered the conversation in a different direction. He checked the list of appointments he had till two, mentally preparing what he'd need.

"Sure," Kailey said. "You had Tiny yesterday?"

He'd left his notes on the desk for Kailey. "Habanero sauce this time. I didn't ask why she had it."

Kailey rolled her eyes. "Mavis has been watching the Food Network again."

Judy was quiet. With her slight build and fair coloring, she could vanish into the back of the clinic without anyone noticing. She was more than competent in her work, and she didn't usually talk a lot, but she was so quiet that he wondered if he'd offended or scared her somehow.

After his interaction with Ms. Van Delton, he began to wonder if he was coming across as overbearing without realizing it. Again.

"Didn't I hear you were going out with Harvey this weekend?" He was trying to be one of the gang, just chatting around the watercooler. The metaphoric watercooler.

The two women exchanged glances.

Nelson felt like he'd stepped in it somehow. "What? What did I say? Did you break up?"

Kailey shook her head. "No." She winked at Judy. "I'd say they were the opposite of breaking up."

Nelson looked at Judy. "Should I ask?"

Judy flushed. "We— I— I mean, we didn't want to make a big deal of it."

Nelson was puzzled. "A big deal about what?"

Judy looked at the floor with a smile crossing her face. "He asked me to move in with him."

Nelson still didn't see the problem. "That's good, right?"

Judy nodded.

"And you don't want to make a big deal out of it because…?" He was out of his depth here.

Judy was still looking at the ground, grinding the toe of her shoe into the floor.

Kailey sighed. "She doesn't want to rub it in."

Nelson looked over at Kailey. "Rub what in? Where?"

Kailey rolled her eyes. "They're getting serious. Like, maybe soon walking-down-the-aisle serious."

Nelson rolled his hand, hoping Kailey would soon get to the point, since Judy must have run out of words.

"Nelson, everyone knows what happened to you. We don't want to make you uncomfortable."

Nelson stepped back. Wow, way to suddenly make him uncomfortable.

"I wasn't, not till you said that."

He paused and braced his hands on his hips.

"Judy, I'm very happy for you. And if Harvey pops the question, I'll be happier. And I hope you have a lovely wedding and live happily-ever-after. If you want to."

Kailey opened her mouth and he held up his hand to stop her.

"I'm not some fragile, broken person here. Yeah, I know my wedding didn't happen. It doesn't mean I want everyone else to be miserable, or that I'm opposed to people dating and being happy together, and I don't need my staff avoiding 'sensitive' topics when I'm around to support my fragile ego. Okay?"

Judy nodded, and headed back to prepare for their first appointments. Kailey, of course, couldn't let it go.

"If you don't want us thinking you're still heartbroken, maybe you should start dating again. Or, I don't know, stop avoiding anything related to weddings."

Nelson threw up his hands. "I missed one wedding because my horse had colic!" He looked at her expression. "Seriously, you think I faked it? Unbelievable."

He stomped back to help Judy. He hadn't realized missing one wedding—*one!*—when his horse was sick had started rumors that he was now a bitter misanthrope.

Sometimes he hated small towns.

"WOW," MARIAH SAID.

Abigail had brought her to the old mill. The place had been shut down for a couple of years, and the outside of the building was industrial, but the setting…incredible. Harking back to the original structure, the building sat beside the river that flowed through the town. The trees surrounding the mill and growing on the hillside behind it wore garlands of yellow, orange and vivid red, the notes of evergreens adding lowlights in contrast.

The natural surroundings were at their peak, helping to sell the mill as a romantic venue. Unfortunately, the mill itself was lacking that natural beauty.

Any of it.

Still, Mariah could look past the gray metal siding. It was a big building, and the parking lot, though untended, also had plenty of room. What could happen from there depended on how much Abigail was willing to invest.

"The location is perfect." Mariah paused.

Abigail nodded. "I couldn't have picked

a better time to bring you here, but I know the building is not anywhere close to what it needs to be. Let's look inside. I had the place assessed, and structurally, it's still sound. But it will need a complete refit to make it what we need."

Mariah followed her to a door. It squeaked, but less in a "you're about to die" creepy way and more in the annoying, needing grease way. Mariah hoped the place hadn't been left to deteriorate.

It hadn't.

Dust motes were dancing in the sunlight coming through the windows, high up. Along the far end, metal stairs led to a second level. Where they stood, the ceiling soared above them, heavy wooden beams at the near end, morphing into steel beams as the space had expanded over its lifetime.

Space. Lots of empty space.

Mariah circled around. She could picture rows of chairs with an aisle to a chuppah, or an arch, where couples could make their vows. Or remake them. Over there they could have a place for the reception with a big dance area, and a kitchen back under the second floor. Upstairs, offices or rooms for the wedding parties to prepare.

Dances, anniversaries, parties—this space

could handle them all. She crossed to one of the few windows on the first-floor level and saw the river outside. If they had sliding doors to open here when the weather was warmer… maybe they could clear some space behind the building for an outdoor patio, as well.

She turned to Abigail.

"No machinery?"

Abigail shook her head. "We had everything that could be salvaged sold off. It was added to the pension fund."

Mariah looked around again. She wasn't an engineer, or an architect, but she could imagine that refitting this space would be expensive. At least, to make it fully functional and anything close to what Mariah was imagining.

"The place has enormous potential." Mariah said, carefully.

"And needs enormous work." Abigail sighed. "I'm inquiring about an architect to come and prepare plans, but I wanted your input into what we need here. What do you imagine this place like?"

Mariah's eyes swept the space again.

"You'll need an industrial kitchen—assuming this would be the place to host receptions, parties, dances, et cetera. I don't imagine there's any place with that capability in town now?"

Abigail shook her head. “We only have a diner, one ‘nicer’ restaurant and the pizza and sub parlor. None of those are designed for catering large events. Anyone local has to travel to Oak Hill, and it’s not that impressive once you do.”

Mariah considered.

“You need the space to be flexible—for services, meals, all with different numbers of guests. I wouldn’t dream of guiding your architect, but I had thought it might be nice if, say, the kitchen was back there, where there’s a second floor, and over it could be offices, rooms for the wedding party to get ready onsite, and then have the events in this space where we could possibly keep these high ceilings.”

Abigail nodded. “That makes sense to me. I hadn’t thought of all that.”

“And, if we’re dreaming big, imagine sliding doors on the wall facing the river. The view would be incredible, and when the weather cooperated, we could open them up, bring all that in.”

Abigail smiled at her. “And we have to do something to the exterior. Would we want outdoor space, for more than parking anyway? Maybe around back?”

Mariah cocked her head. "Are you reading my mind?"

"I hope not. That would be terribly uncomfortable, I'm sure."

Biting the bullet before her imagination got away from her, Mariah decided to be frank.

"It's going to be expensive. I don't know how much you're willing to invest."

Abigail examined the space with a narrowed gaze. "I'll have to see what the architect comes up with. My pockets are undoubtedly shallower than your grandfather's, but I'm willing to do a lot."

Mariah looked around, looking at more of the details. She and Abigail had walked around the interior, but they hadn't left footprints. She could see dust motes in the air, but they weren't breathing in dust and musty smells.

"You've been maintaining this place, haven't you?"

Abigail nodded. "Yes, I have. It was the place that built Carter's Crossing. I hope it can still do that, with a bit of work."

Mariah wondered, for the first time seriously, just how much money Abigail Carter did have. Mariah's grandfather was paying her own salary for this year, while she worked to makeover Carter's Crossing. Abigail was providing room and board, so that Mariah could spend all her time working on this plan. She'd assumed they wanted to do this on a shoestring.

Mariah worked with large and small wedding budgets, so she hadn't been concerned with the idea of going more cheap and cheerful than all out.

But she could only imagine the cost for the renovations on this building. Abigail's home, and the maintenance it would require, wasn't cheap, either.

She also wondered, not for the first time, why her grandfather was doing this. He'd sold Mariah on the idea as a challenge, an apprenticeship. But what was her grandfather getting out of this? Why was he helping an old friend, one who called him Gerry?

Abigail was still a beautiful woman. Perhaps she and her grandfather—

Mariah put a brake on those thoughts. None of that had to do with her job. And she was sure her grandfather wouldn't want her speculating on his past.

Abigail turned to Mariah. "Can you write up a list of everything you think we'd need for me to give to the architect? What things we must have, what we'd like to have and what we might even dream of, if we were to go a little crazy? We can give that to him, have him come and look around and see what we can do."

Mariah nodded. "That's not a problem. I've done weddings in a lot of different spaces, and I have my own ideas of what works best. And what doesn't. Coming up with a list like that will be easy."

Abigail sighed. "It's going to take a while, though, isn't it? Now that I've decided on this, I'm anxious to get going."

"As it happens," Mariah teased her, "I have some ideas about that, as well."

NELSON PULLED THE van into the drive of the old farm. His old farm now. The house was boarded up, but the barn was still functional. In the paddock outside, he counted the five horses.

He parked the van by the barn and made his way into the building. He heard the hoof-beats of the animals coming in the open side door.

One brown head was already bobbing at him as he pulled out a bale of hay, setting it down in the aisle.

He rubbed the horse's forehead, and the horse butted his head against him.

"Yeah, yeah. Hay is coming. You guys behaving?"

Most of them were in the barn now. Nelson ran his gaze over them, checking that they were looking alert, moving smoothly, their hair lying flat and their eyes bright.

He pulled a pocketknife out and slit open the hay bale. Two more heads pushed over the top rail of the big pen.

When he'd decided to use this place for rescued horses, he'd wanted a space that was low maintenance, but provided the animals with shelter, as well as the freedom to enjoy their life without additional restrictions.

Half the barn had been made into a large pen, or box stall, with an open doorway to the paddock. There was a water trough, self-filling, and he augmented the grass with hay and grain as needed.

The rest of the barn included a tack room, feed room and smaller stalls in case the horses needed to be segregated. Nothing fancy, but a safe place for horses that needed it.

Nelson greeted each eager horse, and then tossed hay into the manger. He held one flake in his hands, and finally, the oldest and slowest member of his herd came forward, nudging Nelson with his gray muzzle. Nelson gripped his halter and carefully examined the yellowed teeth, making sure he was still able to eat.

"You're holding on there, Sparky. You make sure these other guys behave."

The final member of the herd hesitated in the doorway. Nelson kept his movements slow, and his gaze away from the chestnut watching him with white-rimmed eyes.

"So, Sparky, how's the new guy doing?"

Sparky took another bite of hay.

"Yeah, we'll let him settle in a little longer. You tell him he's safe here. Maybe next week I'll be able to spend some time with him. Just don't let him talk about weddings, okay?"

MARIAH ENTERED THE kitchen and found Nelson walking through with a basket of apples. She paused.

He flicked a glance her way. "Delivery for Grandmother."

Mariah narrowed her eyes. That tone—yeah, that tone was for her. She was about to respond in kind, when she pulled in a breath.

She wanted to make this plan for Carter's Crossing work. Not just for herself, though that was certainly a big reason. She wanted to do it for Abigail, who was so determined to keep the town alive. And for her grandfather, who had sent her here for his own reasons.

She didn't need to antagonize anyone. Undoubtedly, she'd step on some toes somewhere in this process, but Nelson was Abigail's grandson. He would carry influence in this community. Her plans might not directly affect a veterinary practice, but he was someone in this town. Being on good terms with him would be smart.

Plus, she had been a little…maybe not exactly rude, but a little short. Curt. Testy. And that hadn't been on him. It was a conditioned response from the behavior of other men, but she should clear the air.

However, if he responded like a jerk, she would happily put him in the group with those others and feel free to be curt in the future.

"I'm afraid I wasn't very…gracious when we first met."

He'd taken the apples into a pantry. He turned and stared at her. Yeah, he hadn't expected that.

"Tiny had got away from me, or he wouldn't have been in your face like that. I understand that not everyone likes dogs. And Tiny is big."

She rolled her eyes. Okay, he was heading straight into the holding pen where "those guys" resided in her estimation.

"I told you, I'm not afraid of dogs. I was

startled. And I've had my ability to navigate questioned too often."

He cocked his head. "Do strangers need to offer direction to you frequently?"

Oh, he was in that pen now, and he was going to be the leader of the misogynistic pack.

She glared at him. "Drop me in the middle of the Pacific with only a sextant and a watch and I could tell you where I was and navigate to the nearest safe landfall. However, it seems to be a concept many men can't handle, that I can find my way around without possessing a Y chromosome."

"Wouldn't you need a boat?"

She eyed him suspiciously. He was leaning against the counter now, smirking.

"I can find my way on land, as well, without a boat."

"But if I was dropping you in the middle of the Pacific with only a sextant, you might drown before you found your way to that safe landing."

"Seriously? That's what you're taking out of this? I tell you I'm a proficient navigator, and you want to nitpick the semantics?"

"Well, I wasn't going to out-navigate you but maybe I've got a better sense of humor."

Oh, that had been a joke, had it?

"I have a great sense of humor."

"Right."

"I don't appreciate jokes about my navigational skills. They tend to be a cover for latent misogyny."

"Now you think I'm a misogynist?"

"I'm testing the hypothesis. So far all signs look good."

He stared at the ceiling, jaw tense.

"I think I have a good appreciation of women and what they are capable of. I grew up with Abigail Carter, and there's not much she can't do.

"But the other day? I find a car in my parking lot, out of state, when the clinic is closed. The driver has a map open on her tablet in front of her. I would have offered help to anyone, with or without a gender. It's how I was raised."

Mariah opened her mouth, then closed it. When you put it that way…

"I'm sorry." She could see she'd surprised Nelson again. "I grew up on a boat."

"In the middle of the Pacific?"

She ignored him.

"My mother grew up sailing. My dad didn't. But if we came into a marina with my mother at the helm, every man within hailing distance would come to 'assist,' yelling directions and basically assuming she was incompetent. That did not happen when my dad was at the wheel, though he was the one who'd need help. And even though I spent my life on a boat and was a better navigator than either of my brothers, that bias was still there.

"It's slowly getting better in the sailing community, but I admit, I'm a little testy about that. In this case, I wasn't looking at the map to find out where to go—seriously, this is a small town. It's not that difficult to navigate. I'd just got some ideas buzzing through my brain and I was trying to find the nearest railway stations and airfields. I was caught up in that and didn't realize how it would look to someone else."

He'd been teasing her, for a moment, and she'd felt that they could maybe be friends. He'd had reason to be upset by what she'd accused him of, and he'd let it slide. But now she could see his face close off as he pushed himself to stand.

"Fine. If you see Grandmother, tell her the Fletchers sent the apples."

Right. He wasn't a fan of this wedding/romance idea.

"Why are you opposed to your grandmother's plan?" Would anything change his attitude on that?

"It doesn't matter." His voice was flat.

Sure it didn't.

"Are you going to fight it?" Mariah wasn't sure what he could do, but if he was opposed, she needed to find out. Find out and defend against it.

He paused at the kitchen door. "My grandmother knows how I feel. I would never do anything to hurt her. I'm not going to get involved in this one way or the other. I'm never going to be part of it, but I'm also not going to stand in the way."

Mariah wished that reassured her. She was afraid that his attitude would affect other people in town. And without knowing why he felt this way, there was nothing she could do to offset that reaction.

"She's investing in this, time and money," Mariah said. "I'm going to make sure it works for her."

He looked at her, something sad in his eyes. "I'm sure you will." He turned and left.

Mariah sagged against the counter. Well, she didn't think he was going to hate her for her response to his offer of assistance in his parking lot. He was going to hate her because she was helping his grandmother make Carter's Crossing a wedding and romance venue.

Somehow, not the improvement she'd been hoping for.

CHAPTER THREE

TUESDAY NIGHTS WERE darts nights.

In a town the size of Carter's Crossing, these were important events. Unless there was a birthing emergency, or a horse with colic, Tuesday nights found Nelson at the Goat and Barley with his friends.

The Goat and Barley was halfway between Carter's and Oak Hill. It was a pub, with a half-way decent menu and an excellent selection of draft beer. It was far enough from Carter's that not everyone would know what you'd done, and anyone who came from Carter's wasn't wanting to talk about you because you might talk about them.

In theory. Nelson was pretty sure his grandmother still knew everything that went on here, but she didn't say anything, and he kept his own confidences. He wasn't doing anything beyond playing darts poorly and drinking some beer anyway.

He leaned back in his chair. He and his buddy Dave had just been soundly beaten in darts. Same old same old. While their two friends from Oak Hill were taking a turn, Nelson had his chance to tell Dave about the conversation with his staff yesterday morning.

After his talk with the wedding, sorry, romance planner, he wanted some sympathetic feedback.

He swallowed a mouthful of beer and picked up an onion ring. Dave was watching the hockey scores over the bar.

"Hey!"

Dave turned back. "Hey, yourself."

He'd known Dave since grade school. Maybe before. Long enough ago that they knew each other well.

"I gotta tell you what Kailey and Judy said yesterday."

"This doesn't have anything to do with tapeworms, does it? 'Cause that was just gross, man."

Nelson grinned. Dave was surprisingly squeamish. They'd gone through high school biology together with Nelson dissecting while Dave wrote up notes. Without looking.

"I could tell you about the Fletchers' pig, if you wanted. But no, it wasn't anything to do with work. Did you know Judy and Harvey were getting serious?"

Judy and Harvey were a few years younger than Dave and him, but that didn't matter much now that they were long out of high school.

Dave stopped with his glass halfway to his mouth. "I knew they were going out."

"He asked her to move in with him."

Dave took a careful swallow. "That's your big news?"

Nelson frowned. Dave was looking at him, not with a "hey, that's interesting" face but more like he was waiting for Nelson to start talking about tapeworms.

"No, but Judy and Kailey didn't want to tell me. They were afraid I'd be upset."

"Were you?"

Nelson threw his hands up. "Why would I be? I mean, I like Judy fine, she's a great assistant, even if she hardly talks, but it's nothing to me if she moves in with Harvey."

"That's good," Dave said. "Why are you telling me? I'm not interested in Judy, either."

"They, Kailey and Judy, thought I was too fragile or something. That if someone talks about weddings or engagements I'll freak out."

Dave was still watching him carefully. "You're okay, though?"

Nelson pointed a finger at his friend. "You

think that, too. You think I still haven't gotten over it."

Dave shrugged.

Nelson ran his fingers through his hair. "What is it with people in this town? It's been three years! I'm not going to burst into tears if someone gets married! I'm not upset."

"You kind of seem like it now."

"That's just because everyone thinks I'm a romance invalid. I'm fine!"

"Okay," Dave said soothingly.

Nelson frowned at him. "If you say 'there, there, now' I'm going to hit you."

Dave grinned. "Okay, you're fine."

"Of course I'm fine! What is wrong with people here?"

Dave grabbed his own onion ring and took a bite. "You haven't dated anyone since you've been back."

"I brought Rachel to the concert last year."

Dave rolled his eyes. "You and Rachel have as much chemistry as you and I do. Less. She's been your backup date since you were kids. I mean, you each drove there separately, and your grandmother sat between you."

Nelson crossed his arms. "Still counts."

He knew he was splitting hairs. He'd known Rachel so long as a friend that he sometimes had to remind himself she was a woman. It wasn't that she wasn't pretty, because she was, in a nice, good girl way, but there'd never been a spark between them.

Dave pointed his half-eaten onion ring at him. "And you skipped out on the wedding."

"My horse had colic!"

His voice was loud enough that patrons at the bar turned around to see where the sound was coming from.

Nelson lowered his voice. "Sparky was sick. Colic is serious. I had to deal with him."

"Really?"

"Why would I lie?"

Dave shrugged. "Before the wedding, someone said they bet you'd weasel out with some excuse."

Nelson grit his teeth. "The horse was sick."

"Okay, I believe you, I promise. But that's what everyone thinks."

Nelson let out a breath. "Sometimes this town drives me nuts."

Dave finished his onion ring, looking carefully at Nelson.

"So you'd be okay if I told you something."

"I'd be okay. Fine. Ecstatic. Whatever."

"Jaycee and I are getting serious."

This time it was Nelson with the glass paused halfway to his mouth.

"You and Jaycee? Really? How did I not know this?"

Dave shrugged. "You know how I've been spending Friday nights taking cooking classes?"

Nelson narrowed his gaze. "With Jaycee?"

Dave nodded.

"And you didn't tell me because you thought I'd curl up in the corner?"

Dave shrugged. "You're not going to do that, right?"

Nelson looked away. "You really think I wouldn't be happy for you?"

"You're right. I'm sorry." Dave shoved the basket of onion rings over to him in apology. "That's what Jaycee said, too."

"Jaycee is a smart woman. Except, of course, for that whole getting serious with you part."

Dave grinned. "She is smart. And don't tell her she shouldn't be with me. I know that, but she hasn't figured it out yet."

Nelson looked around the bar. "So how many other people have been hiding their dating lives in case I couldn't handle it?"

"I'll tell Jaycee to spread the word. Are you good if she joins us next Tuesday, then?"

"Absolutely."

He didn't mind, not really. But he had enjoyed his time with just the guys. Obviously, though, that wasn't something he could share, or he'd have people running for cover any time he showed up, expecting his breakdown.

Wait till word got out about the Romance Center in Carter's. He hadn't heard anyone talking about that yet. On the other hand, apparently, no one would talk to him anyway.

The next wedding-type event this town had, he'd better be there front and center or everyone would believe he was permanently damaged.

Small towns.

MARIAH LOOKED AROUND. This was the power center of Carter's Crossing.

It was also the parlor of Mavis Grisham's house. Mariah was reintroduced to Tiny. Tiny apparently considered the encounter at the clinic parking lot to be the beginning of a wonderful friendship. Mariah did her best to push him away while not offending Mavis.

Fortunately, Abigail was on top of this as much as everything else she did. She told Tiny to sit, and he did.

"Good afternoon. We can finally start talking about our plan for Carter's Crossing. It's happening, so let's get things going."

The room quieted as Abigail spoke.

"I think you all know by now that the new face here belongs to Mariah Van Delton. She's been loaned to us for a year to help us implement our plan to make Carter's Crossing a wedding destination."

There was a smattering of applause, and some nods in Mariah's direction.

"Mariah has just arrived, but she's already provided valuable insight, and has, in fact, expanded the original vision we came up with. So, Mariah, why don't you share your idea with us?"

All eyes turned to Mariah, including those of Tiny. His ears even perked up.

Mariah set down her cup of tea.

"Thank you for welcoming me here. As Abigail said, I came to help you develop Carter's Crossing into a wedding destination. I've been a wedding planner for five years, so I have inside knowledge of what people expect when they book a wedding."

She paused and glanced around the room. She was the center of attention. Tiny cocked his head, waiting for her to continue.

"Unfortunately, there are some major drawbacks to your plan."

Everyone froze.

"I know Abigail is going to convert the old

mill, but it's not ready yet, and it's going to take a while. Months at the minimum."

Heads nodded. Tiny cocked his head in the other direction.

"As well, when people come here for a wedding, they'll have guests. This is a little far for people to drive from the city, enjoy a wedding and return in the same day. Currently, there's no hotel or other place for these guests to stay."

Now people began to talk. Abigail raised her hand. "She knows our plans, everyone. Let her finish."

Tiny lay down with a sigh.

"Thank you, Abigail. I know, you have every intention of setting up B&B's, but they also aren't ready yet.

"In any case, that will limit the size of weddings that can be put on here. And it's okay. This isn't going to be the place where the big, five-hundred-guest weddings take place. This isn't that kind of destination."

Mariah heard the rattle of a spoon on a teacup, and Tiny's eyes closed.

"So the idea I had was that instead of making Carter's Crossing a wedding destination, we make it a Center for Romance."

She paused, but the silence was complete.

"Not *just* weddings. Romantic getaways. A

place to come to make the perfect proposal. Anniversaries, vow renewals…and, also, weddings. In fact, if someone came here to propose, it could naturally lead to having the wedding here."

She could feel the attention focused on her.

"The benefits of this kind of plan include taking advantage of the four seasons' worth of beauty that Carter's Crossing offers. Most weddings are summertime events, but if we're a Center for Romance, we can have people here year-round, not just in the summer for a wedding.

"Another advantage is that we don't have to wait until the mill is ready to get things underway. What I'd like to propose is that we plan some events to happen on this upcoming Valentine's Day. Probably involving local people, considering the time and hospitality limits, but if we can get some publicity for this, then people will start looking at Carter's Crossing when they think of a place to go for a romantic getaway. We'll have the initial infrastructure here to support our plans, and we'll have some photos and experience already."

Mariah stopped. She hoped that was enough to get things rolling.

Heads turned now to Abigail. Tiny sat up and looked at Abigail, as well.

Abigail was smiling. "I think this idea is genius, but it will take all of us to make it work."

Heads started nodding, and voices murmured. Then the questions started.

"What kind of events? What would they require? What do we need to do?"

Mariah explained that without the B&Bs ready, they'd need to find romance among the people already in Carter's Crossing or surroundings. Mariah didn't know the area and didn't know the people. If they could find three events to stage for Valentine's Day, the whole package would be a manageable size, while still being large enough to attract attention.

Everyone loved the opportunity to assess the dating activity in town. Mariah heard the women discuss who was together, who'd broken up, who might be getting serious. She didn't know the names yet, but she would.

Mavis spoke up. "What about Gladys and Gord?"

Conversation ceased for a moment.

"It's their fiftieth wedding anniversary on Valentine's Day."

Mariah sat up straighter. "That would be wonderful. Celebrating that milestone would work beautifully. Do you know if they'd be interested in an anniversary party?"

Faces frowned at each other. "I don't know that Gord would want to pay for a big party. Now that the mill is closed—"

Abigail's clear voice spoke through the room. "These first events, for locals, are going to be paid for by the committee. Gord and Gladys won't have to pay for anything."

Eyes widened. Mavis said, "I'll talk to Gladys. I'll tell her we want her anniversary to be the first event for our plan, and then she won't think it's charity."

"Thank you, Mavis," Abigail said. "Now we just need two more romantic events."

"THAT WENT WELL," Abigail said as she and Mariah walked back to the Carter home. Fallen leaves crunched under their feet.

"I think the committee's offer to pay for the events helped a lot."

Abigail smiled. "It seems only fair. We need this to launch our plan, and we need local people to do that. Things have been difficult here, financially, so I—we don't want to make this a hardship."

Mariah looked at the woman walking beside her. She was coming to a better understanding of her partner in this endeavor.

"Tell me about this committee."

Abigail's eyebrows lifted. "That was the committee you just met."

"And what is their budget, so I know what we're spending on these events?"

Abigail shot her a sideways glance.

"I'm that part of the committee."

"And the budget is…" Mariah said.

Abigail shrugged elegantly. "What it needs to be."

Mariah shook her head. "You're investing a lot in this plan."

Abigail nodded. "I was raised to believe that the benefits my family gathered from the mill meant that we also had a responsibility to the town. I want to make sure Carter's Crossing survives."

Mariah wondered how much family pride was driving Abigail. This town was the Carter family's legacy.

"I had a thought," Abigail said. "What would you think, if this plan works, if we changed the name of the town to Cupid's Crossing?"

Mariah paused. "Could you—would you do that?"

Abigail nodded. "I could make it happen. I thought, along with the romance idea, if we had the name, and people could post letters, or use that address for events, it would help with the marketing."

"That sounds like an excellent idea."

Abigail nudged Mariah with her shoulder. "Together, we're going to hit this town so hard it won't know what's happened to it."

NELSON DRIED HIS hands and wandered back out to reception. Kailey and Judy were talking again. They paused when he came up to the desk, but at least they weren't looking guilty.

"Kailey, can you let the rescue people know they can pick up those two cats tomorrow? The usual after care. They should be ready for adoption within the week, just have a little bald spot."

Kailey made a note. "The rescue agency said to tell you they might have another horse needing help."

Nelson considered. "Any more details? I'm still getting the chestnut settled in, so if this one needs a lot of work, I'll have to change some fences at the farm."

Kailey shook her head. "No details, but I'll let you know once I hear. And, speaking of letting people know, why didn't you tell us the romance woman is staying with you?"

Nelson took a step back. "Hold on, no one

is staying with me. Are you talking about Mariah Van Delton? Is she what you call a romance woman?"

Here it was. Word had spread.

Kailey crossed her arms. "You did know. And if she's staying with your grandmother, that's almost as good as staying with you."

Nelson could see a lot of ways that anything going on with his grandmother and her home had nothing to do with him. He refused to stay in the house exactly for that kind of reason. He didn't want to know everything his grandmother was up to, and he certainly didn't want her to know that much about him.

If he hadn't been concerned about her, living alone in that big house and refusing anything like help, he wouldn't even be staying in the carriage house.

And Mariah Van Delton? He wanted to stay as far away from her as possible.

"Why did you call her the romance woman?" He'd been surprised not to hear about this crazy plan of Mariah and his grandmother's before this, and had half hoped that meant they'd reconsidered.

Kailey rolled her eyes and even Judy gave him a skeptical look.

"Are you really trying to tell us you don't know what's going on?"

Nelson shrugged. "I heard a bit—just a bit," he defended himself as Kailey's mouth opened. "And I hoped it would blow over."

Judy gave him a look of pity. "But you said…" Her voice trailed off. It was as much of a personal conversation as he'd had with her since he'd tried to convince them he wasn't a wounded misanthrope.

Apparently, it hadn't been that convincing.

"I'm all for romance, and love, and marriage, and kids, and the American dream, and whatever else. But I think emotional events are best left private."

Kailey turned to Judy. "Told you."

Nelson frowned. "Told you what?"

Kailey shrugged.

"I told Judy she should get Mariah to help her propose to Harvey on Valentine's Day."

"What?" Nelson had a hard time getting his brain wrapped around that. Judy was the quietest and shyest person he knew, so he couldn't picture her proposing. Especially not in an event engineered by Mariah. Because that event would be big and public and focus all kinds of attention on Judy.

"Yeah, I knew it was a long shot. But we need something for Mariah to set up for Valentine's Day. I've been married for years, so there's no chance for me."

"The Donaldsons are doing a vow renewal," Judy interrupted.

Nelson blinked. They were?

Kailey shook her head. "That's different. It's their fiftieth wedding anniversary on February fourteenth. Bert and I got married in June, and it's been seventeen years, so not a milestone."

Nelson could see his grandmother and her crew having their fingers all over the Donaldsons' anniversary. They'd probably talked the couple into it.

"Then there's the Valentine's Day event taken care of." That wasn't too bad. In fact, celebrating that major event was kind of nice.

Kailey shook her head. "We need two more events. We've been running through any couples in town who might be ready to celebrate something, and that's why I was nudging Judy."

Nelson looked at Judy, who was staring at the ground.

"I don't think Judy wants any nudging." Judy shook her head, so this time he figured he had it right.

Kailey sighed. "Okay. How about Dave and Jaycee?"

Nelson shook his head. "What Dave and Jaycee are doing is entirely up to Dave and

Jaycee. I don't think Dave wants to make a spectacle out of their relationship, so why don't we focus on the animals here in Carter's Crossing and leave my grandmother and Ms. Van Delton to worry about their—plans?" He'd almost said *nonsense*.

He wasn't sure about the looks the two women were giving him, even though Kailey had turned around to her computer and Judy was heading back to check on the two cats he'd just spayed for the animal rescue.

"And for the record, if Judy decides to propose to Harvey, I'd be happy to hear about it."

A slight exaggeration, but he didn't need to be handled with kid gloves.

"SO WHAT DO you think?" Dave asked Nelson.

Dave had stopped by the carriage house before they met for darts. He'd told Nelson he had a question for him.

Nelson was still processing the backstory to the question.

"You and Jaycee are that serious."

Dave rolled his eyes. "I told you that at darts last week."

"You said you were serious. You didn't say you were shopping for a ring."

A goofy grin crossed Dave's face. "When you know, you know."

Nelson considered. Dave and Jaycee had grown up here in Carter's, so they'd known each other since they were kids. He didn't think they'd been dating that long, but they'd been friends for years.

"Why not give her the ring some other time than Christmas?"

Dave shook his head. "We talked about it. We can't afford to spend a lot, so the ring is our Christmas present to each other."

"Then why are you asking if you need to get her something else?"

"Because I think she's going to get me something else, and then I'll look like a jerk if I didn't do the same."

Nelson wiped down his countertop. He'd just finished his dinner when Dave stopped by. The neatness he'd had to incorporate into his work spilled over into his personal life. He liked things clean and put away.

"Well, since the ring is a piece of jewelry that she wears, not you, that seems more like a present for her anyway. But if you really want to cover your bases, get her something."

Dave slapped a hand down on the freshly wiped countertop. "But if she didn't get me something, she's going to be mad. It'll make her look bad, and like I'm not listening to her."

Nelson nudged his hand away and rewiped the spot on the countertop.

"You didn't let me finish. You get her something, but don't put it under the tree. You keep it hidden away somewhere and pull it out if needed."

Dave frowned. "Okay, but what if she didn't get me anything? I return it? What if she finds out about that?"

It was a small town. News usually worked its way around.

Nelson lifted a finger. "No, you save it for the next time you're supposed to give her something. Like Valentine's Day."

Dave pumped his fist.

"Genius, man. You are a freaking genius."

Nelson thought of the work he'd done to get his veterinary degree. The animals he'd saved. And Dave was impressed with a bit of gift-giving chicanery. People were weird.

"THANKS FOR INVITING me to join you," Mariah said, looking at Jaycee driving the vehicle, and then Rachel in the back seat of Jaycee's car.

Jaycee shot a look at Rachel. Mariah held in a smile.

She'd been pleased when the two women had invited her to join them for darts night. There were a limited number of women her age in town, and fewer were single women. She'd been working hard, but it was nice to take a break.

Not to mention that she was good at darts. Darts were a staple at so many places around the globe.

The whole town was buzzing with the plans for Valentine's Day. And Jaycee was dating someone, so Mariah suspected Jaycee had a plan she wanted the Romance Committee to assist with.

It didn't hurt that Jaycee had long dark hair offset by golden skin and would look fantastic in promotional materials.

Mariah needed a couple more good events. Her grandfather had promised to provide publicity, if she gave him something worth publicizing. So far everyone who'd approached her wanted a romantic dinner or getaway. Which was fine, but not really the kind of big thing they needed to kick-start their plan for Carter's Crossing.

The vow renewal was sweet, but they also needed to appeal to a younger age demographic. A dinner date was nice, but currently, what Carter's Crossing had to offer along that line wasn't going to bring people in from the city.

She needed something big. Something splashy.

She hoped Jaycee had something more like that in mind.

"Go on, tell her," Rachel said to Jaycee.

"Okay, I hate feeling like I'm using you, but I am glad you're coming along with us tonight because this is the first time I've joined Dave and—"

"Jaycee, cut to the chase!" Rachel shoved Jaycee's shoulder.

"Dave and I are getting engaged this Christmas."

Mariah waited. A Christmas engagement was not a Valentine's Day event.

"We know we want to get married, but we don't have a lot of cash right now. We're getting the ring for Christmas—that's all we're doing for gifts, because we're saving up for a house, and the business..."

Rachel poked her friend again. "Come on, Jaycee. Get to the point. She doesn't need to know all these details right now."

Jaycee huffed a breath as she turned into the parking lot of a brightly lit pub called the Goat and Barley. She pulled the car into an open slot, and then turned to Mariah.

"We're doing everything low-key, because of money, but I would love to have a big engagement party, so that everyone knows. Our first date was on Valentine's Day. I wondered if the Romance Committee might make an engagement party one of their events."

Okay, this was much more what Mariah needed. If she and Abigail could come up with a big enough venue, they could probably get by without professional catering, if they found a good band, and made it mostly about the entertainment. Wait, what about a skating party? Bonfires, a dance…

She realized Jaycee and Rachel were waiting to hear her response.

"Sorry, guys, my brain started firing. This might be just what we need. Do you have anything in mind? Would you want to have the proposal then, too?"

Jaycee shook her head. "Nothing in mind, just having everyone come to celebrate. I don't think Dave's mom approves, so maybe a party will get her on board. And no, I'm not waiting a minute longer than I have to for that ring. If we could afford it now, I'd be wearing it already."

Mariah could believe it. Jaycee's smile, the glow in her dark eyes, the way her fingers were tapping on the steering wheel: everything said she was happy and excited and in love.

Rachel looked just as thrilled for her friend.

Mariah wanted to throw Jaycee and her fiancé a party. She wanted to give them a chance to enjoy themselves with the support of their community, especially if his family wasn't completely on board.

She held up one gloved hand. "It's not my decision alone. And there are things to work out. But it sounds like a great idea to me."

"Yay!" Jaycee and Rachel high-fived.

"Don't say anything till I've talked to Abigail, okay?"

Jaycee pouted. "I have to tell Dave."

Mariah frowned at her. "Can he keep a secret?"

"Of course he can."

Mariah wasn't reassured by the doubtful look on Rachel's face.

Before she could suggest leaving Dave out of the loop, Jaycee squealed. "There they are!"

She flung her door open and raced to meet her Dave. Mariah watched her as she threw herself into the arms of an attractive blond man who got out of the driver's side of a pickup truck, and then stopped, halfway out of the car.

Dave wasn't alone. And she knew the guy he was with.

Rachel spoke from behind her. "That's

Dave, in case you didn't guess. And you know Nelson, right? He's Abigail's grandson. You must have run into him at her place."

Mariah pasted on a smile. It became a lot more genuine when she saw Nelson spot her, and frown. Oh, this was going to be a fun night.

CHAPTER FOUR

THE FIVE OF them entered the Goat and Barley. They found a table, and Nelson avoided Mariah, sitting by Rachel. She nudged him with her shoulder.

"You playing darts?" She was holding back a grin, brown eyes sparkling.

Nelson had done complicated surgery on expensive thoroughbreds without making a wrong move, but he couldn't hit a bull's-eye to save himself. It didn't stop him from trying most nights.

Not tonight, though. He didn't need Mariah getting the best of him. Not when he was absolutely, one hundred percent certain she was a ringer. And no one else caught it.

He was certain when she shrugged and admitted she had played before, while not claiming any special skill. He was certain when Dave offered to play for the next round of drinks. He thought of warning Dave but decided to let him find out what Mariah was really like.

After this, Dave might listen to him if the time came to warn him about something more serious. He wished he'd had someone to talk to when he'd been up to his eyeballs in wedding plans. Someone other than Sherry Anstruthers.

Mariah and Rachel teamed up against Dave and Jaycee. Rachel was almost as bad as Nelson was, but Nelson still would have bet his money on that team. And he was right. Mariah was an ace.

Dave bought the next round when they returned to the table. He was laughing, and making Mariah promise to play with him against the Oak Hill guys.

Nelson was quiet, watching Mariah charm his friends.

Dave shot him glances, and Rachel poked him in the ribs, both concerned with his uncharacteristically quiet behavior. He ignored them and took a break to hit up the men's room.

He took his time, trying to work out a plan of action.

This engagement party had raised all his suspicions. Jaycee blurted out that Mariah was going to throw an engagement party for Dave and her as soon as they'd met in the parking lot.

Dave was obviously surprised by the news. Jaycee had never been much for big parties, so obviously this was Mariah's idea. She needed more events for her Valentine's Day plans, so she'd roped Jaycee into it. He didn't know how she'd done it, or what she'd promised, but he knew how bad things like that could get. He'd been through this before.

He wasn't sure what to say. He hadn't shared all the details about the disastrous end to his wedding, and he didn't want to do so now. But he'd have to explain his problem with Mariah. He could see the worry on his friends' faces.

His reticence had probably contributed to the town's belief that he was still wounded from his aborted wedding ceremony. The truth was that he hadn't wanted anyone to know what a jerk he'd been. He'd hoped to avoid that. Rachel was the only one who knew most of the details, and she still didn't understand.

Why did his grandmother have to decide to make the town a wedding destination—no, a romance destination?

He stopped at the bar to get the next round. Rachel slipped into the seat beside him, strands of her long brown hair falling from her ponytail.

"What's up, Nelson?"

He turned to her, waiting for their drinks.

"Is it the wedding planner thing? Too soon?"

He crossed his arms. He knew exactly what everyone believed the problem was. That he was upset because of Mariah's job. Well, he was, but not the way they thought.

"It's been three years, Rachel. I'm over it."

He could see she didn't believe him. "I'm over being upset about it. But what happened was the result of a bad decision I made, based on bad advice I got. And that bad advice I got was from Mariah's boss."

Rachel's mouth dropped.

"Does she, I mean, does your grandmother—"

"Grandmother thinks Mariah deserves a chance. But I'm a little...skeptical."

Rachel's brows lowered. "I'm sorry, Nelson. I had no idea. Would you rather leave now?"

Part of him did. But he couldn't tell Rachel he didn't want to leave Mariah alone with Dave and Jaycee. Even he could see that would sound a little...paranoid, at best.

But Rachel hadn't been through what he'd been through. He was the one who'd gotten too wrapped up in plans, and he was the one who'd been advised by Mariah's boss that he was right, and that Zoey just had nerves.

He hadn't understood that Sherry's primary interest wasn't in making their wedding day something they'd always look back on and remember with happiness and joy. Sherry had been interested in her fees, her reputation and impressing the next potential client.

Nelson had been stupid and had made the wrong decision. He'd made it because he'd put his goals ahead of what Zoey wanted and needed. He didn't exempt himself from that. But he'd trusted Sherry and relied on her advice, not his own instincts. He thought they both bore blame.

He didn't think every wedding planner was evil. He wasn't that stupid. But he knew, absolutely, that Sherry was selfish and greedy. He'd heard Mariah say she'd learned everything from that same Sherry.

His grandmother thought Mariah deserved a chance. Nelson wasn't sure he agreed, but he'd promised not to interfere. And he wouldn't, unless Mariah's schemes were going to hurt people he cared about.

He finally told Rachel he was happy to stay. When she looked skeptical, he explained, "I need to do this, Rach. It's come to my attention that the people in this town think I missed that last wedding because I couldn't face it, not that Sparky really had colic."

Rachel looked guilty, and he shook his head.

"You, too? My horse was sick. I swear. But if I run away every time Mariah is around, those rumors are going to continue. I don't like her, but I'm not afraid of her. I'll stay and hang out with my friends."

Rachel chewed on her lip, but she didn't get a chance to respond before their drinks were slapped down on the bar top.

Nelson led the way back to their table, happy to see that Mariah had vanished.

It was too much to hope that she'd left, but at least he could enjoy his friends' company without her. Then he saw who she was talking to.

Harvey. Judy's Harvey.

It was a small town, but couldn't she insert herself into the life of someone other than the people he hung out with and worked with? Was it too much to ask?

MARIAH WASN'T SURPRISED when a stranger asked if he could talk to her. It hadn't taken long to discover that she was known to everyone, and everyone knew why she was there.

This time the young man, named Harvey,

had a good idea for her. He wasn't the first to approach her, but his idea was one she could work with.

She sympathized with the many people who'd been undergoing financial hardship and wanted to take their partners out for a dinner on Valentine's Day, but that wasn't what they needed right now as a Valentine's promotion.

She let Abigail know about all these requests, and each time she could see Abigail take that responsibility on her own shoulders. Mariah was impressed by how hard Abigail was working to keep the town alive. And Mariah wanted to help. She was learning to like these people.

She caught a glare from Nelson.

Most of these people.

She wanted this romance plan to work, and to bring life and prosperity back to Carter's Crossing. She needed something better than a dinner out to promote the town. And Harvey had something better.

He wanted to propose to his girlfriend.

These days people didn't just go down on one knee or have a ring show up in a dessert to ask someone to marry them. Proposals had become elaborate, complicated and sometimes expensive. And often went viral.

A proposal that took advantage of what Carter's Crossing had to offer, things that other places didn't, was exactly the kind of event she needed.

Mariah didn't remember hearing about a Harvey when the committee had gone over the dating prospects in town, so she wasn't sure if she'd missed it, or this was one they didn't know about. In any case, she'd happily help Harvey with his proposal.

As always, she cautioned, "It's not just my decision in this. But it sounds really promising. I'd have to get approval, but assuming I did—"

Harvey had an anxious look on his face. "I want to surprise her. I don't want her to hear about it from someone else."

Mariah nodded. It was a valid concern, from her short experience in Carter's Crossing.

"I'll just talk to Abigail for now. But I can't approve this on my own."

"It's okay if Mrs. Carter knows. She'll be careful. But a lot of people talk in this town."

That was the truth.

"Assuming this all works out, what kind of proposal were you thinking of?"

Harvey chewed on a cuticle.

"I want something special. I want her to be

able to tell all her friends about it. I want to show her that she's special."

That was sweet. And perfect.

"Why don't you tell me about her, what makes her so special and what it is that's special between the two of you? What you have in common that other people don't? We want it to be something unique, but also something she loves."

"Sure." Harvey stopped chewing. "Her name is Judy, and she's beautiful. She works at the veterinary clinic."

Mariah closed her eyes. No. Way. Another chance to bump into Nelson Carter? The man made a face like he'd sucked on lemons every time he saw her.

It was annoying. And provoking. And puzzling.

She'd decided she should avoid him as much as possible. And now she had two events that were going to impinge on him. She'd noticed his reaction when Jaycee blurted out about the engagement party. It hadn't exactly been a happy face.

And now a proposal for someone who worked for Nelson. Was this town really that small?

Harvey had stopped.

"Sorry, you were saying Judy works at the vet clinic?"

He nodded. "She's wonderful with animals. Loves them all, and they love her. She can't have a pet at home, because her sister is allergic, but once we get married, we can buy a house and have as many animals as she wants."

Harvey might not be the handsomest man in Carter's Crossing, but he was in the running for sweetest, Mariah thought.

"So are animals the bond that brought you together?"

His eyes widened. "Oh, no. Not that. We're both big fans of *The Walking Dead*. We love that show. We dress up for Halloween, and go to cons together…in fact, that's what I'd like to have for the proposal. Can we do a *Walking Dead* one?"

Mariah blinked, and blinked again. A zombie proposal.

Yeah, that wasn't what she'd been expecting.

THE PROBLEM WITH small towns was that avoiding someone was almost impossible. Well, there were other problems, but this was the one troubling him now. In theory, a wedding or romance planner and a vet shouldn't cross paths often. But the odds were not shaking out in his favor.

It didn't help that his grandmother still expected him to join her for dinners that were no longer for two, but three. He would have liked to avoid them, but as much as he didn't like spending time with Mariah, he still wanted to know what she was up to, and who might be in the path of her impending explosions.

Not that it was much of a secret.

"Nelson." His grandmother caught his attention at the next dinner. Beef bourguignonne. Another dish he liked. Another one he couldn't properly enjoy with Mariah at the table. But he was eating it anyway.

"Yes, Grandmother?" She couldn't complain about him having a tantrum. He was eating, and he wasn't staring at Mariah. At least, not once he realized he was doing it.

"I'm not asking for your assistance, or involvement, but you are aware that Dave and Jaycee have asked to have an engagement party this Valentine's Day?"

He took a moment to make sure his voice was even.

"I heard that their engagement was being considered for one of your parties, yes."

Mariah narrowed her eyes at him. "It was Jaycee's suggestion."

Nelson believed that the words had come from Jaycee, but he had suspicions as to where the idea had come from. Since it wasn't a question, he didn't respond.

"I had no idea their first date had been on Valentine's Day," Mariah continued, glaring at him with a laser focus. Was she reading his mind? No, or she'd be throwing something at him.

Grandmother interrupted the one-sided argument.

"As Dave's friend, we need to know if you're attending, and if you have any suggestions, or comments to offer. This is obviously not an endorsement of my plans," she added, the sarcasm unmistakable, "but it would be appreciated so that we can make this event something that they will both enjoy and remember."

Nelson heard the challenge. She'd said she wouldn't involve him, but it was an empty promise. In a town this small, people he knew would be part of the *Romance Lives in Carter's* thing she and Mariah had going. He couldn't boycott everything they did without hurting people he cared about and who cared about him.

And even if he'd wanted to avoid any event they came up with, he couldn't, because the town already believed he was still scarred from his own aborted wedding. He'd promised himself he wouldn't avoid the next wedding-type get-together.

With jaw gritted, he forced a smile. "Dave is my friend, and if he invites me to his party, of course I'll be there. As far as the event itself, Dave and Jaycee are small-town people. Our events are usually small-town, as well."

Mariah rolled her eyes. Grandmother stared at him under lowered brows.

What did they expect? It's not like he and Dave had ever discussed their dream engagement parties. He was willing to bet all the money his grandmother was investing in this project that Dave didn't have a Pinterest board on the topic.

"Those kinds of events aren't going to keep this town alive, Nelson."

He understood, but he didn't believe their town was going to survive big wedding plans, either.

He wasn't going to bring that up again. He and Grandmother had agreed to disagree.

Nelson had managed to finish his plate, so he stood.

"Dave and I play baseball in the summer, watch hockey in the winter, and drink beers and play darts on Tuesday nights. He doesn't like dressing up, and he hates broccoli. That's all I've got for you, so I'll clean up after myself and let the two of you get to work."

An hour later he was at his farm. The horses had all come into the indoor pen for the night, since temperatures were dropping. He checked that the barn was warm enough and fed them some hay. He noticed that the new chestnut stayed inside while Nelson was in the building now but wouldn't come to get any of the food while he was leaning on the rail.

He stayed where he was. The new guy needed to learn. His frustration with Mariah and his grandmother melted away as he watched his horses.

Sparky was the oldest, and needed the most attention to his physical care, but the chestnut was the most vulnerable right now. Nelson wanted to give him time with a nonaggressive human nearby, letting him know that not all people were bad, and not all of them would hurt him.

He watched his horses eat, rubbed necks and muzzles as they were offered and let the calm and quiet work on his perspective.

One party was not going to destroy the town, or his friends. He'd let Dave know he should feel free to refuse anything that made him uncomfortable. That would take care of him.

Maybe it was time for him to start working on the house here at the farm. If Mariah was living with Grandmother, he didn't need to stay so close. Maybe space would be good for both of them.

He thought he'd made over his life for the better, here in Carter's Crossing. He'd pulled back on his competitive, take-charge side, and found a life beyond his practice. But ever since Mariah Van Delton had stopped in his parking lot, things had gotten complicated.

He wished she really had been lost.

THE NEXT TUESDAY night it was an all-guy dart night, and Nelson was careful not to let on how much that pleased him.

"Did the girls not like playing darts?"

He didn't know why they wouldn't. Thanks to Mariah, the girls beat every comer.

Dave shrugged. "I don't quite get it. Jaycee had wanted to come for weeks, and now all she wants to do is plan this party."

Nelson straightened up. This was his cue.

"Are you sure you want to have this party?" Okay, he'd promised his grandmother he'd stay out of it, but she'd asked him for advice on what Dave liked, so he decided that gave him wiggle room. Maybe what Dave liked was to not have a party.

Dave shrugged. "It was Jaycee's idea, but I'm happy if she is."

"Are you sure?"

Dave gave him a puzzled look. "What do you mean?"

"I wondered if Grandmother and…Mariah had the idea first."

Dave frowned. "I'm not sure. I first heard about it from Jaycee, last week, when we got here. You heard her."

Nelson swallowed some skeptical, and impolite, words. "You don't have to do this if you don't want to, you know."

Dave speared an onion ring. "I don't care, myself. But Jaycee is pretty excited about it."

"Really?" Jaycee had always been a practical, down-to-earth type of person.

Dave nodded, and swallowed. "She thinks it will help my mother come around."

Nelson paused in midreach for his own onion ring.

"Your mother? What's she got to do with it?"

"Jaycee doesn't think Mom likes her."

That surprised Nelson. Jaycee was hardworking, kind and pretty. Watching her with Dave last week had convinced him that the two truly cared for each other.

"Why wouldn't your mom like her?"

Dave's cheeks flushed. "Jaycee has a point. Mom has never gotten over when I dated your sister."

Nelson glared at his friend. "That was junior year of high school, and you swore nothing happened."

It was the single incident that almost ended their friendship. When Dave told Nelson he wanted to ask Delaney out, Nelson almost hit him. Well, once he got over the shock that anyone wanted to date his sister. That shock dealt with, he wanted to wrap her up and keep all guys away from her.

After the short dating event with Dave, Nelson had had to clue in. His sister was a lot prettier than he'd realized, and someone else had wanted to go out with her not long after Dave took her out. Then he and Dave united in trying to keep her safe. Safely single.

He thought Dave was long over that. His sister hadn't been back to Carter's for anything more than a flying visit in years.

Dave held up two fingers. "Nothing happened, scout's honor. But Mom seems to think that something might yet. Jaycee thinks Mom likes the idea of being connected to the Carters."

Nelson almost choked on the beer he'd swallowed.

"Is your mom crazy?"

Yes, Abigail was awesome, but she could focus that awesome on someone in uncomfortable ways. And the rest of them? His parents were working in—was it Azerbaijan now?—and his sister was totally a city girl. His aunts and uncles and cousins had all moved away.

Dave screwed up his lips. "Possibly. Jaycee says in Mom's eyes she's still from the wrong side of the tracks."

"That's messed up, if your mom thinks so." Nelson had friends from both sides of the literal train tracks in town, and the side of the tracks had nothing to do with the character of the resident.

Dave nodded. "I know. I think Jaycee is overreacting, but Mom does like your sister, and tells me everything she hears about her. I figure, if the party makes Jaycee happy, I'll do it. She's promised they'll do all the planning, and I just have to show up."

Those words sounded familiar to Nelson.

Dave bumped his arm. "You'll come, right?"

"Of course," Nelson agreed. "Unless I get a call—"

Dave's brows came down. "You'd better be

there, or I want pictures to prove something was wrong with your horse. I don't want to go through this alone."

Nelson remembered his own engagement party. And to his shame, he remembered how little of it he'd spent with his fiancée.

"I'll be there, unless an animal is dying. And you can come with me for proof if I get a call."

MARIAH SAT DOWN across from Abigail Carter. They each had a notebook, and Mariah had her laptop open. This was business.

"So, Jaycee and Rachel and I sat down and did some brainstorming last night."

Abigail nodded. "You came up with something promising, right?"

Mariah tapped a pen on her notepad, which was covered in scribbles.

"I think so. Can you assure me that the mill stream will be frozen solid by mid-February?"

Abigail stared past her. It took her a minute to respond.

"I can remember only two years where the stream didn't freeze. And I remember a long way back. I'd say there's probably a ninety-five percent certainty that the water will be frozen. It's not too deep there, so it freezes more quickly than south of town."

Mariah bit her lip. "Then we'll need a plan B, but I'm hoping a skating party will work."

Abigail sat back. "A skating party. I didn't expect that."

"We want to invite most of the town. We can't do an event for everyone who asks, but almost everyone can come to this. Jaycee and Dave know a lot of people, and since we're going to use this to promote Carter's Crossing, we need to show something big. We want the whole town to feel a part of this. Jaycee is on board for that.

"Since we don't have a big indoor facility—"

"Not yet," Abigail said.

"A skating party would be a good outdoor event. If we do it at the mill, we can stage everything there, and if needed, provide indoor space. The stream is beautiful, and we can do it up with lights and music. There's enough potential ice space to have more than one 'rink,' so different ages and skill levels can be separated."

"Lights. An evening event?"

"Afternoon-to-evening event, but days are short here in winter, and we don't want things to look dark. We don't have the facilities to provide full catering, but we could have hot chocolate and cider, fire pits to cook s'mores and hot dogs on sticks and, of course, some champagne to toast the happy couple. Then there are the practical things to think of, like heaters and Porta-Potties."

"A skating party seems very retro, kind of Norman Rockwell."

Mariah nodded. "That's something we can make the most of about the town. With the older homes, the lack of chain stores and restaurants, we need to focus on what makes this place special. I think the skating party works for that, and Jaycee assures me she and Dave can skate. She's even considering a skate/dance for the two of them to their song."

"What's their song?" Abigail asked.

Mariah bit back a grin. "Jaycee is still deciding on that."

"I thought songs were supposed to arise spontaneously from a particular moment."

"Jaycee is going to make the moment happen."

Abigail smiled. "I do like that girl. It's a wonderful idea, and we should be able to pull it off. Let me know what you need, and I'll get the committee working on it."

Mariah looked down. "I'll take the notes we made last night and work them up. Then we can discuss with the committee what we can do, and when."

Abigail ticked off a line on her own notebook.

"Now, about this proposal you mentioned."

Mariah crossed her arms. "This one is a little more difficult. Harvey wants to use a *Walking Dead* theme."

Abigail tilted her head. "Excuse me?"

"Apparently, he and Judy are big fans of the TV show. It's what brought them together, so he wants to use that in the proposal."

"I'm not familiar with this particular show. What's it about?" Abigail had a wary look on her face.

Mariah screwed up her nose. "Why don't I play the first episode for you?"

Abigail came around the table to sit beside her while Mariah moved her cursor until she found where she'd located the pilot episode.

Mariah had never dreamed that setting up Carter's Crossing as Cupid's Crossing would entail watching a zombie show with Abigail Carter.

She hit Play and waited to see how Abigail would respond.

She was quiet until the credits rolled.

"No."

Mariah had been racking her brain for

ideas for a zombie proposal. Trying to make it suitable for Valentine's Day, rather than Halloween, had been a challenge. She hadn't expected Abigail to have much in the way of ideas for the proposal, but she hadn't expected a no, either.

"No, we aren't doing the proposal?" Mariah wanted it clarified. A proposal on Valentine's Day was a truly romantic event. But the zombie part was trouble.

"No, we aren't doing a zombie proposal."

Mariah opened her mouth, but Abigail continued before she could interrupt.

"I know Judy. She and Harvey may love that television show, but Judy does not want dead people proposing to her. I know a couple of young women who would enjoy something a little shocking for an event like that, but Judy is not one of them."

Mariah blinked. She'd been assuming Harvey knew what his fiancée wanted, but Abigail could be right.

"If Harvey believes this is what Judy wants, and he wants to surprise her, how do we check out what Judy really does want? Does she have a close friend we could ask who could keep the secret?"

Abigail considered, and shook her head.

"I wouldn't trust her sisters, and she doesn't

have a lot of friends. She's very reserved. Harvey is a good match for her, but he is not a man of imagination."

Mariah tapped her notebook again. She had to question Abigail's statement, because a zombie proposal sounded like something that required a lot of imagination, maybe more than Mariah had.

She wanted to make this proposal work, but she didn't know how. Normally, she just asked her client. She'd never planned a proposal before where she was in the dark as to what the askee liked.

"Her mother?"

Abigail shook her head. "Kailey is our best bet."

"Kailey?"

"Kailey works with Judy at Nelson's clinic. Kailey is older and settled and can keep a secret. And most important, she has access to Judy forty hours a week. If Kailey can't get the information out of her, I don't know anyone who can."

Abigail frowned, and Mariah could imagine the planning going on in that well-coiffed head.

"It would be best if you took Kailey out for lunch. She's busy outside work with three kids and a husband to take care of. Nelson's staff gets an hour for lunch."

Abigail smiled at Mariah. Mariah smiled back, less happily.

Nelson avoided her, and barely talked to her when he couldn't. Mariah knew there was a story there, but Abigail wouldn't tell her, and Nelson never hung around long enough for her to ask him again. Even if she asked, she couldn't imagine him telling her.

She did her best to keep away from him. She didn't want to stir up any more animosity. Abigail swore he wouldn't get in the way, but Mariah was learning how impossible it was, in a town this size, to avoid someone.

He was going to flip when he found out she was spending time with one of his employees. And she could imagine no scenario in which he didn't find out.

CHAPTER FIVE

He didn't just find out, he was standing in the reception area, wearing those blue scrubs again, when she walked in to meet Kailey.

There were two women there. One improbable redhead with a matronly figure and an air of confidence. The other a petite blonde who appeared to want to blend into the woodwork.

Mariah knew the older of the two was her lunch date, but even if she hadn't been able to figure that out, Kailey had a coat on over her own scrubs.

The blonde must be Judy.

Doing her best to ignore Nelson while greeting Kailey and trying to study Judy was difficult. More like impossible. Mariah's eyes started to cross.

"Mariah?" Nelson asked, surprise in his voice.

"I told you I was going out to lunch, Nelson." Kailey's tone told him she was taking no flack.

"But I thought you were meeting Bert."

"You obviously thought wrong, Nelson. I'm having lunch with Mariah. I won't introduce you, since you two live together."

"We don't—" Both Mariah and Nelson reacted to that statement, but Kailey ignored them.

"And this is Judy, Mariah." Mariah smiled at the younger woman, who looked down at her feet.

"Kailey…" Nelson spoke in a warning voice.

"Nelson…" Kailey echoed.

"Are you getting involved in something you shouldn't?" Nelson looked at Judy, and back at Kailey.

Did Nelson know what was going on? Mariah expected a full-on hissy fit.

Kailey put her hands on her hips. "Nelson, I'm your receptionist, not your daughter. You can tell me what to do while I'm behind that desk, but you need to ask nicely, and you stop when I walk out those doors."

She pointed at Nelson.

"And you'd better not think I would do anything to hurt or embarrass my friends."

A confused look passed over his face.

"Then why…?" he started.

Kailey marched to the door. "I'm walking out the door, Nelson. Time's up!"

Mariah followed Kailey out the door with a glance back. Kailey had just rocketed up the list of people she liked. She understood now the confidence Abigail had in Kailey.

"ABIGAIL SAID YOU had something to talk to me about."

Kailey had waited only till they were safely in the car and the engine on.

"Don't tell me my Bert wants to do something romantic."

Mariah choked out a laugh. "I haven't met your Bert yet."

Kailey wasn't upset. "I'd have to send him for a medical checkup if he had. Bert is a wonderful husband, but he doesn't have a romantic bone in his body."

Mariah didn't know how to respond to that.

"It's okay, though, because I don't, either. Romantic doesn't pay the mortgage or feed the kids."

"Oh." Since Mariah's whole purpose in Carter's Crossing was to focus attention on romance, she wasn't sure that Kailey was the right person to help her.

"But I can enjoy other people being romantic, and I absolutely want this plan to work in Carter's. I love this town, and I want my kids to have the option to stay here. So how can I help you?"

Mariah pulled into a parking slot in front of the diner.

"It's about Judy."

"Please tell me she called you to ask for help proposing to Harvey." Kailey's face had lit up.

Mariah shook her head. "No, it was actually Harvey."

Kailey burst out laughing. "Let's go in and order some food. Then I'll tell you why that's funny."

Once they'd ordered and were on their own, Kailey explained how she'd suggested Judy propose as one of the events for Valentine's Day.

"Do you think she wants to marry Harvey?" Mariah asked.

"Oh, definitely. But she's too shy to ask him herself. And I think she'd like a more conventional proposal, with Harvey asking the question, not her, so this works out perfectly."

Mariah sighed. "About that. Harvey suggested a *Walking Dead* proposal."

Kailey looked shocked. "What in the—oh, you mean, the TV show?"

Mariah nodded. Kailey shook her head.

"No, I don't think that's what Judy would want. She might like that show, but she also reads a lot of romance novels."

Mariah relaxed. "Okay, that's good to hear. Abigail has already vetoed the zombie proposal. Can you tell me what she would like?"

Kailey gave a nod. "That's what this is about, then."

"I need someone who can tell me what Judy likes, what would make this a proposal she'd enjoy and remember, and it has to be a secret."

Kailey held up a hand. A moment later the waitress put their plates in front of them.

"Anything else?" the woman asked.

"We're good, thanks."

After she left, Kailey leaned forward. "I'll keep it quiet, no problem. I don't know the answers right now, but I can find out."

Mariah picked up her fork. "And she won't figure out what you're doing?"

Kailey grinned. "I can use the excitement over Jaycee and Dave's party to draw her out. The girl is not a big talker, so she's used to me asking her a lot of questions."

Mariah chewed, and then asked, "Will she be okay with something public like this? If she's that shy?" Everyone mentioned that Judy was quiet and shy, and Mariah didn't want to embarrass her. She never wanted to do that to someone, and in this case, when they were trying to get publicity for Carter's Crossing, a disastrous event would be worse than no event.

Kailey considered. "If it's romantic enough, I think she'll be fine. Nothing embarrassing, but I know she wants to marry Harvey, and I think she'll feel special knowing he went to this much trouble to make it memorable for her."

"That sounds good. But I need to ask, is Nelson going to be a problem?"

Kailey picked up a forkful of her dish. "He's got a bit of a thing about weddings, of course, but don't worry, I can handle Nelson."

Mariah wished she could say the same.

NELSON WAS RELIEVED that Mariah didn't stay in town for the holidays. Grandmother asked her, while the three were dining *à trois*, what her plans were for Thanksgiving.

Nelson had closed his eyes, bracing himself to hear that she would be part of their celebration. But Mariah was returning to New York. She'd spend the holiday weekend with her own family, whatever members weren't sailing around the planet somewhere, and update her grandfather on the plans for Valentine's Day in Carter's Crossing.

Nelson didn't ask for details on those.

He spent his own holiday with Grandmother and an assortment of the town orphans; mostly elderly women who would otherwise spend the day alone. Nelson would deny it with his dying breath, but he kinda liked these get-togethers. The women fussed over him, and while he'd hate that on a constant basis, once in a long while it was nice.

And after dinner his grandmother would relax, and he'd hear the stories she'd rather he not know.

Like now.

"So have you heard any more from Gerry?" Mavis Grisham had asked. Fortunately, she'd left Tiny behind. Tiny had once embarrassed himself with the turkey, so he was no longer invited to holiday dinners.

Nelson almost asked who Gerry was, but bit his tongue. If the women forgot about him, they were much more revealing.

Grandmother shook her head. "No, Mariah usually talks to him."

Ah, right. Mariah's grandfather. He'd forgotten.

"Does she know about...you know, you and him?"

Oh, this was getting good. Grandmother had a history with Mariah's grandfather? That would explain the man's willingness to help. Or would it?

"I don't know what she knows. I haven't told her anything."

"Do you have any regrets? Wonder what would have happened if you'd made different decisions?"

Nelson didn't intend it, but surprise had him dropping the fork in his hand.

Six pairs of eyes swiveled in his direction, all with accusing looks.

That wasn't fair. It wasn't as if he'd sneaked in to eavesdrop. They'd just forgotten about him.

"Are you done with your pie, Nelson?"

From the tight-lipped expressions he saw aimed his way, he wasn't hearing any more tonight.

He nodded. "I should probably head out now. Thank you all so much for a lovely day and a wonderful dinner. Happy Thanksgiving!"

He left cheerfully, but determined to return in the morning and ask his grandmother some questions. Mariah Van Delton was stirring things up in Carter's Crossing, and it appeared that part of that was a result of a past relationship between Abigail Carter and Gerry Van Delton. He thought he had the right to know more about this thing that was causing him stress.

Plus, he was curious. Who knew his grandmother had a past?

Scratch that. Abigail Carter was exactly the kind of woman who would have a past.

HE WAS IN the kitchen making coffee when his grandmother came downstairs the next morning.

"Good morning, Nelson. You're up early."

He passed her a cup, made the way she liked it.

"I wanted to catch you before you got busy."

Her eyebrows arched. "Oh, really?" There was amusement in her voice.

"I didn't know you and Mr. Van Delton had known each other, romantically. I was curious."

Abigail stared at him for a moment. Nelson knew she would only tell him what she wanted, and he didn't have a lot of leverage to try to change her mind. He'd hoped she'd be less discreet before she had an injection of caffeine.

"Gerry and I dated in college."

"Was it serious?" he asked, intrigued by the idea of his grandmother with a slew of boyfriends. He'd seen pictures of her when she was young. She'd been beautiful. Still was.

She nodded. Her gaze drifted over his shoulder, her mind obviously in the past.

"I had two serious suitors, Gerry and your grandfather. My father wanted my husband to take the Carter name and settle here, in Carter's Crossing. Take over the management of the mill."

Nelson knew his grandfather had done just that.

"Gerry didn't want to do that?"

She shook her head.

"What did you want?"

He was intrigued by the image of a young Abigail, torn between the two men. He knew the Van Deltons had businesses in New York. They were wealthy on a big scale. He could easily picture Abigail there, attending galas and running charities.

Had she wanted that, all those years ago? Had she chosen duty?

"I wanted someone who loved me enough to put me first. Your grandfather did that. Gerry did not."

Her gaze focused again, and she looked at him.

"I don't regret the choices I made. But I do wonder if Gerry does."

"Why?"

"He's been divorced twice and is single now. Mariah's father is estranged from him, and I'm not sure how close he is to his daughters. Mariah hardly knows him."

Nelson suspected there was a tinge of satisfaction in his grandmother's voice.

His grandmother was not sweet and shy. She was strong and proud, willing to make hard choices and stand by the consequences. She would not like being someone's second choice.

Interesting. If, or when, the two of them met up again…

Nelson stopped himself.

He was not getting involved. He didn't want Mariah here. He didn't want her grandfather here, either.

"I'm going to check on the horses. Is there anything you need me to do for you?"

Abigail shook her head. "No, I've got everything under control."

He wished he could say the same.

NEW YORK WAS an adjustment.

It had been an adjustment when she'd first left the boat and settled in Richmond, Virginia. A home that stayed still, all the time. People, always around. More noise, pollution and people. After living in a relatively small space with five people, she was alone, in the midst of many.

New York took that to an exponential degree. Especially after months in Carter's Crossing. The crowds, the noise, the smell—it was all an assault on her senses.

Then there was her grandfather's home.

Abigail's house was large, beautiful and certainly not crowded with just the two of them living there. But her grandfather's house was larger, had more expensive furnishings and felt emptier, despite the live-in servants.

Her grandfather was very wealthy. He was also, she suspected, lonely.

He still put in long hours at work; he wasn't home when she arrived, and she didn't see him till the next day. Of his three children, none of his relationships were close.

Her father was his only son. The last she'd talked to her parents, they were in Indonesia. She wasn't sure her grandfather knew what country they were in. Her dad rarely spoke to his father.

The breach had happened before Mariah was born. Her dad had wanted to marry her mother, buy a boat and sail the world, giving up on the business life her grandfather had groomed him for. Her dad was tired of the long hours, constant phone and email demands, and had fallen in love with her mother and with the ocean.

Her grandfather had not taken it well. He told her father that the only way he could touch his trust fund was if his son promised he would never marry the woman his father considered to be scheming for a rich husband.

Her father had given his promise to never marry her mother. He got his trust fund money, used it to buy the boat and sail away with her mother. To this day, her parents weren't married.

Over the years that heated anger had dissipated, giving way to cold hurt. Her grandfather had apologized and retracted the promise he'd forced. Her father hadn't. Her dad kept in touch with his parents, but as acquaintances, not family. He hadn't forgiven.

As she grew up, Mariah discovered how much it hurt her mother that her father wouldn't marry her. Her mother hadn't forgiven her grandfather, either.

Not a happy family. She had two paternal aunts. One had broken off all contact with Gerald. The other had married another wealthy businessman and was now divorced.

She relied on her father for financial support. Her son worked for the company. He was presumably the heir apparent. Her cousin and aunt both suspected Mariah wanted to supplant him.

Mariah recognized both the strengths and flaws Gerald possessed. While she didn't want the life her parents had, she didn't want the life her grandfather had, either. She wanted something that fell between those two extremes.

She wanted a simpler life than her grandfather's, with family and friends. She wanted friends and neighbors who stayed put. She'd been lonely growing up, making friends only to have them leave, or to leave them behind as her parents continued their wandering life.

She wanted a position with her grandfather's company that she'd earned, that she could count on, and a place here in New York, where she would never feel lonely and left behind.

She knew she wasn't going to find it in her grandfather's house. But she would get her own place, settle down and grow roots that would never be dug up.

This had been her plan for the past five years. She'd spent them in Richmond, learning how to plan events, how to make sure things ran well and got done. The opportunities that opened for her had been in wedding planning, but she didn't want to be limited to that.

She'd done this on her own. She hadn't asked her grandfather for a handout. He'd respected that.

This fall he'd given her an offer. If she'd work in Carter's Crossing for a year, making it a successful wedding destination, he'd give her a partnership in his event-planning company.

As much as she knew his faults, and how he'd hurt her parents, she also understood he wanted to do better. He just didn't know how.

The family, those in the city and still on good terms with her grandfather, gathered for an elaborate Thanksgiving dinner in the formal dining room.

It was a small party. Her grandfather, her aunt Genevieve and her cousin, Pierre. Mariah had prepared herself for a long, dull dinner. With the suspicions Aunt Genevieve and Pierre harbored, she didn't want to talk about anything related to business at dinner, and there was nothing she had in common with them. Tomorrow she should be able to talk to her grandfather about Carter's, and she could wait for that.

Her grandfather hugged her, with warmth,

her cousin kissed her cheek formally and her aunt gave her a languid wave. They took their seats around the table, well spaced, even though the additional leaves weren't in. A typical family gathering for the Van Deltons.

The staff brought in the first course. Aunt Genevieve opened the conversation with complaints about her housekeeper, and a problem at the last charity ball. Mariah was quiet. She didn't have a housekeeper, didn't want one, and was more interested in planning a ball than attending.

Her aunt would think she was crazy.

Pierre interrupted to bring up some issue at work.

"We can discuss that at work, Pierre. This is a holiday. I want to hear how Mariah has been enjoying small-town life."

Her grandfather smiled at her, and it was sincere. Pierre frowned, slightly, and Aunt Genevieve didn't pretend to have any interest.

Mariah smiled back at her grandfather. "It's been interesting. It's much different than here, or even Richmond, but I've enjoyed the people I've met."

"How is Abigail?"

"Who's Abigail?" Pierre asked, his voice suspicious. It must be exhausting to be looking for competitors everywhere.

"Abigail is an old friend from college," Gerald answered, attention still focused on Mariah. Pierre relaxed and looked bored.

"Abigail is a force of nature." Mariah noticed how intently her grandfather was listening.

"She always was."

"Her husband died while her children were still young, and she took over responsibility for the mill and her family then. It's part of the town lore."

Her grandfather nodded. "I'm not surprised she finally had to close her mill. Lumber isn't the same business anymore. Cheap imports, protective tariffs—I knew she wouldn't be able to maintain it."

Mariah wondered if he'd been keeping track of Abigail.

"I'll tell you tomorrow how the wedding/romance event plan is going, but I find it hard to believe it could fail with Abigail involved."

Gerald nodded. "I wanted her to come to New York, back when we were in school together."

Pierre almost choked on his food. That brought his mother's attention back to the conversation.

"What did you want that for?" Pierre asked.

Gerald shot him a glance. "I wanted to marry her. She'd have excelled here."

Genevieve's eyes widened. "What?"

Her grandfather had a twinkle in his eye, one that Genevieve and Pierre missed. Mariah watched him warily, not sure what mischief he was up to.

"What do you think, Mariah? You know her now. Wouldn't Abigail have taken to New York?"

Mariah shook her head. Her grandfather might be playing with her aunt and cousin, but she was going to give an honest answer.

"She has an absolute loyalty to Carter's Crossing. To her, it's not an obligation, but her calling. She's determined to make the town a success, somehow, by sheer force of will if nothing else. If anyone can do it, she can. But she has control there. I'm not sure New York, with all the competition, would suit her."

Genevieve nodded. "Someone from a little town in the middle of nowhere wouldn't know what to do here. It would be a disaster."

She shot a worried glance at her father. Mariah suspected her aunt lived in dread of a third marriage.

"Abigail would play this town like a fiddle. Wouldn't she, Mariah?"

He was definitely stirring up trouble. But was that all he was doing?

"She could, I'm sure. But she wouldn't want to deal with the…the pettiness. The jostling for status. She's happy where she is, able to run things as she likes.

"At least, that's what I think. But who knows?" Mariah shrugged.

Her grandfather had his head tilted, considering her words.

"You think she's happy where she is?"

Mariah suspected he was more invested in his question than she was comfortable taking responsibility for.

"She appears to be. But I'm not sure anyone would know if she wasn't."

Her grandfather let the topic of Abigail Carter drop, but she was sure her aunt had added Abigail to her list of worries.

The next day Mariah finally had a chance to sit down and talk with her grandfather about what she was doing in Carter's Crossing.

"You're exactly right, Mariah. The lack of rooms for out-of-town guests will limit the size of any events, no matter how many B&Bs they come up with. Not everyone wants to stay in someone's home. Is there any other space that could function as a hotel? I might be willing to invest in that."

Mariah blossomed in his praise.

"Abigail's house would make a lovely small hotel, but I don't think she'd consider giving it up. It's been her home her whole life. Downtown doesn't currently have appropriate vacant space, and I don't think you'd want to locate a hotel on the literal wrong side of the railroad tracks. That's where the loss of employment has been the most obvious.

"You could buy land outside town, I suppose. I don't know the zoning rules, though."

Her grandfather shook his head. "I'll wait to see how things go. I think right now this idea of making it a 'Romance Center' takes advantage of what the town can offer and exploits its assets year-round, just as you concluded.

"Tell me about what you have planned for Valentine's Day."

Mariah straightened her notebook, though she didn't need it. "We have a fiftieth wedding anniversary and vow renewal. The couple was married on Valentine's Day and have lived in Carter's Crossing their whole lives. Abigail's committee is doing most of the legwork on that. They're tracking down the minister who officiated, to see if he's still alive, and have found most of the remaining wedding attendants. The church they married in is still in town, so they're using that space for the celebration.

"I don't expect a lot of people will necessarily want to celebrate a fiftieth going forward, not in Carter's, but it shows that romance can start and last there, so it's a feel-good story, and sets the tone."

Her grandfather leaned back in his chair. "Okay, have you got something splashier?"

"Absolutely. An engagement party. The mill isn't renovated yet, but we can use the space for staging. We're having an outdoor, old-fashioned skating party on the part of the river that goes by the mill."

"Weather?"

"It would be extremely unlikely that the river won't be frozen, and we can handle a snowfall or cold snap with lots of heaters and covers. We're still working on the indoor plan B if the weather suddenly gets unreasonably warm or rainy."

"Get lots of video—that should have a lot of appeal."

"Of course. And the final event is a proposal. You know how they've gone viral if done right."

He smiled at her. "And you'll make sure it's done right."

"Thanks to Abigail. We're going to use the gazebo in the middle of the town green. We're stealthily getting information on the woman's favorites, so the details are still being worked on."

Her grandfather tapped a finger on the desk. "The couple is reasonably attractive? They'll look good?"

"Not drop-dead gorgeous, but she's pretty, and he's totally in love with her, and it shows. They look like real people, which might be better than if they were too picture-perfect. She works for the local vet, so we could bring in animals, and he's a schoolteacher in the next town."

"I'm proud of you, Mariah. This all looks great. I look forward to having you working for me."

Mariah must have been tired, because she wasn't as excited over that affirmation as she should be.

"I'm looking forward to that, as well."

"You sure you don't want something more? You've got a good head on your shoulders. I can see a lot of myself in you."

Mariah put a hand over his. "I may not want to be just like my parents, but I do want to make sure I keep enough time to enjoy my life. I don't want to take over the world."

Her grandfather's smile was twisted. "I get it. I've made mistakes. It might be time for me to try to enjoy some of my life, as well."

CHAPTER SIX

NEW YEAR'S EVE was a bust.

Nelson had been looking forward to a night of fun with his friends. He had a rare night where he planned to not be on call. Mariah had gone to New York again not long before Christmas, and was staying through the New Year, helping with her grandfather's company and its many events.

He'd been relieved that he could enjoy the holidays without her. Somehow, he was thinking about her even when she wasn't around.

Worrying about what she might do to his friends. That was all. But for the night, he could push thoughts of her aside.

Then, just as he was heading out the door, he'd gotten a call from the answering service.

A dog, hit by a car. The family was in tears. There wasn't time to get the vet from Oak Hill.

He quickly changed to scrubs and raced to the clinic.

The damage to the golden retriever was extensive. There was massive internal bleeding. The owners insisted he do anything he could.

He called in Judy, apologizing for disturbing her New Year's. She shook her head. She loved all animals and was as determined to save this one as he was.

They tried. The surgery lasted four hours. He knew it was still touch and go. He offered to let Judy leave, but she wouldn't go till she knew if the dog would survive.

The dog didn't make it.

Nelson hated it. Hated that a beautiful animal was dead. Hated that he'd exhausted himself and Judy and hadn't been able to save him. Hated having to tell the news to the family.

It was a crappy New Year's.

By the time he'd wrapped up at the clinic, the ball had dropped in New York City, everyone had kissed whoever they were kissing and, while there was still partying going on, Nelson was heading home.

He was in no mood to party. He had a glass of whiskey on his own at home, as a salute to a lovely dog who'd no longer be a loving part of his family.

Then he went to bed and did his best to forget the whole evening.

A week later Dave told him they were having a do-over on Nelson's ruined New Year's Eve.

"A do-over," Nelson repeated, voice flat.

"Yep. You deserve a night to have a good time. Jaycee and the women are planning that party still, so we, the guys, are going out to the Goat and Barley and getting drunk and celebrating."

"What are we celebrating?" Nelson didn't have a lot to celebrate right now.

"A new year, good things coming. I know you had a crappy night, but that doesn't mean the whole year is going to suck."

Nelson managed not to promise. He didn't often let himself loose. He was the only vet in town.

When the family of the golden retriever he couldn't save reached out to ask for time to cover their bill, the one he had to send because, unfortunately, he had a business and had to pay for Judy's time and the materials he'd used, he agreed, and cut back the bill. Then he texted Dave to tell him he'd be coming.

He needed a break. He wasn't worried about the rest of the New Year. He just wanted to forget the now.

NELSON WAS DRUNK. He hadn't been this drunk in a long time. Words were coming out of his mouth before he had time to censor them.

This was a really bad idea in a small town,

where he had a reputation to uphold, and where his grandmother always found out everything that was going on. Tonight, however, he just didn't care. He needed to forget about the dog and the family, and alcohol was the only weapon he had for that right now.

Yeah, he was drunk. And so was Dave. Otherwise, Dave wouldn't be telling him about his problems with his engagement party. Using large gestures.

"Hey, I like to skate. I mean, regular skate. Like, hockey skate. Ya know?"

Nelson nodded, his head feeling loose on his neck.

"Fairly nights. I mean, fairy lights. Yeah. Those things. I said no problem. Hot chocolate, good."

"You like hot cholate," Nelson agreed. He had a sense that was the wrong word, but it didn't matter, becausc Dave kept going.

"I know. You're a good friend, Nelz'n."

Nelson reached out to slap Dave's arm, but got his head instead.

"Sorry, man."

Dave giggled. "It's okay. It's all okay. Except for the dancin'."

Nelson pointed his finger in Dave's general direction. "You don't like dancin' now? You did in high school."

Dave grabbed at Nelson's finger. "Don't point at me. Not nice."

"Sorry, dude. I'm drunk."

Dave stared at him. "You're a genius. A frickin' genius. That's how they'll get me to dance on skates. They'll have to make me drunk. I just have to stop drinking and I'm safe." Dave was nodding and didn't stop.

It seemed like a good plan to Nelson. But one part didn't make sense.

"Why are you dancing on skates? You play hockey on skates."

"Ezactly. Zactly. Right."

"We don't dance when we play hockey. 'Less we score. Then we cel'brate. But you don't dance."

"I *know*. But Jaycee wants me to dance on skates. At the party. Like they dance at weddings. But this isn't the wedding. It's the party. The skating party. So we have to dance on skates. It's all part of the plan."

Nelson took a moment, and then figured it out. The plan. Planning. Party planning. Wedding planning. Mariah Van frickin Delton.

That was the problem. Jaycee didn't want Dave to dance on skates. Jaycee had never asked Dave to dance on skates. Right?

"Dave," Nelson said. This felt like a very

important question. "Have you and Jaycee ever danced on skates?"

Dave shook his head violently and grabbed at the bar when he almost fell off his chair.

"No, skates are for hockey, not dancin'. Wait, they want us to dance on skates at the party."

"Zactly. Did Jaycee ever ask you to dance on skates before?"

"Never." Dave banged his fist on the table.

"Then the problem is Marijah."

Dave focused on his face with extreme effort. "Who?"

"Mahira… Marij… Wedding planner."

"Oh, right. Her. She's the one who wants to dance on skates?"

"She's the one that wants *you* to dance on skates."

"You sure about that? She didn't say anything."

Nelson frowned. "No, that's not how they do it. She tells Jaycee, and then Jaycee tells you."

Dave blinked owlishly. "That's sneaky, man. Really sneaky."

"I know. That's what they did to me." Nelson tried another head shake. Still loose.

Dave's jaw had dropped. "Jaycee asked you

to dance on skates, too? Wha— Are you trying to take over my party?"

Nelson concentrated and managed to put a hand on Dave's leg. "No, not Jaycee. Not your party. My party. My weddin'."

"Whoa, man," Dave said. "Is that what happened? Dancing on skates? But that doesn't make sense."

"I'll tell you what happened. But ssshhh. Don't tell everyone." He meant to put his finger on his lips, but it ended up on his nose. Weird.

Nelson had a suspicion that this wasn't the discreet place he should be talking about this. But he had to save Dave. Dave shouldn't lose Jaycee because of the wedding and the wedding planner. Or party planner. Whatevs.

"So I was getting married. Right?"

"That's right," Dave agreed.

"And then Sherry and I ruined it."

Dave blinked. "I thought it was Zoey. Was this another wedding?"

"I was marrying Zoey. Sherry was the wedding planner."

"Okay." Dave nodded. "Marry Zoey, plan Sherry."

Close enough. "And we had a big plan. Big, fancy wedding. Lots of guests. Important guests. I wanted it to be perfect."

Nelson wasn't sure why he was waving his arms around, but Dave was following his argument.

"Right."

Nelson sent a message to his voice to lower. Less volume. When Dave flinched, he wondered if it didn't happen right.

"Zoey didn't like it. She said we should 'lope."

"'Lope," Dave echoed.

"But there were all these people, right? We'd spent money, right? I mean, if we 'loped, everyone would be mad.

"So I said, Sherry. Sherry. Sherry."

"Sherry, Sherry, Sherry." Dave sang it back to him.

"Sherry was my wedding planner."

"I know. But you had a problem."

"Right. Right. Sherry, we have a problem. Zoey wants to 'lope. Not get married. Wait, elope married. Not a wedding. She said it was too much. Too stresssssful."

"Just like this skating party!" Dave shouted.

"And Sherry said, not a problem. She said brides were like this. Zoey would be glad when it was over. So I said, nope." That final *p* popped with a satisfying snap of his lips. "No eloping."

"Aww."

Nelson nodded his head. It was hard to make it stop, but he had to because he couldn't see Dave when he was nodding.

"Sherry was wrong."

"No." Dave looked shocked.

Suddenly, Nelson's head cleared as memories of that black day came back, escaping the wall he normally had solidly erected against their return.

"Zoey didn't show up for the wedding."

Dave lunged to hug him. "I'm sorry, man. That's awful. I wish I coulda been there, but Austalia…Stalia…it was too far."

Nelson closed his eyes, shoving aside the moment of clarity, welcoming the numbing confusion of the alcohol back.

"Yeah. So I gotta tell ya. Eloping is better than a big wedding. I should have eloped when she asked. Don't let Mariah plan a big wedding. Just elope. Much better."

Dave nodded. And nodded and started to tip out of his seat. Suddenly, the bartender was there, saying things like they'd had enough, and it was time to go.

Even the haze of alcohol couldn't remove the gloom that settled over Nelson as he remembered that time.

He shouldn't have gotten drunk. He needed

to keep control. Keep the bad memories away. He stood, and the room swirled around him.

Yet another mistake. He wondered sometimes if he'd ever learn.

NELSON'S HEAD WAS POUNDING. His mouth tasted like the bottom of a kennel, and his head pounded. And pounded.

When his head started to yell "Nelson" he realized it wasn't just his head pounding. It was his door. No, someone pounding *on* the door.

He pulled a pillow over his head to drown out the noise, and the movement made him queasy.

The pounding and yelling didn't stop.

After a struggle, he identified the yeller as Mariah.

He waited for her to go away, but she didn't. And he realized she wasn't going to.

That was some angry yelling she was doing. No one was stopping her, but the only person who could was his grandmother, and she was probably in on it.

Nelson groaned and shoved the pillow off. He pushed against the mattress and forced himself upright.

He wanted to fall back down, but the yelling was getting louder.

She probably learned to yell on a boat.

He managed to get to his feet, and finally, reluctantly, opened his eyes. He winced, even though the day was overcast, and not much light made its way into his bedroom. He reached a hand out to a wall and started to stumble to the door.

He finally got to the doorknob and twisted it. The door pushed back so quickly it hit his arm.

"Stop it," he croaked.

Miraculously, the pounding outside his head and the yelling stopped for a moment. He turned to feel his way to the kitchen. He'd just managed to turn on the tap when the door slammed, and he closed his eyes and groaned.

The water turned off, and he found a glass of water thrust in front of him. He gulped half of it down and took a breath.

"Aspirin?"

The voice was still loud with that question, but not as painful as it had been.

He furrowed his brow, thinking through the haze in his head. "Bathroom."

He swallowed the rest of the water and carefully placed the glass in the sink, as gently as possible. The noises from the bathroom as Mariah hopefully located the medication were still loud and echoing in his head.

Her footsteps clacked in the hallway, and she thrust a couple of pills at him.

He swallowed them dry. Then, feeling dizzy, he stumbled to his couch and half sat, half fell on it. He let his head rest on the back as he tried to will the aspirin to hurry through his system and provide some relief.

The footsteps clacked and stopped in front of him. He kept his eyes closed, hoping against hope that she'd vanish, in a puff of smoke.

Futile wishing. There was obviously something big bothering her. Big enough that she'd pounded on his door for what felt like hours.

"So I guess your excuse is that you were drunk?"

Sure. Make that his excuse. He had no idea what she was talking about, and he was in no condition to deal with it anyway.

"I don't care if you were drunk. I don't care if you were temporarily insane. I don't care if it was a full moon and you were about to turn into a werewolf. You made this problem, and now you need to fix it."

Nelson didn't know what the problem was.

He held up his hand. "Give me time for the aspirin to work."

She huffed, something he'd never imagined

sounding so loud, and then dropped into the chair across from his seat.

What he wanted to do was crawl back into bed and sleep until his hangover was gone, but he knew enough about Mariah to know that wasn't going to happen. She'd pounded on his door, gotten him water and aspirin, and then plunked herself down on his chair.

She wasn't leaving.

He tried to take advantage of the temporary quiet to figure out what the problem was.

She considered his being drunk an excuse. He thought back, and yep, she'd said that. Which probably meant something had happened last night.

He and Dave…

Oh, no. He'd been talking to Dave. Talking a lot. Talking without a filter, in the way that one did when drunk.

What had he said to Dave?

He couldn't hold back a groan when he remembered what he'd revealed. He'd told Dave, and possibly anyone else at the Goat and Barley last night, about his own aborted wedding. About Zoey asking him to elope. He'd said something about eloping being the right option.

Had Dave eloped with Jaycee? That would create a problem for Mariah. Maybe Dave had just refused to have the engagement party. There'd been something about dancing on skates, but it didn't make a lot of sense. Why would anyone want Dave to dance…?

"What exactly did you do last night?"

Nelson opened his eyes. He took his first real look at Mariah this morning.

She was wearing jeans, hair back in a ponytail. He didn't notice any makeup. With a flicker of pain, he figured she'd rushed over here without taking time to get ready. And still managed to look good.

He glanced at his watch, realizing he was wearing the same clothes he'd had on last night. They were wrinkled and untucked. He imagined he looked bad.

That didn't explain the look on her face. She was angry. No, she was furious.

How to put this so she didn't start yelling at him? The aspirin was dulling the edges of the pounding in his head, but he'd only had a few hours of sleep. He was in no shape for a fight.

"Dave and I went out."

She interrupted, "That much I know. Why?"

"I missed New Year's." And he had that whole issue with the retriever…

"Fine. You had to catch up on a chance to get drunk."

That wasn't fair. He didn't do this regularly. Not since Zoey—but he clamped that thought down.

"So Dave and I went out—"

"To the Goat and Barley. I know."

If she knew so much, why was she here yelling at him?

Crap. Dave must have eloped, so she couldn't find him to ask. Probably couldn't find Jaycee, either, and if they were on a plane on their way to get married, they wouldn't answer their phones.

How had Dave managed to get on a plane? He'd been as drunk as Nelson, and Nelson was having a hard time staying upright on the couch.

"We had some shots, talked a bit..."

"What did you talk about?" Her voice was still dialed up to much too high a volume, but he could think, a bit.

"Dave was upset about dancing. Yeah, he didn't want to dance. It all started from that."

Honestly, if she and Jaycee hadn't tried to make him dance on skates, Nelson would never have ended up advising him to elope.

"Dave's a big boy. He could have refused the dance."

Oh. They really did want Dave to dance. He'd have to figure out why later.

"Things went from there, and I might have told him to elope."

He looked over. Mariah had her arms crossed, but she wasn't yelling at him. Why wasn't she yelling at him?

"Okay, fine, we'll deal with that later, but when did you talk to Harvey?"

Nelson felt his mouth open, and he quickly shut it. Too quickly. It hurt.

He repeated her question in his head. Still didn't make any sense.

"Did I talk to Harvey? I was pretty sure Dave and I left together after that."

"Pretty sure?" Now she was getting closer to that yelling volume. "Well, I'm 'pretty sure' that Harvey and Judy just eloped. No, not just pretty sure since Harvey left me a voice mail!"

He pressed his hands over his ears, trying to control the volume shrieking into his poor, abused brain.

"Why do you care? They love each other—do you have to corner every possible wedding within a certain radius of Carter's Crossing?"

"I care—" His hands couldn't block out that volume level. "I care because our third event for Valentine's Day was Harvey's proposal to Judy!"

"What?" This made no sense. He'd talked

to Kailey. Judy hadn't wanted to propose to Harvey… Wait, Harvey was going to propose to Judy?

"I'd convinced him to do something better than the zombie thing, but he told me he'd decided to elope to Vegas instead, thanks to you."

Nelson couldn't understand. He hadn't talked to Harvey—unless Harvey had been at the bar? Would Harvey have heard them?

Yeah, they'd been a little loud. But what was the thing about zombies?

"I didn't talk to Harvey. I mean, if he was at the bar, he might have overheard us—"

"You think? Yesterday he's fine, we've got almost everything settled, and this morning he's on a plane to Vegas, and says it's because of you. Sounds like the explanation to me."

"I didn't know you were doing any proposal. Especially not with my staff."

"It was supposed to be a surprise. Have you noticed how news flies around this town?"

That, he had.

"We have five weeks till Valentine's Day. I told my grandfather we had three events lined up. Now you've cost us one. How are you going to fix that?"

He wasn't going to be able to fix anything until he'd had a lot more sleep and his brain was working better.

"How am I supposed to fix an elopement? I'm too late to fly to Vegas to object to their wedding."

There was silence, and he risked opening his eyes. He regretted it. The light had brightened and shot painfully through his aching head. And he didn't like the expression on Mariah's face.

He closed his eyes again.

"You're going to find me another proposal."

He almost laughed. He was the last person in town anyone would tell about a proposed proposal.

"Right." If Mariah wanted to talk about crazy…

The next thing he heard was the slamming of the door.

He relaxed, allowing his abused body to lie down on the couch. Thank goodness she was gone.

He'd have to talk to her about this…encounter they'd had, but first, he needed sleep. And finally, he was alone and could get that.

"WE HAVE A PROBLEM."

Mariah met with Rachel and Jaycee in the back booth of the diner. This had become their unofficial planning space. The Goat and Barley was the guys' place, and if Jaycee and

Dave were in the same vicinity, Jaycee tended to be distracted by her fiancé. They were now officially engaged, and Jaycee was showing off her ring any chance she got.

At the diner, though, Jaycee was focused and intent. The news of the engagement had not gone well at Christmas. Jaycee's mother-in-law-to-be had been all politeness on the outside but managed to get in some digs. Dave hadn't noticed but they had hit Jaycee. Why the rush to get married? Was there a reason?

Dave said he couldn't wait to make Jaycee his wife. Jaycee saw her MILTB looking at her stomach, as if Jaycee had planned a pregnancy to trap her son.

Jaycee was determined to prove she was going to be a great wife to Dave and had decided that the perfect engagement party would be the first step. Mariah was happy to help her. She thought Jaycee was a wonderful person, and that Dave's mother needed to see that. But she was getting a little worried about Jaycee.

The party was supposed to be a celebration of their engagement. It was supposed to be fun. Jaycee had promised that she and Dave loved to skate. But Jaycee was getting a little lost in the details. Like this dance on skates. Mariah thought it was a fun idea, but it sounded like Dave was dragging his blades, so to speak. Jaycee was starting to clench her teeth when she talked about it.

That problem could wait for now. The anniversary party was well underway, with the committee, under Abigail's supervision, taking care of most of the details. Mariah was overseeing that one on a much bigger picture scale.

Now she needed to see if Jaycee and Rachel could help her with the aborted proposal. She wasn't sure how much she trusted Nelson to fix the mess he'd made.

"What's the problem?" Jaycee asked, looking a little frantic.

Mariah put a hand on Jaycee's. "Nothing to do with your party, so just breathe, okay?"

Jaycee took a long breath.

"Told you." Rachel shook her head at her friend. "Mariah's got it all under control."

The waitress stopped by, and they placed an order.

Once the drinks arrived, Mariah filled them in.

"There was a third event lined up for Valentine's Day—it was a surprise, so I couldn't tell you about it. But it's not happening now, thanks to Nelson Carter, so I was hoping you two could help me out."

Jaycee and Rachel looked at each other. "Nelson? What did he do?"

Mariah carefully did not grind her teeth. "You know Harvey and Judy?"

They nodded.

"Harvey wanted to propose to Judy. A beautiful, romantic, surprise proposal."

"Aww." Rachel smiled.

Jaycee frowned. "How did Nelson mess it up?"

Mariah pursed her lips. "You know he and Dave went out last night?"

Jaycee nodded, looking worried.

"Harvey was at the bar, heard Nelson talk about weddings and something about how eloping was better, so Harvey and Judy flew to Vegas this morning."

Rachel snorted a laugh. "Seriously?"

Jaycee appreciated the seriousness. "I guess that means the proposal is off."

Mariah nodded. "I need a third event. I've told my grandfather about our plans, and he's arranged publicity. I need to show him I can pull this off."

"Could Judy and Harvey have a reception on Valentine's Day instead?"

Mariah shook her head. "That's not going

to work for a few reasons. First, our other two events are already for things that happened previously, so I really wanted something that was happening on Valentine's Day.

"If Carter's Crossing is going to be a place where people come for romance, we should be able to have a romantic event happen on the actual Valentine's Day. Nothing against your party, Jaycee, but I want something that isn't a celebration where the really romantic part happened off camera, so to speak.

"Secondly, there aren't a lot of venues in Carter's right now. The engagement skating party is happening at the mill. It's not ready yet, but it does have a roof and walls. The anniversary party is at St. Christopher's reception hall. That's the only full-size space the churches have between them.

"The proposal was supposed to take place at the bandstand in the park. I can't have a wedding reception at the park in the middle of February. Everyone would freeze. The proposal was perfect for that space."

Jaycee bit her lip. Rachel nodded.

"Okay, I see why that won't work. How can we help?"

Mariah clenched her hands under the table. "Can you think of someone who might be ready to propose? It just fit so perfectly, and

I've got everything ready to make the bandstand beautiful. I could adapt it with different flowers, or music, or whatever, but starting from scratch would be a problem."

Rachel looked at Jaycee. "I can't think of anyone offhand. Can you?"

Jaycee twisted up her lips. "Tanya broke up with Kevin, right?"

Rachel nodded. Jaycee shook her head. "I'll try to think of someone, but honestly, the dating pool is a little shallow here."

Rachel rolled her eyes. "Tell me about it."

Jaycee blew out a breath. "Sorry, Mariah. We'd love to help, but this is a tricky one."

Mariah sighed. "I was afraid of that. Well, I told Nelson he has to fix it, so I hope he can come up with something."

"What about a pet wedding? That Nelson would know about."

Mariah frowned. It was meant to be a joke, she knew. But this was serious business. Her job wasn't a joke. And the thought of letting her grandfather down made her anxious and tense.

The lessons she'd learned growing up—don't make a promise unless you can keep it; and if at all possible, don't promise anything, because you might have to break your word.

She'd never used the word *promise* with

her grandfather, but she thought he was taking it as a serious commitment. She needed to make this work.

She was an outsider, so she had a disadvantage. But Mr. Elopement Carter was not. He'd better step up.

CHAPTER SEVEN

"HE'LL COME CLOSE to eat but backs off right away."

Rachel stood beside him, watching the skittish chestnut.

"That's better than when you first got him, though, right?"

Nelson's gaze was focused on the horse. "It is. I need to be patient, but I don't want to take in another until he's settled."

Rachel nudged him. "You asked me out here to give advice on your horses?"

He shot a glance her way and saw the smirk on her face.

"Are you telling me you don't have any?"

"Come on, Nelson. We know each other. This is the place you come to think. If you wanted me out here, you've got something you're thinking about, and you want to talk about it in private."

This just might work, Nelson thought.

He'd had a difficult week. Getting drunk and hungover on his days off was not a great way to start. Finding out just how much he'd told Dave, and apparently everyone else at the Goat and Barley, about what had happened at his non-wedding made it worse. And then, Mariah.

Mariah's visit had been a little hazy in his memory, but she'd reminded him that he'd agreed to fix his mistake, or he'd be destroying Carter's Crossing's future and his grandmother's dream.

He didn't remember agreeing to that. Mariah didn't care.

He should have told her to run with the two events she had and leave him alone.

Except…

Except that he'd promised his grandmother he wouldn't ruin everything. He wouldn't sneak into town and steal the Christmas presents and decorations and food.

And though he hadn't done it intentionally, he had allowed, under the influence of too much to drink, his own viewpoint and history to spill over and upset their plans.

He hadn't had any intentions of influencing Harvey. But he had wanted to let Dave know that Dave had a say in his wedding and engagement, and that fancy parties might damage his relationship with Jaycee.

He should probably thank his lucky stars

that Dave hadn't run off to elope with Jaycee. Nelson suspected that Jaycee wouldn't have run. She was pretty wrapped up in this party planning.

Not that Nelson was going to offer any more advice. He'd done enough already.

Instead, he'd tried to find out what dating life was like in Carter's Crossing. Not to participate, but to find out if anyone was ready to make things serious. He was restricted by the fact that no one thought he wanted to know. And no one wanted to tell him.

He'd talked to the owners of his patients, which had led to more than one awkward conversation, and two offers of blind dates, for Nelson himself. He'd asked Kailey, giving her ammunition for months when it came to keeping him in what she considered to be his place.

He'd been forced to face the same truth that Mariah and her committee had. There were not a lot of dating locals, and none were ready to get married, except for Dave and Jaycee, and Harvey and Judy, who were now already married.

Thanks to him.

The elopement had been nothing but great for Judy. She had a smile on her face, most of the time, and now volunteered comments without prompting. It didn't help Nelson in his quest, however.

He'd come to the end of his ideas. He just had one, mostly crazy, hail-Mary, last-chance idea. And he needed Rachel on board.

He tried to put the words together.

"Are you involved in any of this romance stuff?"

He felt her shoulders shrug beside him.

"I'm helping with Jaycee's party."

Yeah, it was more Jaycee's party than Dave's, but that wasn't something he could fix, as much as he might want to.

"Did you know about the proposal Mariah had planned?" She'd said it was a secret, but Rachel and Jaycee had been spending a lot of time with Mariah.

He'd apparently taken more notice of it than he'd realized.

"Harvey and Judy, yeah. We heard about it after the elopement. Mariah asked if we knew anyone else who might be interested, but we couldn't think of anyone."

Of course not. That would be just too easy.

"Mariah blames me for the two of them eloping."

"I know."

Nelson shook his head. No secrets in a small town.

"Nelson." Rachel sounded insistent. He turned to look at her.

"I know why you don't like Mariah and her plans." She did. Before he shot off his mouth at the Goat and Barley, Rachel had been the only person with whom he'd shared any details of his almost-wedding. Because they were friends, and because the town wanted to pair them up.

He'd been avoiding dating for several reasons. He needed to understand how he'd allowed himself to be so cruel to someone he loved. Someone he'd wanted to marry. He wanted to be sure he'd never do that again. He'd removed himself from situations where he could take over like that, and, as a result, possibly ignored figuring out why.

"But, Nelson, Mariah isn't like your wedding planner. I swear. She isn't like how you described that Sherry woman."

Nelson drew in a breath. He'd promised not to interfere, but Rachel was a good friend. He needed to be able to tell someone.

"Mariah not only worked for Sherry. I heard her tell Grandmother that she'd learned everything from her."

Rachel was speechless. Her mouth opened and shut, and she finally shook her head.

"Nelson, I don't know. I don't know what

you heard. But seriously, she's trying to rein Jaycee in from being too crazy over this. She's being considerate, and really nice. I like her."

There it was. If there was a contest, with Nelson on one side and Mariah on the other, Mariah was going to win. Even Rachel, who knew his story, liked Mariah.

Well, until Mariah screwed them over. He didn't want that to happen, but it didn't seem like anyone would listen to him. If Rachel and Grandmother wouldn't, who would?

He might as well see if Rachel would help him with his crazy idea. At least Rachel shouldn't get hurt over this.

"Let's see how things go, okay? What I wanted to talk to you about, well, what I wanted to ask you, was about a way to help Mariah. And Grandmother."

Three guesses who he really wanted to help.

Rachel shrugged. "Okay. I'm happy to help."

She always was. Rachel was the nicest person he knew.

"Mariah wants another proposal to plan. And no one is ready to propose. So what if I propose to you?"

He watched Rachel's face. Surprise. Shock. Suspicion.

"You want to propose to me?" she asked, carefully.

He puffed a cloudy breath into the cold January air.

"I don't want to be involved in any of this at all. But I'm supposed to fix my mistake."

Rachel was still speaking precisely. "You want to marry me to fix your mistake?"

Nelson almost stepped back. "No, no, not marry you."

"Of course, how silly of me. Just propose."

He relaxed, slightly. Now she got it, and she hadn't yelled.

"Right. I'll propose, you'll say yes and then, after things die down, we'll break up."

Rachel crossed her arms. Her lips were pressed tightly together.

"Let me see if I understand this. We'll pretend to start dating."

Right. They should do that first.

"Sure." Nelson nodded. "That's not a problem."

"Well, good. I'd hate to have our fake relationship be a problem."

Okay, Rachel was not taking this well.

"Then you'll fake propose on Valentine's Day. With a fake diamond, I assume?"

"We can use a real diamond. Really, we can pick a ring, and you can keep it. I hadn't thought that far ahead because I wasn't sure you'd agree to it."

"There is that pesky agreement to get through, isn't there? But I have more questions. How long are we fake engaged?"

Nelson tried to think of an appropriate time range. It had to be long enough that no one suspected it was fake, but not so long that they had to make serious plans.

"And who's going to break it off? Are you ready to be jilted again, or am I supposed to take one for the team?"

He hadn't thought that far ahead, either. Obviously, having two women jilt him was not going to do his reputation any good. On the other hand, if Rachel did this favor, he couldn't insist that he be the jilter.

"We could make it a mutual decision."

Rachel rolled her eyes. "Right. If that's the case, then we need to set a timeline before either of us starts dating again, because whoever dates first would be the winner."

Nelson began to understand the magnitude of stupidity his fake engagement idea entailed. He'd thought that since he and Rachel were friends, and kind of dated, whenever one of them needed a plus one, that this was something he could pull off.

But there were ramifications and subtexts

behind all these decisions that he hadn't understood.

"My dad would talk for the rest of his life, or my life, whichever was longer, about how I'd blown my chance. You do understand that half this town thinks I should be trying to get you to propose to me for real, don't you?"

No, he did not. Not completely. But he did understand that he'd hurt his friend. He needed to let it drop, right now.

"Rachel."

He waited this time until her gaze returned to his.

"I'm sorry. It was a stupid idea. I thought, since we were friends, that we could pull this off, but I don't want to make your life more difficult. It's my problem, not yours."

Rachel looked away again.

"I have my own problems, Nelson. I just—really, I can't take on yours, too."

He examined Rachel, while she watched the chestnut. He'd assumed Rachel was happy, contented, living in Carter's Crossing, taking care of her dad, working for her uncle, helping everyone in town.

He'd shared his problems with her. He hadn't been a good friend, though, because he hadn't helped with hers.

"Rachel, if you need something, just ask,

okay? You've been a good friend to me, but I haven't been as good to you."

Rachel let out a long breath of cold air. "It's okay. I'm just—I don't know. Having a midlife crisis or something."

"Rachel, you're not even thirty yet. I don't think you can call yourself midlife."

"I'm advanced for my age, I guess."

MARIAH KNOCKED ON Nelson's door. This time she heard steps coming her way and didn't have to yell and pound.

Since she was no longer blazing angry, that was just as well. She didn't have any pounding and yelling in her today.

Just a desperate flicker of hope that somehow, Nelson had come through. He'd asked to talk to her, so she hoped he'd found someone ready to propose.

That was plan A. The next plan she had was a plan F at best.

Nelson wasn't in wrinkled clothing, and he didn't stink of whiskey, so things were looking up already. He didn't look excited, like he had a great idea, but she didn't think he'd be excited even if he did find someone for her.

He didn't like her. Or at least, he didn't like what she was doing, and he hadn't been willing to look past that.

It bothered her more than it should. Despite their rocky beginning, she had to recognize that he was a good guy. To everyone except wedding planners anyway.

He was a crappy darts player, but he cared about his friends and grandmother. He was a good vet, according to anyone she'd heard talking about him. He even rescued horses.

And yes, he was good-looking. But none of that mattered. He wanted nothing to do with her. She had less than a year here anyway, so it really shouldn't bother her.

"Come in." He stood back to let her enter.

She hadn't paid much attention to his place last time. She'd been frustrated, angry and convinced she was going to fail. She'd wanted to make him feel some of that pain.

Today she noticed that the apartment was extremely tidy and finished in a way that reflected his grandmother's house. Like he wasn't the one who'd bothered to pick out the furniture and curtains.

She was probably just trying to find things not to like about the man.

"Have a seat. Can I get you anything?"

Two people who want to get married? She shook her head. She wasn't interested in anything else.

She sat on a chair, and Nelson sat on the

couch across from her. Exactly like they had a week ago.

He drew in a breath and exhaled again.

"I'm sorry. I wasn't able to find anyone."

She clenched her fists. No, no, no. He couldn't do this. She needed this, so much. She'd made a commitment. Almost a promise. She had to come through.

He shook his head. "This is a small town. Kids who grow up here often move away. There just isn't a big dating pool, and no one in it is ready to make the leap to the married pool."

"Except for Harvey and Judy." She knew she was being bitchy. She didn't care right now.

"I promise, I tried. I asked every client I saw this week. I asked Kailey, and what she doesn't know, or Grandmother, doesn't happen in this town."

She frowned at him. He said he was sorry, but he wasn't invested in this.

"I know you don't like what we're planning for Carter's Crossing. And deep down, you probably hope it fails. But the town needs this."

She saw anger on his face.

"I know the town needs outside business to survive. I might not be a big fan of this particular idea, but I didn't plan to sabotage it. I really tried to find someone who would like to take advantage of your proposal. I even asked Rachel if she'd agree to a fake engagement, just so you'd have someone to get a ring on February fourteenth. But it was a stupid idea, and she said no."

Mariah blinked at him. A fake engagement? He'd really tried to arrange a fake engagement?

That could have worked. It's not like engagements didn't get broken. The big thing for now was to show a romantic proposal, one that would entice people from out of town to come here to replicate.

Maybe she could get Rachel to change her mind?

Mind buzzing again, she made sure. "Rachel said no?"

"She had good reasons. I hadn't thought it through."

Right. Mariah wouldn't push Rachel into this. But it was a smidgeon of hope. A possibility. If there was someone else who would agree to a fake proposal with Nelson.

Someone desperate. Someone motivated.

She sighed. She knew of only one person right now that desperate and motivated. Could she make it work?

"I'm sorry, really. I tried. But there's nothing more I can do."

He stood up, waiting for her to leave, convinced he was off the hook.

No, she wasn't giving up on that hook.

"I'll do it." She almost called the words back. This was crossing lines, smudging borders.

Nelson's brow creased. "You'll do what?"

"I'll accept your fake proposal. We can get engaged for Valentine's Day."

NELSON SHOOK HIS HEAD. Then pinched himself for good measure.

She thought they were going to get engaged on Valentine's Day? Okay, now he knew. She was crazy. Certifiable.

She flipped open her notebook.

"We're going to need to set some rules and make a plan. If we suddenly act like we're madly in love, it will look suspicious."

Nelson choked.

Mariah narrowed her eyes. "There's no way we can do this otherwise. No one will believe it."

Now she was making some sense.

"No one will believe it. With Rachel, at least we've been friends since we were kids. Like Dave and Jaycee. But us…"

He didn't think he needed to clarify just how much the two of them had been anything but friendly.

"Exactly. The first rule is that we're going to need to spend most of the next few weeks before Valentine's Day together."

Strange how she could start that sentence saying "Exactly" and then take it in *exactly* the wrong direction.

"I have a practice to maintain." He hoped she didn't miss that edge he added. What, was she going to sit in on his day-to-day work? If so, he hoped the Fletchers needed more visits to their pigs. He could almost smile at the picture of Mariah hanging out at a pigsty.

"Right. And I have a lot of planning to do. But we have weekends and evenings."

Nah ah.

"I have other things to do on weekends and evenings." Things he enjoyed. Things that relaxed him.

She looked up at him. "I'm sure I can survive spending a few evenings at the Goat and Barley."

Did she think that was all he did in his free time?

"I'm working with rescue horses on my time off." Sure, Mariah grew up on a boat and could apparently find herself anywhere in the world with a sextant and who knows, a box of nails, and she was killer at darts, but he was pretty sure a life on a boat didn't give her a chance to become a horse whisperer.

"That will work!"

Oh, no, she really was a horse whisperer. Kill him now.

"We'll go out for dinner tonight. The Moonstone. I want to talk to you about using your horses in my plans for the town. We can work out the details on that. Then we'll discover that we actually 'like' each other and start dating. I can offer to teach you how to play darts, and—"

"No."

Nelson used to be like Mariah. He'd run his plans all over poor Zoey, with his wedding planner urging him on. He wasn't going to do that now, and he wasn't going to let anyone do it to him. Especially not to his horses.

Mariah had already sailed quite a distance past him. "No?"

"No, you're not using my horses."

Mariah rolled her eyes. "Tell me about that tonight, not now. You have dated before, right? You know what you're doing? I don't have to coach you?"

"Uh, yeah. I've dated." She'd been upset that he assumed she was lost but she could assume he'd never gone on a date? He'd dated, proposed and almost got married. He knew how to woo a woman. When he wanted to.

"Okay, then. I'll leave you to make the reservation. You can pick me up just before seven. The sweater you wore that first night I was here was nice—you could wear that again."

Nelson opened his mouth to answer when her phone chimed. She glanced at it and stood up. "Sorry, I need to take this. I'll see you at seven and we can hammer out the rest of the details."

And while Nelson mentally mustered up his arguments, she was gone.

He stood, listening to the door close. Except for the whisper of perfume in the air, it was as if she'd never been there.

But she had. He could try to pretend, but she'd been there, told him they were dating and would be getting engaged in a few weeks.

She was definitely in the right career for her. Bossy, managing, planning, riding roughshod over others.

He had to follow her over to Grandmother's house and make her sit and listen to reason. Or just flat-out tell her he wasn't doing it. But when he got to the door, he saw her car pulling out.

Okay, he could go over there at seven and

tell her it wasn't happening and why. With Grandmother listening in.

No, he couldn't do that. Mariah was right; he wanted to make up for his mistake. He didn't want the chaos and stresses of big weddings messing up his town and his friends, but he didn't want Grandmother to lose everything investing in a disaster. She was committed to saving Carter's Crossing.

This whole idea had been a conflict for him since Mariah arrived.

Fine, they could talk tonight at Moonstone. He'd make the reservation, but it was going to cause a lot of gossip.

He texted Jaycee, since he didn't want to talk to anyone. He told her he wanted a table for two at seven. Sure enough, she responded right away.

You've got it—best table in the house! Looking forward to seeing your date! We're all rooting for you.

Right. He'd forgotten for a while that he was a damaged husk of a man after his non-wedding.

That was when the beauty of it struck him. He'd been told he needed to date again so that people would stop feeling sorry for him.

He needed to show everyone in town that he wasn't traumatized by weddings.

Okay, then. Mariah wanted her event. If he dated her, the romance planner, he'd show people he was fine. He was over the jilting of the past. They could start treating him like a grown-up again.

But he had one important rule for Ms. Van Delton. He was not going through this whole poor-baby routine again. This time he got to be the jilter. And that was nonnegotiable.

MARIAH HAD BEEN confident when she ordered Nelson to pick her up, but now, with the clock ticking down toward seven, she wasn't sure he'd show. If he did, she wondered whether he'd play along with her. She didn't like the idea of a fake engagement, but she also wasn't thrilled about falling short of her commitment.

And, she argued to herself, so many engagements didn't last. It wasn't a big deal if this one didn't. She could stage a fake proposal to promote Carter's Crossing without claiming it was real, just a publicity event. It would market better if everyone thought it was real, that was all.

She wasn't happy with the arguments she was using to convince herself. She wasn't going to give up on finding another proposal or similar event that would be real. But having this in her pocket, ready to go if needed, made sure things were going to work out.

She wanted Nelson to agree for that reason, but she had another reason she wasn't going to share with him. Nelson demonstrably had influence in Carter's Crossing. He'd already managed to blow up one event she'd planned. She didn't intend to let him have the chance to mess up anything else. If they spent all their free time together, then she could make sure he didn't do any more influencing.

That was why she tried on four outfits before finding one that looked good without trying too hard. And took time to curl her hair and apply extra makeup. She had a fake romance to sell, so she was working hard on selling it.

It was not to impress Nelson. They were coconspirators here, not dates.

When Nelson did pull up in front of his grandmother's house, at seven exactly, in a car that wasn't the clinic van, she was pleased to see, underneath his jacket, that he was wearing that sweater. The one she'd told him to wear. It wasn't because it made his eyes look extra blue, or that it outlined what was undoubtedly an attractive chest. No, it just meant he was going to do what she'd asked.

Suggested. No, demanded.

She had to work a little harder to explain the pleasure that sizzled down her spine when his eyes widened in appreciation when he saw her. She hadn't wasted her efforts. Right.

He followed her out to the car and opened the door for her. She thanked him. Then he walked around the hood to the driver's side and slid behind the wheel. He'd left the engine running, so the interior had warmed up.

As he put the car in gear, he shot a glance at her. "How did you get Grandmother out of the way?"

She shrugged. "I lucked out. She got a call—about the architect, I think."

She noticed Nelson's frown. Probably better not to talk about that. Renovating the mill was going to push all the buttons he had against this project. Another reason to make sure he was on board. She'd half expected him to bail, but he was here.

"We'll have to tell her the truth."

Mariah stifled a grin, as something warmed her from the inside. If he was laying down rules about telling Abigail, he was in. This was good.

"We can lay down the guidelines when we're at the restaurant."

Nelson shook his head. "Not really."

Mariah sat straighter. "No? Any good reason for that other than contradicting me?"

He pulled into a parking space, not far from the restaurant. It was a small town, and they were already here.

"If we're lost at sea, I'll be sure to do what you tell me to. But Carter's Crossing is different, and here I can navigate better than you.

"I made the reservation with Jaycee. I didn't tell her who I was bringing, but I'm willing to bet any amount you want that she's going to be there, watching every move we make. We can't be overheard making rules about dating, or no one is going to buy what we're selling."

Mariah squinched up her nose. "Fine. We can't talk about dating in there."

"I have two stipulations." Nelson moved his body over, leaning against the door, watching her face in the light from the storefront in front of them.

Mariah frowned. She didn't want to argue this. She just wanted it done. This was her job—couldn't he just let her do it?

"What are the two things you want to stipulate?" She wasn't going to accept anything blindly.

"The first is telling Grandmother."

Mariah nodded. She hadn't been looking forward to pretending to fall in love with Nelson in front of Abigail. She was a party planner, not an actress. Keeping up the front in public would be hard enough. She wasn't sure she could sell Abigail.

No, she was sure she couldn't.

"And secondly, I end it."

Mariah shifted back in her seat. She hadn't seen that one coming.

"You end it? You get to unilaterally decide when and how?"

Nelson huffed. "No, we should agree on that. But I'm the one who breaks it off, as far as everyone knows."

Her mind struggled to wrap around this stipulation. Did he have that fragile an ego? He couldn't bear to have a woman end things with him?

As she opened her mouth to tell him what he could do with that stipulation, she suddenly understood.

Mariah was leaving Carter's Crossing in the fall. Once she had everything underway, Abigail and her committee could take over. Mariah might offer some assistance from afar, but she'd be gone from Carter's.

Nelson would be here still. She could put it all behind her, but he couldn't. If he didn't want to be the jiltee it made sense, even if it wasn't the gentlemanly behavior she'd expected from him. He wouldn't have to pretend to be heartbroken once they were done and she was gone.

So instead of arguing, she agreed. Though she would have liked to argue on principle.

He sighed. "Do you have more rules to add?"

She nodded and watched his mouth quirk up. He wasn't surprised she had rules. He wasn't stupid, either.

"I plan the proposal, but you do the asking."

He rubbed his jaw, freshly shaven, she noticed.

"No problem. I don't want to *plan* anything."

He was more forceful in that comment than she'd expected. He really didn't want anything to do with the Romance Center idea.

"I'm going to keep looking for another option, and if I find one, we cool off on the 'dating.' But if we do have to roll out this proposal, it needs to be done well, and that's my forte. I'll do the planning, but ask Abigail to front for it, so we can pretend that you're behind it. I can't appear to be planning something for myself."

Nelson's gaze was centered on the dash of his car. Mariah wondered what he was thinking.

"I want to hear about it beforehand. If it's supposed to be coming from me, it needs to look like something I'd actually do."

That might limit her. This proposal had a primary purpose, which was promoting Carter's Crossing as a romantic destination.

"Will people believe you planned a truly romantic proposal? Something beyond asking if I wouldn't mind?"

Nelson's gaze drifted over her shoulder, and it didn't look like he was seeing the hardware store across the street.

"If it doesn't include me making a fool of myself, then yes, people here will believe I could pull something together. Something nice.

"We should head in now. Jaycee will be looking for us."

He'd cut off the conversation, and there was a lot behind his statement that he wasn't sharing. She remembered that first dinner and knowing that there was more going on with Nelson than she knew.

She was tempted to tell him he had to let her in on whatever it was, or she wouldn't go through with this. Because as gossipy as this town could be, no one had shared with her what had happened to Nelson. And she hadn't asked, because, well, what reason would she have beyond a personal interest in the man? Which she didn't have, obviously. Not before.

She had no leverage to make him open up. He'd agreed to this fake dating and proposal, presumably to help his grandmother, but she didn't think he wouldn't happily opt out if possible.

She was taking a risk here, and she didn't like that. Not at all.

CHAPTER EIGHT

JAYCEE'S MOUTH DROPPED as the two of them entered the front door of the restaurant together. It was a quiet night—there were only two other occupied tables, but those parties also stopped and stared.

He'd known this would happen. He was prepared. But he wasn't happy about it.

For the next several weeks he was going to have to spend all his free time with Mariah. And even after that, he understood, once they were "engaged," they'd still need to spend time together. Would they even have something to talk about?

But no one could say he hadn't gotten over his aborted wedding after this, or that he was against weddings. And once they'd broken it off, people would be off his back for a while.

Jaycee took their coats and led them to a table, right in the window. Nelson rolled his eyes mentally. This town was too involved in everyone's lives. It would serve their purpose, though. The town would talk about them dating.

Jaycee pulled out a chair for Mariah.

"I had no idea you were the person Nelson was bringing to dinner tonight."

Nelson broke in before Mariah could respond.

"Mariah wanted to talk about my horses. She thought they might be useful in her plans."

Jaycee's forehead creased. "But—"

Nelson grabbed the menus from Jaycee's limp hands. "I know. I'll tell her."

Mariah shot a glance between them.

"Ooookay, then," Jaycee said. "Can I get you something to drink?"

Nelson shook his head, while Mariah asked for white wine. Jaycee left with a puzzled look.

Mariah leaned forward. "What is it about your horses?"

He leaned forward, too. "I'll tell you after you've got your drink and we've ordered."

Mariah sat back and frowned. She flipped open the menu and scanned the contents. After making a decision, she set it down and stared at his still-closed menu.

"Aren't you going to order anything?"

He shrugged. "The menu hasn't changed for a while."

"Why aren't you drinking?"

"I'm the only vet available tonight. I limit my drinking times. I'm not a saint, but I try not to be out of commission too often."

"The other night wasn't something you do often?"

He groaned and dropped his head. "I haven't been that drunk in years."

"Did something happen?"

His chin firmed. "Bad case."

Jaycee came back then with their drinks. Nelson ordered a steak; Mariah opted for pasta.

After Jaycee left, Mariah leaned forward again.

"Okay, enough stalling. What's the story about your horses?"

"It's not anything big. I have some rescue horses."

He left it there. Mariah waited for a moment, then said, "Okay, you have rescue horses. You're giving them a home, I guess?"

Nelson nodded.

"Is this a state secret? What is it about these horses?"

"The place I provide is for them to recover, relax and live out their lives in peace. They aren't workhorses."

"No one rides them or anything like that?"

He shook his head.

"Why not?"

"Some of them are old. Very old."

"And the rest?"

If he gave points for persistence, she'd be a high scorer.

"They've been abused. I'm trying to teach them to trust people again."

"And are you successful?"

"Moderately." He was very good, but he'd made new habits, and downplaying his achievements was among those.

"But not enough that they'd be of any use to people coming to Carter's Crossing?"

Did she think he wasn't doing his job?

"What would people want from them? I'm not providing carriage rides around town or trail rides on the farm."

Mariah held up her hands. "I don't know anything about horses. I just wondered. That's part of my job. You said you're trying to get them trusting people. I'm going to bring people into town, so I wondered if there was a way to help each other."

Jaycee brought over their plates before he could tell her there was no way her plans were going to help his horses.

He took advantage of the distraction to remind himself to relax. He didn't understand why, but everything Mariah said made him want to argue.

After Jaycee left, Mariah leaned forward again. "Can you try not to look like you want to snap my head off? We're supposed to like each other enough to start dating. Serious dating."

Nelson ground his teeth together. She was right. He needed to behave.

"I'm sorry." He gritted the words out, annoyed that he needed to say that. "Why don't you come and see the horses? Then you'll understand."

Mariah narrowed her eyes. "Are they going to bite me? Knock me into the mud?"

Nelson held in a laugh. He'd found something Mariah was not an expert about. "No, you don't have to get close enough to be bitten or knocked down. They're behind fences, and you can stay outside those."

"Okay, then."

She still looked so uncharacteristically nervous that he reached over and squeezed her hand. "You'll be perfectly safe. I go there all the time just to chill."

Jaycee came over to ask how their meals were, and Nelson drew back his hand. Jaycee had been staring at their hands.

Why had he done that? He shook his head.

Jaycee looked sold on their date being real, so he was getting caught up in the act. That was all. Otherwise, he was getting soft on Mariah. Not a good idea.

Nelson managed to turn the conversation to places she'd traveled while growing up. Since she'd been almost everywhere, conversation never lagged again. They did argue, once or twice, but it didn't veer into personal territory. He might have even enjoyed someone who pushed back, someone other than his grandmother.

As they got in his car for the short drive back to his grandmother's, Nelson was surprised to note that, for the most part, he'd enjoyed his evening. It had been a while since he'd spent time with anyone who hadn't grown up with him in Carter's Crossing. It had been fun. Maybe this fake dating thing wouldn't be too painful.

IT WAS A short date. No, Mariah corrected herself. It was a short predate.

Seven wasn't a late start for a dinner in many places. New York, French islands in the Caribbean, Europe. But in Carter's Crossing, it was a late start, and Nelson had to get to his clinic in the morning.

Mariah was back by nine. Abigail was still up.

"Was that Nelson who dropped you off? Not that I mean to pry, but yes, I'm prying."

Mariah laughed. "Yes, it was Nelson, and I'll tell you all about it. How was your call with the architect?"

"He's coming out tomorrow to look at the mill and assess if we can work together."

"That's great news. And your contractor can start soon?"

Abigail nodded. "Winter is slow for her, so she's glad to have a chance to put her crew to work. Would you like some tea?"

Mariah agreed, and after hanging up her coat, followed Abigail into the kitchen.

Abigail plugged in the kettle and brought out the teapot. Mariah, familiar by now with the routine, found the cups and tea. Then she sat at the table while Abigail fussed with napkins and spoons, milk and sugar, lemon and honey.

Once the kettle had boiled, and Abigail steeped the tea, she sat across from Mariah.

"You were out with Nelson?"

"You haven't heard already?" Mariah was sure the news had started the rounds.

Abigail merely poured tea into two cups and passed one toward her.

Mariah added some milk. "You know how upset I was when Harvey and Judy eloped."

"And you blamed Nelson."

Mariah shrugged. "The message Harvey left me said it was because of something Nelson said. I think blaming him was an obvious choice. And, to be blunt, he was drunk."

Abigail grimaced. "Nelson doesn't usually allow himself to lose control that way."

"He said he'd had a bad case."

Abigail nodded. "A beautiful family pet hit by a car. He couldn't save the dog, and the family was devastated."

Mariah learned more from Abigail about what had happened than she had from Nelson. Because he wouldn't confide in her? Or because it still upset him?

"I went to see Nelson."

Abigail smiled. Mariah suspected this wasn't news.

"I told him he needed to find a replacement proposal for the one he'd lost us." She swallowed. "I was not very nice."

"He's a big boy."

Mariah expelled a breath. She was lucky Abigail wasn't more protective of Nelson.

"He did try. He even spoke to a friend, asked her to pretend to get engaged to him."

This caught Abigail's attention. "Rachel?"

Again, Mariah wasn't surprised by Abigail's knowledge of her town and its people.

"She said no, so, I uh, I said I'd be willing to be fake engaged to him."

Mariah waited for Abigail's response. Would she think it silly? Dishonest?

"I assume he agreed, and that's why you were out tonight?"

Apparently, neither silly nor dishonest bothered the woman.

"He insisted that we tell you what was going on, but we don't plan to tell anyone else. If I can find another event, we'll forget this, but we're running out of time, and I told Grandfather…"

Abigail was staring past Mariah, a small smile on her face. Mariah had the feeling there was a joke that she was missing.

"Thank you for telling me, and I'll respect your confidence. Does this mean Nelson is now part of the proposal planning?"

Mariah shook her head, and she could have sworn Abigail was disappointed.

"I think it's best if I plan it, and let you execute it? Then we can pretend it's coming from Nelson, but make sure it comes out the way we need. We aren't hurting anyone, are we?"

Abigail smiled. "No, I can't imagine anyone being hurt. Unless of course, you or Nelson…?"

Mariah's eyes widened. "I'm not sure Nelson is going to be able to convince anyone he even likes me. And I'm not looking for anyone right now. I need to get Carter's Crossing set up and settle in with Grandfather's company. We'll be good."

"Then this should all be fine," Abigail agreed. But somehow, Mariah still felt like she was missing the punchline on a joke. One at her expense.

NELSON WASN'T SURPRISED to find that his dinner with Mariah had already become common knowledge and was now of more interest to his staff than Judy's elopement.

Judy had been considerate enough to only miss two days of work, so he hadn't had much to complain about. And while she didn't talk much more to him than previously, she was smiling most of the time.

Kailey was also smiling when he came in the door of the clinic. In theory, the three of them started work at the same time. Most days Nelson was the first in. But he swore Judy and Kailey must coordinate on days when they wanted to embarrass him, because then he'd walk in to the two of them staring at him.

"Now what?" he asked, grumpily. He hadn't slept well last night. Some instinct of self-preservation told him he'd been incredibly stupid to fall in with Mariah's fake engagement plan.

"So is it serious?" Kailey's eyes were sparkling. "How long have you two been together? Does this mean she's staying in Carter's Crossing?"

He sighed. He didn't want to feed their nosiness, but this was supposed to be the start of a relationship with Mariah. He couldn't be too grumpy, but if he didn't object to some degree, they'd get suspicious. At least, they should.

"I presume you're talking about the fact that Mariah and I had dinner together last night."

Kailey squealed. He raised his hand to stop her.

"She wanted to talk about my rescue horses. She had some crazy idea about using them in her plans for the town, so I told her no. That's all it was."

Kailey shook her head. "I don't think so. You could have talked about that at your place. Come on, boss, you can tell us."

Sure. Then he decided he could have some fun with this.

"I told Mariah that, but she wanted to go to Moonstone."

He scowled, but inside he was grinning.

They hadn't decided who was going to be the initiator of this dating thing, so he'd start the ball rolling. That was as far as he was going to go for now, though.

"Don't you two have real work to do?"

Judy headed to the back, a smile on her face, though Nelson wasn't sure if it was about his having dinner with Mariah, or just the same newlywed glow she was wearing these days.

Kailey leaned over, glancing to make sure Judy was gone.

"Seriously, boss, I'm happy for you. Even if this doesn't work out, you're putting yourself out there."

Nelson headed to the back to get ready for his first appointment. He didn't respond to Kailey, but inside, he was smug. This was going to work out well. Well enough that Kailey wouldn't be the only one who'd stop worrying about his social life.

And he felt a little warm inside. Sure, small towns were nosy, but they cared.

He wondered what Dave would say at the next dart night.

CHAPTER NINE

MARIAH WANTED TO get the next event in Project Proposal underway. They had only a limited time to fall madly in love in front of the town, but she had a planning meeting tonight. She, Rachel and Jaycee now had a standing date to meet and go over the details for the engagement party on Tuesdays while Dave was at darts night with Nelson.

She was happy to be part of girls' night, even if it was work related.

Growing up on a sailboat, traveling all around the world, had obvious advantages. If she'd been given one of those world maps, the kind where you color in every place you've been, Mariah would have been kept busy for a long time and used up most of the crayons. Pretty well any place that touched water, she'd been.

She'd seen different kinds of people, and a variety of lifestyles. She'd picked up bits of many languages and lost her breath at incredible beauty.

But she'd been the only girl. Her brothers hadn't left her out maliciously, but they'd had more things in common and were closer in age to each other. She met girls her age on other boats, not that many, since full-time cruisers tended more to retirees than young families, but she had met some.

When she was younger, finding another girl to play with had been a highlight. As she grew older, it was rarer to find one who shared her interests and became a friend, not an acquaintance. But while the two families might travel to a few places together, eventually they'd part ways. Everyone promised they'd meet up again, and occasionally they would, but it was random, rare and at the mercy of weather and her parents' plans.

Rachel and Jaycee were best friends and had grown up together. Mariah envied them their long friendship. She couldn't imagine how secure it would feel to have friends who'd known her since before kindergarten. Who shared stories from her whole life. Who were there. All the time.

When the planning meetings got sidetracked into other topics, Mariah was happy to follow along. She basked in the feeling of being included. This was what she wanted. When this project was done, and she settled in New York City, she could have her own place, set down her own roots and make her own circle of friends.

In Virginia, she'd been so career focused that she hadn't made an effort to find friends. She wasn't sure she knew how. Here in Carter's Crossing, she was learning. She was looking forward to finally finding her place, and her people. She might not have someone who knew her growing up, but she could make friends who would last the rest of her life.

She'd idealized friendships. Someone to spend time with. Go shopping with, go out with, talk over things with. She hadn't considered that there were things about having good friends, involved friends, that might not be as wonderful. She'd ignored the part about talking things over that she might not want to talk about so much. Concern that headed into nosy territory.

Jaycee hadn't even said hello before she started. "What's up with you and Nelson? How long has this been going on?"

Rachel was the voice of reason. "Jaycee—don't get carried away. You don't know anything other than they had dinner together."

Mariah set down her notebook and pens. She met two pairs of eyes, zeroed in on her. They weren't going to back down; she could tell.

Huh. This was part of being a friend, as well. Good thing she wanted to talk.

"First of all, we've had dinner together before. Abigail has Nelson over a couple times a week. Last night Abigail was dealing with the architect who's coming to look at the mill, so we went out because I wanted to ask about his horses."

Jaycee wasn't convinced. "You didn't have to come to Moonstone to do that."

"Nelson didn't want to disturb Abigail, and what, was I supposed to go to his place? Like that wouldn't have got everyone talking?"

Yeah, make it sound like Nelson came up with the idea.

Rachel gave Jaycee a knowing look. "I told you so."

Jaycee pouted. "I hoped Nelson was dating again."

Since Mariah was the one who was going to be dumped, she didn't need to look like she was chasing him now. She had some pride. But she was puzzled. Why wasn't he dating? If he was, he wouldn't have asked Rachel to pretend to get engaged to him. And she wouldn't be starting a fake romance. Was there no one around he was interested in? Unrequited love?

There was a story about Nelson. She wished

these gossipy people would talk about it, but they either knew already and were all talked out, or they didn't want to tell her. She almost asked. These two would know what the story was. But it felt wrong. Gossipy. Prying.

Like she wanted to know because she was interested in him. But she was supposed to be, right? But what if it got back to Nelson?

The person she should ask was Nelson. After all, if they were going to fall in love, she should know his past, especially as it related to love affairs. Was it a love affair? Some past dating thing? Would he even tell her?

Why did it feel important that he be the one to tell her?

She mentally shook her head and caught up with the conversation between Jaycee and Rachel.

"Dave's mom has been talking about her own engagement party, and how they had a sit-down dinner. Maybe we should try something like that? I mean, is this skating party too informal?"

Mariah snapped into planning mode. A sit-down dinner was not the kind of event that would promote Carter's Crossing. It was also nothing like Jaycee and Dave. They were active, fun people, and deserved a party that people would remember and talk about, not a cookie-cutter dinner.

Jaycee was a confident, outgoing woman, with a clear idea of what she liked, but Dave's mother was her weakness. Mariah was just beginning to understand the social divide the railroad tracks made in this little town.

The wrong side of the tracks was more than just an expression.

"Jaycee, I want you to have the best engagement party ever. I don't want to make it the party I want. I want it to be the party you and Dave want. You sounded excited about a skating party. Neither of you even talked about a formal dinner. Isn't that the kind of thing you said you hate?"

Jaycee played with a strand of her hair and nodded.

"Dave's mother may not have enough imagination to see this, but your party is going to be fun, unforgettable and in excellent taste. Abigail supports this. Remind Dave's mom about that if she gets to be too much.

"Now, how's the song choice going?"

MARIAH KEPT GLANCING at her watch. Nelson was taking her to see his horses, and she somehow found herself ready early.

She tried to tell herself she wanted to make

sure he hadn't caused any trouble last night out on his own, but if she was honest, she was looking forward to the trip just for the chance to see his place and his horses. She wanted to know why they were verboten for anything she had planned. She was curious about what his farm was like.

She wanted to understand him better.

Um…

Because of the fake proposal. They needed to set up more dates and work out the logistics for this "relationship." She had a rough plan worked out, but she didn't know if he'd agree to everything.

She'd dealt with all types of people planning events, mostly weddings. There were guys like Dave, who were easygoing and didn't care much about the details.

There were people like Jaycee, in the middle of the spectrum, who had a good idea of what they wanted, but still needed support for their ideas. They would listen to suggestions and accept guidance.

And on the other end, the bridezillas.

Mariah was good at identifying the types. Nelson wasn't an easy guy to figure out.

Nelson was easygoing at times, but not like Dave. He had more confidence than Jaycee, but while he'd certainly pushed a lot of her buttons, he hadn't gone into bridezilla territory.

Not knowing was making her a little nervous.

He'd told her to dress warmly, so she had long johns on under her jeans and sweater. In New York at Thanksgiving, she'd stocked up on warm clothing, so she had a new, warmer coat, as well. This far from the moderating effect of the ocean, things got much colder. The stream by the mill was frozen already, and she kept her fingers crossed that it would last.

Except when she was outside because her fingers got too cold to move.

Nelson pulled up in front of the house in his clinic van. Mariah didn't wait for him to get out. She scrambled to open the door as quickly as she could, grateful that the van was warm.

Nelson was grinning. He was still dressed in his work clothes, but he looked comfortable in the cold. He would.

"Blood still thin?"

She wanted to make a smart comment back, but it was obvious she wasn't comfortable in the cold. Her teeth were chattering. She rubbed her hands on her arms and leaned into the warm air coming from the vents.

"It's not this cold in Virginia, where I've

been working these past few years, and on the boat, we stayed where it was warm."

Nelson leaned over and turned up the heat. "Did you never head north, or south, when it was colder?" He glanced at her before pulling the van into gear and heading to the mysterious farm.

Mariah shook her head. "We traveled up the coast of the US and Europe, down Africa and South America, Australia—pretty well anywhere we could get on saltwater, but we went when those places were having summer. It's more difficult to keep a boat warm when the water is cold, and we can't move where there's ice. So no, I'm not used to this cold."

He took his attention off the road long enough to run his gaze over her. She felt it, moving over her skin along with the heat coming from the vents.

"Did you dress warmly? The barn is a little drafty."

Mariah glanced down at herself. "Long johns, sweater, hat, scarf and mitts. I hope that's enough."

"Let me know if it gets too cold and we can come back."

She nodded. "I will." She wouldn't. She had things to do, and a little cold wasn't going to stop her.

"Tell me about your horses. How did you start rescuing them?"

Nelson had driven them out of town, away from the mill. He pulled off onto a side road. "I worked at an equine practice when I first graduated. It was my specialty. I've always liked horses. Helping horses was natural, once I had my own place back here in Carter's."

"You didn't want to stay with Abigail?"

He shook his head. "When I came back, I didn't like the idea of Grandmother living on her own. I know she has staff, but they're only there in the daytime. I didn't want to share the house with her, though. I mean, I love her, but..."

"I guess that makes sense." Mariah was enjoying her time with Abigail, but it was temporary. If she was going to live in Carter's she'd probably like her own space.

Whoa. Where had that thought come from?

"Believe me, it would have been a disaster. Grandmother knows everything that goes on in this town, and believes she knows what's best for people. We needed space or she'd have driven me up the wall.

"I bought a farm. The house needs to be completely redone. I should maybe just knock it down and rebuild, but I've been working on the barn."

Nelson turned onto a side road. This was the most Nelson had shared with her since she'd arrived in Carter's Crossing. It was almost like they were friends. She waited to see if he'd keep talking.

"Not long after I got here, I was called in on a case. An old man, a recluse, had died, and his horse had been tied up in the barn without food or water for days. The horse was old, and I'd been asked to put him down.

"Despite what he'd been through, he was still affectionate, and other than the malnutrition, healthy. But he was too old to be of any use to anyone. I took him to the farm. Then I started repairing the barn, making it a home for him.

"Once the rescue people heard about that, I became their contact when they come across a horse in need of a home. A couple of the horses I've had have been rehomed, but the ones that are too old, or too abused, they stay here."

Nelson turned the van into a long driveway. Mariah saw the dilapidated house, and on the other side of the drive, the barn.

The house had boarded-up windows, and the porch floor had collapsed. The barn, on the other hand, looked sturdy and warm.

Mariah noticed a couple of horses in the field, watching the van pull in.

"This is it. I've got some stuff in the back to carry in. If you go in that barn door, you'll be warmer."

Mariah looked at the door. Were there horses in there? Were they loose?

Nelson must have understood her hesitation. "When you enter the barn, you're in an aisle, separated from the horses by a fence."

Mariah's breath was a white cloud as she sped to the barn door and pushed it open.

She heard a rustling as she rushed in. A couple of horses leaped to the doorway at the other end of the barn, startling her. A third stood by the partition nearest her, watching her with patient curiosity. Mariah heard Nelson approaching, and stepped back, away from the horses, looking around to make sure there weren't any others.

Nelson pushed the barn door open, carrying a bale of hay. Mariah closed the door behind him.

"Thanks. I've got a feed delivery coming, but not till tomorrow. You guys still want to eat, right, Sparky?"

The horse who'd been watching Mariah had turned his attention to Nelson and stretched his head over the wall.

Nelson dropped the hay bale and reached to scratch behind the horse's ears.

"Sparky?" Mariah asked.

Nelson looked over his shoulder at her. "Do you want to meet him?"

Mariah hesitated. She had never been around large animals. Not wanting to give Nelson fodder for mocking her, she forced herself to walk over.

"This is Sparky. He's the first horse I mentioned."

Sparky was rubbing his head on Nelson's sleeve. Mariah noticed the gray around Sparky's muzzle and eyes. The two other horses she'd startled had come back, heading to Nelson and the food he offered.

"How old is he?"

"He's almost thirty."

She took another look at the horse. Was Nelson serious?

"Really? I didn't know horses lived that long."

"Sparky's enjoying himself too much to give up."

Then the two horses who had been outdoors came around the open doorway. That made five. Was that all of them?

Nelson followed her gaze.

"The chestnut, the light, reddish-brown

horse, is the newest, and he's very skittish." Nelson's voice was calm and level. "Don't make sudden moves or loud noises, if you don't mind. He's still getting used to me."

Mariah nodded slowly. She watched the horse, noticing how he hung back, ears flickering, eyes focused on the humans.

Mariah thought her own ears would be flickering if they were able. She felt as uncomfortable as the horse looked.

Nelson continued to introduce her to the horses as he opened the hay bale and dropped chunks of it in the manger.

"The gray is Juno. She injured a tendon and has a limp. She'll never be able to carry a rider or travel too far. The bay is Star. He's blind but knows this field and barn well enough to make it around on his own. Juno normally travels with him and keeps him safe.

"Toby is the chestnut, and with him is Maggie. Maggie is another senior citizen, but she calms Toby down. He'll finally let me touch him, but probably not today while you're here."

"What happened to Maggie?"

"She was another victim of neglect. Her hooves hadn't been tended to for so long they'd grown out to where she couldn't walk on them anymore. It took a while, but she's okay now. She's also developing osteoarthritis, so requires extra care."

While Mariah watched, Toby followed Maggie as she came closer. He stayed just out of reach but finally came close enough to get his share of the food.

Mariah carefully sidestepped down the aisle in front of the partition, slightly away from Nelson, wanting to give him space to touch Toby if possible. She didn't want to disrupt his plans for the horse.

Nelson was right. None of these horses were going to be of any use in making Carter's Crossing a Romance Center. Two old horses, one blind one and one crippled. None of them provided the image that visitors would be looking for, let alone the ability to pull a sleigh or wagon. The final horse was afraid of people.

She hadn't really expected anything. It had been a means to an end, to start the love story of Mariah and Nelson.

If they wanted to promote Nelson as a romantic lead, however, this would certainly fit the bill. Watching him with his horses, talking to them, running his hands over their necks, scratching their ears—it was enough to make a woman feel a little swoony.

She shook herself. She couldn't get carried away. They were going to pretend to date and get engaged. It was good that she didn't find him repulsive, but there was no need to go overboard.

This was what Nelson had meant about his farm. It was a place of refuge for these animals. Not recreation for people.

"Don't move." She realized Nelson was talking to her. His voice had been in the background, talking to the horses, but now it was pitched toward her. It was still level and calm, but there was an underlying note of caution.

Mariah froze. "Is there a spider on me? You don't have poisonous spiders up here, right? You aren't running a black widow refuge, as well?"

Maybe she had a thing about spiders.

A corner of his mouth quirked. "No, not the season for spiders. Nothing's wrong. It's just that Toby is approaching you."

Toby? The skittish one?

"Did I upset him?" She stayed still, but her muscles were tense, ready to move. She trusted Nelson on this, but only so far.

"No." The smile was growing. "I think he likes you."

At that, Mariah looked out the corner of her eye. Toby was two feet away, on the other side of the partition, watching her.

"What should I do?"

"Just what you're doing."

Mariah didn't want to stand in place indefinitely. It was warmer in the barn than outside, but she was still cool. She turned her head, slowly, and Toby stayed in place.

She turned her body, just as slowly, and watched him back.

"I don't know what you want, horse. I don't have any food."

Toby snorted at her. He took a hesitant step closer.

"Whoa there, buddy. I'm not a horse person. Unless you want to get married, we have nothing in common."

He shook his head, and Mariah tensed. He stretched out his nose, and she leaned back.

"Toby." Nelson took a couple of steps toward her. The horse held his ground but brought his muzzle back toward his chest. Nelson stopped his advance but kept talking. Mariah was feeling it; that low, comforting tone inserting itself under her skin.

She totally got how he charmed his horses.

"You like it when a girl plays hard to get, is that it, Toby? It's okay. You can flirt with her, but I gotta warn you, I don't think you're her type."

Nelson maintained the low voice and leaned

his arms on the partition. Toby flickered his ears.

"Would you step up here beside me, Mariah? Nice and easy. He won't bite, but I want to see if he'll come closer."

Mariah had some second and third thoughts about this idea, but with Toby's eyes on her, she came up beside Nelson. She kept her arms safely down at her sides and looked at Nelson for guidance.

He was watching the horse but must have been aware of what she was doing. "That's good. Ignore him. He's taking a step toward you. Don't move—he's just curious. He won't hurt you."

With no change of tone, he talked to Toby. "You're not used to someone like Mariah, are you, Toby? Did you know she grew up on a boat? And she can find where she is, even in the middle of an ocean? That's what she told me."

Mariah felt warm air on her cheek. She almost swore she felt a velvety softness, and then it backed away.

"So that's it, Toby, is it? You're a ladies' horse? Well, if you're nice, maybe Mariah will come around again."

She heard muffled hoofbeats and turned

to see Toby backing off. The air swooshed out of her lungs.

"What was that?"

"I have no idea. But I've never seen Toby approach a person before. Apparently, he likes you."

CHAPTER TEN

"I'VE NEVER SEEN anything like it." Nelson paused to finish his beer.

Dave gave him a strange look.

"Really?"

"Really. I once saw one of those horse whisperers, and it was amazing. But Mariah isn't a horse person. At least, she said she'd never been around them, and she acted like they might be dangerous. But Toby..."

Nelson was still in disbelief over the whole thing.

"Not just Toby," Dave said into his mug.

Nelson raised his fist, then set it back down, frustrated. "Don't go making something out of this. It was just...something I hadn't ever seen before. It's not like—"

He broke off, since he'd been about to say that it wasn't like he was rushing to marry Mariah. Because, in actual fact, he had a countdown to when he was going to ask the woman to marry him.

A fake proposal, but still. Everyone was

supposed to believe it was real. He'd thought it would be a hard sell, and he hadn't been sure he could pull it off.

Maybe not. Maybe he had untapped acting skills. He decided to push.

"Tell me something, the truth."

Dave put his glass down. "Like what?"

"You reacted like Judy and Kailey did. Like you thought there was something going on with Mariah and me. Do you? Think that?"

Dave picked up his glass and took another swallow. Nelson suspected he was buying time. Which meant his answer wasn't no.

"I don't know if I thought there was something happening, but you're different with her."

That was not the answer he expected.

"Different?"

"Yeah. She bugs you. I get it. But it's like there's something more. You can't ignore her. So maybe it's one of those love-to-hate things." Dave shrugged. "That's what Jaycee said."

Nelson closed his eyes and took a long breath. This might make the proposal harder to sell, but he needed to be honest with his best friend.

"I didn't tell you this, but Mariah worked

for the wedding planner who organized my wedding."

Dave's eyes widened. "Really? Did Mariah work on your wedding?"

Nelson shook his head. "I heard her telling Grandmother that she'd learned everything she needed to know from her boss."

"You mean the woman who did your wedding."

Nelson nodded. "I said something to Grandmother about it, and she told me she trusted Mariah. And that Mariah had planned Zoey's wedding just before coming here."

Dave's eyes nearly bugged out of his head. "Your Zoey?"

"My Zoey. So she might have some magical spell on Toby, but I have a hard time trusting her."

Dave nodded. "I get that. Why didn't you tell me before?"

"It's not my favorite topic—how I ruined my own wedding and chased off my fiancée. And, maybe Grandmother was right. Maybe Mariah's better now. I can't imagine Zoey working with her otherwise. But..."

"Yeah. That's a big but." Dave stared down at the table.

Nelson shouldn't have brought this up. It was unfair to Mariah. He knew he was anything but impartial. And it was going to make it harder to sell a big love affair with Mariah these next few weeks.

But he'd also been concerned about Dave. Dave hadn't complained, lately, about his engagement party, but Nelson knew something wasn't quite right. When the topic came up, times when they were hanging out with the girls, Dave's expression tightened. Nelson couldn't understand why Jaycee didn't see it.

Dave and Jaycee had started to practice their dance. Jaycee had brought it up, not Dave. In fact, all Jaycee talked about these days was the party.

Nelson would have liked to talk to Jaycee, ask her if she was considering how Dave felt about all these decisions she was making, and the time and energy she was spending on it. But he'd promised not to interfere.

He'd compromised, telling Dave why he was skeptical about Mariah. He'd be there for his friend if Dave needed him. He was not going to charge in, telling people what they should do.

He'd been that guy and it cost him his fiancée, so he couldn't be that guy again. For three years it had been easy. Now he was going to need dental work from grinding his teeth.

"Another game of darts?" It was time to

distract his friend. Nelson had dropped his hint, and now he'd leave it up to Dave.

Dave blinked, obviously miles away. "Sure."

NELSON MIGHT HAVE doubts about Mariah as a wedding planner or romance coordinator, but he wanted her help with Toby. If she could bring Toby close enough for him to touch again it would advance his rehab. Unlike the other horses, Toby had a chance at a second life with people. The right kind of people this time.

It was worth asking her.

He wasn't sure if she'd be interested in a return trip to the barn. It might not fit into her dating timeline since it wasn't someplace people would see them. When she agreed, he wasn't going to second-guess the opportunity, though, so he picked her up on his next afternoon off.

He'd brought a space heater, to keep the barn warmer. He hoped to spend some time with Toby, if Mariah's magic worked again, and it wouldn't help anything if Mariah turned into an icicle in the meantime.

Her one condition had been that he go with her to a couple of locations she needed to scout before they went to the farm.

Nelson almost bit his lip hard enough to draw blood, holding back the mocking question about whether she needed his help to navigate. She'd never admit it, he knew, and she'd probably claim this was to sell the dating story, but he liked his version better—that Mariah, the mighty navigator, needed his help to find her way around New York state.

He pulled up in front of his grandmother's house, in what was becoming a familiar move. Mariah was ready. He had to give her points for promptness—she never kept him waiting. She was wearing a red coat that made her look pretty. She was carrying a briefcase and a duffel bag.

He got out of his car to open the trunk for her.

"Thanks." She dropped the duffel bag into the trunk. "I brought a change of clothes for the barn."

"You couldn't have just worn something more casual?"

She frowned at him. "I need to look professional."

Nelson was wearing jeans and boots with a jacket. He was dressed for warmth. No one had mentioned needing to look professional. "What exactly are we doing?"

"I'm doing research, looking for activities,

points of interest and other locations for out-of-town visitors."

Nelson sighed.

Mariah shot him a glance. "I'm not going to ask you to do anything, well, anything major. But you can give me a male reaction—just 'I'd hate that' or 'I'd like to do this.' I need more feedback. If you and I are going to convince people that we're dating, I can't very well ask some other guy from town to drive me around."

He didn't want to admit it, but she had a point.

"Plus, if I'm helping you with your horse, you should be able to help me in return."

She shot him a challenging glance.

Nelson couldn't think of anyone else who'd say something like that to him, and he had no idea why he liked it. "Where do you want to go?"

Mariah opened her briefcase and pulled out a sheaf of papers and her phone.

"I've got the first location here on my phone app. In case we lose connection, I printed out directions."

Was she serious? She was angry when he offered a stranger direction, but she didn't think he could find his way around the place he lived?

"No sextant?"

"I'm keeping that as a treat for the next time."

An annoying voice on her phone instructed him to turn left as he pulled away from his grandmother's house.

Once they'd left town, Nelson was able to ask where they were going. Mariah might have her app and her printouts, but he'd grown up here. He'd be able to navigate to anyplace around here better than an app.

Mariah fiddled with the scarf around her neck.

"A place called Evertons?"

Nelson took his gaze from the road to check if she was serious.

"Evertons?"

She nodded.

"I was told they have a corn maze in the fall and make maple syrup."

"Yeah…did Grandmother tell you to go there?"

Mariah shook her head. "No, I found out about it from someone else. Abigail said she couldn't help me but didn't want to tell me why. She thought I should go in unbiased."

Nelson sighed. "You should go in without me, then. The Evertons aren't fond of my family."

Mariah shook her head again. "No, I won't present myself under false pretenses. I'm working with Abigail. I won't hide that."

"Then you're not going to get very far."

Mariah looked at him. "Let me guess. Long, long ago, a Carter and an Everton wanted the same land. They flipped for it, and after the Carter won, it was revealed that it was a two-headed coin. Ever since then—"

Nelson laughed and shook his head. Mariah tried again. "The Evertons started the mill and the Carters won the deed in a poker game?"

Nelson couldn't help looking at her again. There was a teasing glint in those eyes. She might actually have a sense of humor under all her lists and plans. He wanted to find out. But the Everton story wasn't a funny one.

"There was an accident at the mill about fifteen years ago. Mrs. Everton was hurt and died a few years later. The Evertons blame the Carters."

Mariah was quiet for a moment.

"And what do the Carters say?"

Nelson took a long breath. "That Mrs. Everton was in a place she shouldn't have been. If you want to be unbiased, I'll leave it at that."

"Thanks." Mariah looked down at her

notes. "I understand why Abigail didn't want to influence me, but I feel better coming in with an idea of what's going on."

Nelson slowed, ignoring the voice on the phone app. "We're almost there, so I hope you're ready."

Mariah gave him a worried look. "They're not going to come out with a shotgun, are they?"

Nelson toyed with the idea of saying yes, just to see her reaction, but he wasn't that mean. There didn't need to be any more bad blood between the Evertons and the Carters.

"No. I don't know of anyone around here who's likely to greet visitors with a gun. But give them time—they don't know you yet."

The worry vanished from her eyes, replaced with a spark.

"If you haven't driven them to it after all these years, I think I'll be okay."

Nelson hid his grin. He wouldn't admit it to anyone, but he liked that she pushed back at him. After the fiasco with Zoey, Mariah was a relief. No one was going to push her into anything she didn't like. He could relax and be himself.

He turned into the driveway, toward a house set back in the trees. As he pulled the car to a stop, a man his own age stepped out.

He was dressed in work clothes and heavy boots, and a bushy beard covered the lower half of his face.

He had a dog on a tight lead beside him, something related to a German shepherd, and the animal was focused on them with a laser gaze.

Nelson had never seen this dog before, unsurprisingly, but he recognized it as a guard dog, undoubtedly dangerous in the right circumstances.

Jordan spoke, and the dog sat.

He wasn't carrying any other kind of weapon, but the expression on his face was so far from welcoming as to make Mariah's concern plausible.

Well, that and the dog.

Mariah was reaching for the door release, so Nelson quickly got out of the car. He didn't want her to face the wrath of the Evertons on her own. Especially not with a guard dog at the ready.

"Nelson." The bearded man's voice was cold.

Nelson nodded. "Jordan. How're things?"

Jordan ignored him to examine Mariah. Nelson had to fight an urge to stand between the two. "Mariah, this is Jordan Everton."

Mariah stepped forward, hand outstretched. "I'm Mariah Van Delton, Mr. Everton."

Jordan stood in place, ignoring her hand. The dog curled a lip.

"I've heard of you."

His tone didn't indicate that he was very happy with what he'd heard.

Mariah was unfazed. She dropped her hand with no indication of embarrassment.

"I don't know what you've heard, so let me give you an introduction. I'm here to set up a new business in Carter's Crossing. The business is intended to benefit everyone. I plan to make this place a destination for everything related to romance—weddings, anniversaries, proposals, weekend getaways. The town looks like a Norman Rockwell painting, has four seasons for variety and is located within a few hours of several large cities, so I have every confidence I can make this happen.

"I'm paid by my grandfather, who handles events in New York City, among other things. My room and board are provided by Abigail Carter, as I'm sure you're aware. However, this is *my* project. And the project is for the benefit of everyone in the area.

"I intend to take advantage of everything the town has available—bed-and-breakfasts, restaurants, activities, special locations. Currently, Carter's Crossing is almost invisible online, and there's very little promotion for what Carter's Crossing has to offer. That is going to change. I hope to get people to come here, provide business for those who live here and attract more investment and expansion in the town.

"I understand that you have a corn maze on your property in the fall and make maple syrup in the spring. I think both of those activities would work as an attraction for visitors, and I would like to work with you so that I promote your enterprise. I don't mean to tell you how to run your business, but I can advise you as to what is likely to be lucrative with the people we're bringing in."

Mariah brought her pitch to a close and waited. Jordan stood, watching her.

"If I don't cooperate, what then?"

Nelson had been impressed by Mariah's spiel, though he'd never tell her that. She had some good arguments, but he also knew how stubborn the Evertons were. Jordan's father was convinced that the mill was at fault for what had happened with his wife, and he'd passed that belief on to his son.

"Nothing will happen if you don't want to be part of what we're doing. You won't be featured on our website. I won't share with you my ideas to make your events mesh with our romance theme. I won't tell you how I think you could keep people coming in during summer and winter.

"We won't shun you. We won't discourage people from coming here or spread rumors about your place. But I need partners in this enterprise, and I'll focus my attention on them.

"If we bring in more people, I'm sure that will still benefit you, but not as much as you could if you cooperate with us. I do understand that there are things of more value than money, so I'm not going to pressure you. I would like you to work with us, but that's your call.

"One last thing I'd like to mention. I've been working closely with Abigail Carter, as the original idea was hers. She's determined to make this work and has plans to change the name of the town to Cupid's Crossing, to help with marketing. That means your business would not be connected with the name Carter."

Nelson shook his head slightly; not sure he was hearing correctly. Grandmother was going to take the Carter name away from the town?

Was Mariah serious? Or was she manipulating Jordan?

Jordan had his arms crossed, a frown on his face. "Your sidekick here doesn't seem to be aware of that."

Nelson clenched his jaw. He didn't like being called a sidekick, and he didn't like being caught unprepared. Not about something big like this, something that would affect not only him but also everyone else in town.

"I don't think Abigail has told anyone but me. She wants to be sure this idea succeeds before she changes the name."

Jordan shot a smirk at Nelson, enjoying his irritation.

"Well, Ms. Van Delton, I'll consider what you've said. Perhaps you and I could talk about this further, if I decide I'm interested."

Nelson didn't like being cut out. He almost argued the point, but then paused, unsure why he felt this way.

He'd asked to be left out of the romance idea. He had no reason to think Mariah's spending time with Jordan was a bad idea, even if Jordan did look like he was interested in more than talking business with Mariah.

He wasn't her boyfriend…or was he?

They were supposed to be pretend dating.

He moved a few steps closer to Mariah. He didn't think he could get away with wrapping an arm around her, but he reached out and tugged on her scarf.

"We should get going. You still had a couple of stops you wanted to make before we see the horses."

Jordan gave them a mocking salute. "Call me in a week or so, Mariah, and I'll let you know."

"Thanks for listening to me, Mr. Everton."

"Jordan, please."

Mariah nodded. "I hope we can find a way to work together."

"Me, too."

Nelson wanted to tug Mariah and stuff her into his car. Jordan had no intentions of working with anyone connected to a Carter. He was just messing with Nelson. And unfortunately, Nelson was upset by that, because he'd agreed to a fake engagement because…it took him a few beats. Because he'd had a part in Harvey and Judy's elopement and didn't want his grandmother to lose everything in this plan she had to revitalize Carter's Crossing, or Cupid's Crossing, or whatever name they came up with.

And Mariah was supposed to help with his horses.

Mariah finally sat in the car, after he'd held the door open for her, and they left the Everton farm behind them, Jordan watching them drive away, the dog now on its feet.

He'd have to tell Dave about this. Jordan and Dave and Nelson had all been in the same grade going through school and been friends—until the accident. Jordan's dad had pulled him out of school. It had been the end of their friendship.

That one, at least, wasn't Nelson's fault.

MARIAH WAS NERVOUS about going back to Nelson's farm.

It was flattering, and a definite ego boost to be the horse whisperer her last time here, but she didn't have any abilities in that regard. It must have been a fluke. She was going to feel awkward and out of place if the horse ignored her this time.

Too late to worry about that. They were at the farm, and it was time to discover if she had equine superpowers or not.

She opened her door without waiting for Nelson. She grabbed her bag from the trunk and changed her coat and boots, shivering in the cold.

"You could change in the barn—it would be warmer."

Mariah finished buttoning up her coat. "It's okay. I'm done now." She wasn't sure why, but she hadn't wanted to change in the barn, in front of the horses.

Nelson stood staring at her.

"Is something wrong?" Was she dressed wrong? She'd brought the same clothes as last time. Maybe the horse had just liked her coat.

"Are you okay? You don't really have to do this."

Mariah let out a breath. Was she that transparent? "I'm afraid I might not be able to do it again."

She closed her eyes. Why was she admitting this? She didn't want to appear weak in front of Nelson. So often it felt like they were opponents. And this was being…vulnerable.

His response surprised her.

"You don't have to do anything. Maybe Toby was just curious about you because you were new. If so, no harm. I still got closer to him than I've been able to when he's loose.

"If he does want to come to you, that's a bonus."

Maybe they weren't opponents. Maybe they were just people with different goals. Except for the next few weeks. Unless she found another couple ready for a proposal, they had a shared goal of appearing to fall in love.

Guess she should start with Toby.

"Okay, then, let's see if I'm irresistible to horses."

Mariah headed to the barn, but Nelson put a hand on her arm.

"If you're warm enough, let's just stand at the fence. The horses are outside, so we'll see if you're irresistible out here, as well."

Nelson rubbed his hands up and down her sleeves. It was a nice gesture. And she couldn't think of an ulterior motive for it. There was no one here to see them. He was being…nice.

The friction did help. She finally batted him away.

"Okay, I'm good now. I'll go try my magic at your fence."

She followed him to the fence, where they could see the five horses under some trees on the far side. A couple had their heads down, looking at something on the ground. Two had their heads on each other's backs, and one was staring at them.

Within a couple of minutes the herd had started their way.

"Is that me?"

Nelson rested his forearms on the top rail. "Would you be devastated to know that the four of them always come to see anybody who stops by?"

"No. I don't need to be the pied piper of the equine world. It's just if Toby comes, right?"

Nelson's eyes were glued to his horses. "Right."

"Should I hold out my hand or wave or something?"

The corners of his mouth quirked, but he kept his eyes on the animals walking toward them.

"No, just the power of your presence should do it. Sudden noises or movements are more likely to startle them."

All five horses were heading this way. Was it working? She felt a tug of affection for Toby.

"So what will you do with Toby if he gets over his fear? Will he stay here with the others?"

"It depends on how well he does. If he could be useful, and enjoy himself, I'd try to find him a home. I have limited room here, and I can only keep so many horses. I need to be sure I have space for those who have no other options."

This was a side to Nelson she hadn't known before. She hadn't realized the horses were a key to the Nelson lock.

"There's no chance I could talk you into expanding to have regular horses, as well, to ride or do wagon rides or sleigh rides on your farm, is there?"

Nelson shook his head slowly. The horses were almost within reach. Toby was with the herd but hanging back.

"I'm not running a business out here. Having horses for those activities would require a lot of time and money. I have a job, one I'm quite happy with."

Mariah turned sideways to watch him. The first couple of horses had stretched their heads out to touch him.

"Did you always want to be a vet?"

The first nose had reached Nelson, and he ran his gloved hand up the side of the horse's face, rubbing behind the ears. The horse shoved his head against Nelson's body, obviously enjoying the attention. The next horse reached in, wanting the same.

Mariah wondered how he could handle all four if they crowded around him. She wouldn't be comfortable with that.

"As long as I can remember. I like animals."

Then she felt warm air against her cheek. She stayed still.

"Did I do it again?" She kept her voice low and calm, imitating Nelson to the best of her ability.

Nelson had a warm grin on his face, one she couldn't help responding to.

"You sure did."

Then she felt a push, gentle, but still a push, that felt very much like what she imagined Nelson had felt when the first horse rubbed up against him.

"What should I do?" she asked, uncomfortably out of her element.

Nelson had better have been telling the truth about the horses not biting.

"Hold out your glove and see what he does."

Mariah could do this. She braced herself and slowly held out her hand. A chestnut muzzle moved over it, snuffling a cloud of warm breath over her cold glove.

Mariah watched for a moment, mesmerized. Was this really her, charming a horse? Who knew? She looked back to Nelson.

"Don't rub his nose—that can be sensitive. But if you're okay with it, run your hand up his cheek."

Nelson demonstrated on the closest head to him. That horse enjoyed the attention.

Mariah turned her glance to Toby again. Slowly, she moved her hand up to his cheek, expecting him to bolt any moment. Bolt or bite. Instead, after a slight hesitation, he leaned into her caress.

Mariah stroked back and forth for a couple of minutes, then turned to Nelson. “It’s working. I’m doing it!”

She felt a sense of accomplishment out of all proportion to the activity.

But Nelson grinned back, just as happy. At that moment she felt something.

Her smile faltered, but Nelson was pushing aside the heads next to him.

“Are you okay for a couple of minutes? I’m going to go grab some treats. We want to reward Toby for this.”

“Sure.” Mariah heard Nelson leave, while she focused back on Toby. She kept rubbing his cheek.

“Toby, it’s nice to know that someone here likes me, but what the heck was that with Nelson? It was just weird. Don’t tell anyone, okay, horse? Because Nelson might be happy that you like me, but he doesn’t like me or my job, at all.

“Do you know why that is?” she continued, stroking the horse, hand moving to his neck, which he allowed, as well.

“Nah, you’re new here, too, aren’t you? Well, if he does tell you, would you mind sharing it with me? Because it would be a whole lot easier to fake date this guy if he didn't despise me."

He hadn't looked like he despised her a few minutes ago. But this thing with Toby? It was all Toby. She hadn't done anything to merit this. She was just the person Toby decided to trust.

It was too bad Nelson couldn't trust her, as well.

CHAPTER ELEVEN

NELSON WAS HAPPY that darts night was just the guys again. Ever since the engagement party had been greenlit, Jaycee had kept Mariah and Rachel busy with party plans. Unfortunately, the plans were stressing Dave, a lot.

"You're really dancing on skates." Nelson had a hard time picturing that.

Dave nodded. Instead of watching the hockey game over the bar, he was picking the label off his beer bottle.

"It's not that bad. It's more skating than dancing. But Jaycee is making such a thing of it. I mean, it's not like we're in the Olympics where someone is judging every little thing."

Nelson almost bit his tongue, but he managed to keep his comments to himself. It wasn't easy. He saw so much of himself in what Jaycee was doing.

This was what he had against these events. It could bring out a side to a person that could never be unseen. People could be hurt. Things were said that could never be unsaid.

Nelson had learned it all firsthand. But he'd learned other lessons, as well. One was that he didn't always know best. And that even though he could charm, argue or coerce people into doing things, that didn't mean he should.

He'd vowed to himself that he'd never do that again, and he wasn't going to. He'd made a promise to his grandmother to stay out of the romance plan. He'd pushed those limits already, between his drunken diatribe and revealing Mariah's connection to Sherry Anstruthers to Rachel and Dave. He couldn't in good conscience do anything more.

Instead of telling Dave what to do, he asked him if he wanted another beer.

Dave shook his head. "No, I'm good. And sorry, didn't mean to whine. I want to ask you something."

Nelson had been about to go to the bar, but he waited.

"You've been spending a lot of time with Mariah."

Yes, the small-town grapevine was in fine form. He'd refused to tell Kailey and Judy anything except that Mariah was helping with the horses, but he knew they suspected there was more to it. Everyone did.

And there was. They had the proposal coming up in a couple of weeks. He and Mariah were spending most of their free time together, except for dart nights, and other planning emergencies with Jaycee. And it had been, well, not as horrible as he'd feared.

"I told you—when she's there, Toby is a different horse."

"That wasn't just a fluke?"

Nelson grinned. "Toby has a crush on her."

Dave blinked. "Is that a real thing with horses?"

"It is with Toby. Every time she shows up, he comes right over."

Dave had helped Nelson transport Toby to the farm. He understood just how big a deal that was.

"No kidding. So does she work with him?"

Nelson shook his head. "She doesn't know anything about horses. But while she's there, he sticks around, and I've been able to groom him, check his feet. It's been pretty incredible."

"It's just been about Toby?"

Nelson could feel the heat in his cheeks as he paused.

Dave started to grin.

"Oh, so maybe this wedding planner isn't so bad?"

Nelson would have loved to contradict him, but he couldn't.

It wasn't just that he was trying to make people believe that he and Mariah could be in love by Valentine's Day.

It was because they weren't just spending time with Toby together. And he didn't hate it.

Mariah, in a move that was typical, had come up with a program for their time together, one that would help them appear like a dating couple. Since they'd be learning about each other if they were really dating, they spent every free night together doing research.

Research in this case meant watching the other person's three favorite movies. And part of the other's favorite TV shows. And he had to read her favorite books while she read his.

They shouldn't have had too much time for talking, except that they managed to argue about the movies, TV shows and books. She was appalled by the lack of female representation in his choices. He thought hers were too serious and had no humor.

Needless to say, there was no overlap in their choices.

He enjoyed the sparring. He'd thought, after his wedding fiasco, that disagreements and arguments were the last thing he'd enjoy, but somehow, he did.

Because he was a Carter and had always been one of the smartest kids in school, and the most ambitious, people tended to defer to him. When he was treating his animals, no one contradicted him. When he made recommendations, for meals or movies or vacation spots, people listened.

Mariah, however, hadn't been impressed with him since they met. He suspected that sometimes she argued against him, not because she thought he was wrong as much as because she believed he needed to be put in his place.

Somehow, he liked it. And upon occasion, he'd argue a position he didn't honestly support, just to make her sit up, eyes sparkling, cheeks flushed, and go after him.

"She's..." She was what? How would he describe Mariah?

Aggravating and independent. Way too sure of herself. Pretty. Smart. Strong. Brave and patient with Toby. Kind and respectful with Grandmother.

Dave was waving a hand in front of him, waiting for an answer to his question.

"She's not so bad," he muttered.

Dave laughed, looking carefree for the first time in weeks.

"You look like that was painful to say. I knew you weren't just spending time with her for your horses."

"Jeez, Dave, could you say that a little louder? I don't know if the kitchen staff heard you."

He squirmed on his seat, uncomfortable. But this was what he was supposed to do. And it made Dave laugh. It shouldn't bother him so much.

"COME ON, SPILL. You aren't spending all that time with Nelson just working with his horses, now, are you?"

Mariah was impressed that it had taken this long before Jaycee and Rachel asked about what was going on between Nelson and her.

Rachel was nice. It wasn't a surprise that she hadn't pried. But Jaycee was different. It was only the pressure of the engagement party distracting her that had bought Mariah time.

She didn't need time, not really. But it had been a relief, all the same.

Mariah wasn't an actor, but she was trying to act. Whether she could convince these two women that she and Nelson were really falling for each other would be a real test.

Apparently, she was acing it.

"I asked him to take me to some places around here, things that might help with my planning."

"Sure. Is that why you've been spending nights at his place?" How did Jaycee know that? Mariah was still getting used to small-town gossip.

"I have not been spending the night at his place." Not at all. She always came back to Abigail's to sleep.

"Okay, fine, spending the evening. I know he doesn't have any horses up there."

Mariah felt her cheeks flushing. This was good, really. She needed people to believe they were dating.

"We've been…hanging out." It would be better to be vague, and let people imagine what they wanted. Then she wasn't lying, and the rumors would still spread.

"Hanging out, as in making out on his couch?"

Mariah rolled her eyes, but she wondered if this is what she'd missed, with the way she'd been raised. The teasing, about boys and whatever else.

"None of your business." It was supposed

to stop the conversation. Instead, it made Jaycee clap.

"Is he a good kisser? I've always thought he would be. I'm not sure why. I never thought Dave would be, but it turns out he's fantastic."

Mariah tried to get Jaycee back on track. "We're not here to talk about whether Nelson is a good kisser."

But now the question was in her head. Did Jaycee really have to bring it up? But then again, this was part of dating. If they really wanted to sell this…

Rachel was quiet. "You're leaving in the fall, right?"

Mariah nodded.

"Nelson knows you're leaving, too?"

Right. They needed to have a story for that to really sell the proposal.

"Nelson knows what my plans are."

Rachel smiled deprecatingly. "It's just, Nelson had a bad time, and it's taken him a while to get over it. He's my friend, and I worry about him."

Mariah appreciated that. She wanted friends like that, friends who knew you, knew where you'd been and what you'd done and worried about you.

"Rachel, I promise I'll be honest with Nelson. He may be an opinionated, arrogant know-it-all, but if he's your friend, I know there's good down there somewhere."

Jaycee offered her a high five. "You are exactly what Nelson needs. Rachel is way too nice to him."

Rachel smiled, but Mariah could see the worry underneath. Rachel was a lovely person. Quietly pretty, in a way that deflected attention. Kind, generous, helpful… Why had Nelson overlooked her? Nelson said they were friends—did Rachel want more?

Mariah hoped this proposal wouldn't hurt Rachel. But if Nelson didn't care for her, and she cared for him, it was better to know and deal with it.

Maybe, after Nelson broke up the engagement, something could work out between them. She didn't understand why that thought bothered her.

She wasn't here to play Cupid for the residents of Carter's Crossing. She was here to build a business. And that she would do.

After what Rachel said, she had to finally press Nelson on what had happened to him in the past. If they were going to sell this romance, it was something she needed to know.

She just hoped it wouldn't end the fun they'd been having together.

DESPITE JAYCEE'S IMAGINATION, Mariah and Nelson always sat a decorous distance apart when they were in his apartment, doing research.

Mariah could only imagine what Jaycee would think if she heard they were doing "research."

She hadn't pushed Nelson on his life story. If she was honest with herself, she didn't want to share her own in detail, so it hadn't seemed fair to ask him to do so. But she needed to know. There was something connected with weddings and romance and that was much too close to her job for her to ignore.

And, they needed to demonstrate some PDA. That wasn't going to be easy to bring up, but they were running out of time, and it wasn't going to happen organically. Not when they weren't really dating.

Since she hadn't been able to find a replacement event for the proposal at this late date, it appeared that they were going to have to do this thing.

Mariah had brought her laptop and notebook to Nelson's apartment. It was a familiar space by now. The first couple of visits, she thought he had cleaned up for her, but now she realized he just was that tidy. It was a trait she appreciated. Growing up with five people on a boat, the only way to find anything and stay safe was to have a place for everything and everything in its place.

Nelson turned on the hockey game. Mariah knew his favorite team, and more than she wanted about its history and how this season was going.

"You don't mind?" he had said the same the last time they got together, when she had some sourcing to do online, and they weren't actively "researching."

Then she'd said she didn't mind. This time she reached over and turned off the game.

He looked annoyed but didn't say anything. He wasn't stupid.

"I was talking to Jaycee and Rachel, and I realized…we have to work on kissing."

NELSON TOOK A moment to hear what Mariah had just said and understand the meaning.

"Kissing? For this fake proposal, you mean? Is there a kissing part?"

Mariah shook her head.

He felt something drop in his chest. He was disappointed. Working on kissing sounded like fun.

"It's for now. If we want people to believe we're so in love that we want to get married, we have to show some affection in public. Unless that crosses some kind of line for you?"

That would be a no. He was a fan of kissing, and he'd missed it.

Mariah kept her eyes on her notes as she continued, "So that means hand-holding, touching and kissing. And yes, if two people are crazy about each other and one proposes, then there would be kissing at the proposal. I didn't script it—I just assumed it was going to happen."

Nelson didn't respond immediately. He hadn't thought about that part of the fake dating: her list of hand-holding, touching and kissing. Especially kissing. Not as far as actually making the moves necessary for their lips to meet. He'd thought Mariah was pretty, and, well, those lips had inspired some thoughts about how they'd feel…

Yeah, he'd thought about kissing Mariah. But not seriously. Always in the abstract. The idea of taking those thoughts and putting them into action? Not a place he'd allowed himself to go. Now he was going there, pushed on by Mariah herself.

"To be clear, you want me to kiss you the next time we're out together. Like, where there are people around." He didn't think the farm would count.

And, totally unrelated, he wondered if they should go out somewhere tonight, someplace where people were around.

"No, I think we need to practice first."

Practice? Nelson straightened on the couch. Oh, yeah, he was up for that.

"I'm good, but if you want a chance to make sure you're up to speed..." He raised his eyebrows. This research was sounding better all the time.

"Of course you think you're a good kisser. All guys do."

There she went, giving him grief again.

"I am a good kisser. Do you need references?"

Mariah waved off his assertion. "You really think any woman would tell you if you were bad? We're brought up to be nice."

If this was Mariah being nice...

"You think you need to teach me how to kiss?" Seriously, this woman was enough to drive a man to frustration. Frequently.

She was sitting upright, chin raised. "I don't know if I need to teach you or not. But I'd like to try it in private first, in case we need to work on it."

What, she was going to critique his kissing performance? Not happening. He'd make sure she had no complaints. And he needed to derail this line of thought right now.

"Mariah, I don't know what kind of 'working on this' you think we might need, but if you want to kiss me you could just say so."

Mariah lifted her hand and started counting off on her fingers. "Too much saliva, too much pressure, too much tongue, licking, scraping teeth, bad breath—"

"Okay, okay, I get it," Nelson broke in. She really did have a list on this. And then he wondered if he had breath mints around. What had he eaten for dinner?

He wanted to assure her he didn't do any of that, but now he began to second-guess himself. Would anyone have told him if he'd gotten it wrong? He couldn't remember any of his dates trying to avoid his kiss…

"It would look bad if one of us was flinching away from the other when we kissed in public. I just thought we should try a kiss in private first, so we can do it right."

Nelson looked at Mariah, her cheeks slightly pink, her gaze on her notebook and her teeth biting her bottom lip. Maybe it was all this talk of kissing, but right now he wanted to kiss Mariah.

Not theoretical, kissing would be great, but kissing the woman sitting there, the one trying to make kissing an item on her list, something they could practice in order to demonstrate to people that they were falling for each other.

Maybe some people kissed like that. But Nelson never had. He didn't kiss for anyone but himself and the woman he was interested in. He wanted to kiss Mariah but kiss her so that she wanted to kiss him again, not to impress anyone else or critique his technique.

He was going to make her love his kisses.

Being overeager was something that would be on the bad kissing list, so Nelson shrugged.

"Okay, then. Let's do it." He patted the couch beside him.

He watched Mariah. He saw her swallow. Her teeth were scraping her lip now. She set her computer and notebooks down on the floor beside her chair.

"I guess we should go ahead and get this taken care of."

Was she nervous? She totally was.

"Mark it off your list."

She narrowed her eyes, looking like she suspected something. He smiled back at her.

"Come on. No time like the present. Then I can get back to the game."

Her shoulders snapped back, and her teeth were no longer worrying her lip. He held back a grin. Unless he mistook the expression on her face, she was determined that he wasn't going to shrug off this kiss and turn on the TV.

Good. They were on the same page about it.

She stood and crossed to the couch, dropping on the cushion beside him. He watched the expressions swirling over her face. She was staring at his lips, and then she leaned forward, starting to pucker. He could almost read the checklist in her mind.

Uh-uh. Kissing wasn't a checklist.

He put a hand on her cheek, soft under his palm, and kept her at a distance.

"Hold on, Mariah. You all but accused me of being a bad kisser. I can't have that. We're going to do this right."

Her brow creased. "What do you mean?"

His thumb brushed over her cheek. She blinked. His other hand brushed her arm, fingers running up and down from shoulder to wrist and back. Her gaze followed his hand, her expression confused.

His fingers slid up her shoulder, across to her neck, gently stroking. He felt her soften under his touch. Soon he had both hands cradling her face. She drew in a breath, watching him intently. He caressed her bottom lip with one thumb, and her mouth parted.

Bingo.

He leaned forward and pressed a gentle kiss to her forehead. Her skin was warm and smooth under his lips. Her perfume tickled his nose, and he could hear her breathing. He felt his own breath speed up. Mariah's eyes fluttered closed as his lips traced a path down her nose, across her cheek, to one corner of the delectable lips.

She sighed, relaxing fully into his hold.

Then he touched her lips with his, softly. He pulled away, just enough to catch his breath, and she moved closer, seeking more.

He pressed forward again, brushing his lips against hers, back and forth, as she pushed closer to him. His hands slid into her hair, and hers moved up his chest, gripping his sweater.

Now he increased the pressure, feeling the texture of her lips, the brush of her breath, the slight moan that escaped her.

Or maybe that was him. Because kissing Mariah was a pleasure he'd have hated to miss.

Her lips parted, inviting him in, but he made himself pull back. It was more difficult than it should have been, because after all, this was Mariah, his fake date. But the kiss felt real, and that was a problem. It shouldn't. This was all pretend.

She was still there, eyes closed. Right, his hands, in her hair. He made himself loosen his hold, drop his hands, lean back to his side of the couch.

"So," he started, but his voice was rough. He cleared his throat. "Is that good enough?"

Her eyes were open now, and she was holding herself stiffly upright.

She took a trembling breath. "That…that will do."

Nice try. He'd felt her response, and it made the caveman in him want to sit up and beat on his chest.

"You're sure? You don't have any tips? Need to give me some lessons?"

He couldn't let her know how real that had felt.

Her eyes flashed. "Nelson, I'm not here to stroke your ego. We both did good enough. Lessons and further practice are unnecessary."

"All right. Have you got a schedule for kissing now? I'm sure you wrote down just how often we need to kiss in front of people to make this look good."

He wasn't sure why he was pushing this. If he was smart, he'd find a way to put kissing completely off the table. More kissing was just going to cause more problems.

Perhaps his intelligence was overrated.

"I'll let you know. After all, I can initiate a kiss myself."

Oh, that would be interesting.

"Good to know."

Mariah stood and crossed back over to her chair, picking up her notepad with shaking hands. Her hair was mussed from his fingers, and her lipstick smudged. Her cheeks were flushed.

Yeah, he felt confident that he could kiss her well enough.

MARIAH COULD FEEL Nelson's smugness, see it on his face, hear it in his voice.

Yes, that kiss had been…unsettling.

Mariah would admit when it came to kissing, making out, she was inexperienced. Not completely, but she hadn't had a lot of opportunities to practice. There wasn't a lot for her to compare that kiss to.

She only knew that if Nelson hadn't pulled away, she'd have done her best to wrap herself as close to him as she could to continue that kiss. The one that made her forget where she was, what she was doing and why. The one she was already missing.

But even if Nelson was a more than adequate kisser, she couldn't let him have the upper hand. She had to do something so that she wouldn't throw herself back on the couch to continue that kiss.

Her notepad saved her, as it often had. "There's something I need to know if we're getting engaged. Why are you so against people getting married?"

Nelson stiffened, no longer relaxed. He appeared to choose his words carefully. "I'm not against people getting married."

Mariah raised an eyebrow. "Really. How can you even try to make me believe that?"

Nelson clenched his jaw. "I'm not against marriage, or dating, or love, or any of those things. I'm not a fan of elaborate weddings."

Hair splitting.

"Okay, tell me how you split that fine hair."

He narrowed his eyes. She kept her chin up.

"Can you honestly tell me that some weddings haven't been disasters? That some brides or grooms focus only on the big event, and bulldoze over everyone and everything in their way? They make life miserable for everyone around them in service for their big party? You've helped plan some of those, right?"

Oof. Mariah sat back. That was very...

impassioned. Accusatory. And somehow, very personal.

"You're right. There are some people like that. But that isn't everyone, or even most people. My job was to try to find balance—make my clients' wishes come true, but as considerately as possible."

She could see the disbelief in his expression.

"Why do you look like you think I'm lying? What is your problem? Have I ever done anything to make you believe otherwise?"

"Don't you get paid to make sure the big event comes off, no matter what?"

She shook her head. "No, I don't make that my only focus. I need people to refer me to friends, so it's not in my best interest to allow the wedding to make everyone miserable. I try to deliver the event they want, but it's not a thing in isolation. And I don't encourage my clients to believe their wedding is the center of the universe."

His expression hadn't changed.

"I heard you tell Grandmother, the first night I met you, that you'd worked for Sherry Anstruthers and learned everything you needed to know from her."

Mariah sat back. Okay, this might explain some things.

"You didn't hear exactly that. I did work for Sherry, but only for a short while. I didn't like the way she worked. What I told your grandmother was that I'd learned everything I needed to know about how *not* to do my job from her. She was a nightmare.

"But obviously, I don't need to tell you that. You know. You just assumed all wedding planners were like her. Why? What did she do to you?"

NELSON TOOK A moment to consider what he wanted to say. And to consider what Mariah had said.

He couldn't remember exactly what he'd heard at his grandmother's, not at this late date. It wouldn't be hard to find out how long she'd worked for Sherry, or when. Grandmother probably had her résumé somewhere around. And the only way he could believe Zoey would have worked with Mariah was if she was the anti-wedding planner.

Unless Zoey had been steamrolled again.

"I knew someone who used her as their wedding planner. It didn't work out well."

MARIAH WAS FULL of questions, but she restrained herself. This was important to work out with Nelson.

"I've heard some stories, about weddings that were nightmares. While I like to believe all of mine went well, I know I'm not perfect. And I know some of Sherry Anstruthers's weddings went badly.

"The last wedding I worked on, before coming here to Carter's, was for someone who'd planned a wedding with Sherry, and she said it had been a disaster. Her fiancé turned into a groomzilla, and she ended up not showing for her own wedding."

"You mean Zoey."

Mariah opened her mouth, and then closed it again. He knew Zoey? Obviously. He must have known about her first wedding. That went a long way to explaining his attitude toward her. Zoey had interviewed Mariah five times before finally trusting her to take care of her wedding.

"Are you a friend of Zoey's? Were you at her wedding?" Had Nelson been there, and Mariah hadn't recognized him when she saw him again?

There was a bleak expression in his eyes. "No, I wasn't at her last wedding. And I can't say I'm a friend of hers, not anymore."

There was a wealth of meaning behind those words. Mariah tried to decipher it. Had he been a friend of the groom's? Had there been a break, after the wedding, between the groom's friends and Zoey's?

Zoey was such a kind, sweet, shy woman. It was hard to imagine her carrying a grudge. Unless Nelson had been close to her first fiancé. Nelson was a vet, and he'd said he worked with horses. Zoey's father had an equine veterinary practice. One of the best in the country. In vet circles, he was a big deal.

Zoey's fiancé had been a vet, too.

An idea flashed across her brain, but no. Zoey's fiancé had been a Theo, not a Nelson.

"Did you know Theo?"

Nelson shot her a glance, then stared at the blank television. "You could say that. I am Theo."

Mariah shook her head. "What? You're not making a lot of sense. Your name is Nelson. Zoey's ex was Theo—I know, we talked about her first wedding, and what we needed to do differently."

Nelson fiddled with the TV remote. "Grandmother was an only child. She was the last Carter of Carter's Crossing. When she married, her husband took her last name.

"His name was Theodore Nelson. After he married Grandmother, he became Theodore Nelson Carter. My father was Theodore Nelson Carter the second. I'm Theodore Nelson Carter the third."

Mariah felt like a vital part of her torso had taken the first dip on a roller coaster while the rest of her was still waiting at the top of the ride. She held up a hand, trying to come to grips with this information.

Nelson kept talking. "Grandfather was known as Teddy to everyone. Dad was Theo. I was named Theodore Nelson the third so that Grandfather's name didn't die out, but instead of confusing everyone with another Theo, they called me by my middle name. Nelson.

"Until I went to school in California. There was another Nelson in my class, so people called me Theo. When I graduated and was looking to work in some of the top veterinary practices, that 'third' helped with the snob value.

"I'm Theo, the groomzilla. And your former boss was the one who cheered me on, every step of the selfish, vainglorious way."

CHAPTER TWELVE

NELSON PULLED UP in front of the Goat and Barley. Tonight he and Mariah were on their first official fake date.

Mariah had planned out a schedule of dates. On a spreadsheet. This first one was to play darts, on a Thursday night. Nelson recognized immediately that she wanted to do something where she felt in control. She would easily win any dart competition against him. That would give her the upper hand.

Mariah had her lists, but Nelson had insider knowledge. And even though he was surprised that he enjoyed Mariah bossing him into this date, he'd insisted he got to plan the second one.

He had some surprises lined up for her tonight, as well.

It was cold outside, but he was waiting for her in the parking lot. Once her car pulled in, he walked over to open her door for her.

It was easy to read the surprise on her face.

This wasn't part of her script. Neither was the kiss.

The kiss was purportedly to sell them as a couple. Nelson had his own reasons to surprise Mariah with some kissing action.

He'd hoped his memory had exaggerated how enjoyable their first kiss had been. After all, this was Mariah. They'd been at odds with each other for months. He didn't like the idea that she was holding on to the best kiss title he had to give out.

Unfortunately, when he pulled her shocked body close to his, it was his breath that hitched. When she looked up at him in surprise and licked her bottom lip, he forgot who was watching, and why he didn't want this to be so good.

Then their lips met, and he forgot everything but kissing Mariah.

Eventually, the pesky need for oxygen made itself known and he pulled back, his breath shaky. In the background he could hear comments from other patrons.

Right. This was to sell their fake date. He didn't dare let her know how much that kiss had rocked his axis.

"Appropriate use of PDA?" he asked, his voice husky.

It took her a moment longer to come back

to the here and now. The kiss had thrown her off, and he liked a flustered Mariah. She could deny it all she wanted, but he knew she enjoyed the kissing, as well. She had opened to him, fitting herself against his body in a most satisfying way.

"Right," she finally said, looking around at their audience.

There were a lot of people arriving, and they'd all seen the kiss. That was a reason she couldn't argue. She'd resist any intimation that they were kissing because they enjoyed it.

He wasn't fond of the idea, either, but surely, they'd get used to it after some time passed.

She pulled away, her lips pleasantly pink, her breath puffing in the cold. "Yes, just what we wanted."

Mariah was a lot of things, but she wasn't ready to admit she liked him, for real.

"Come on, we don't want to be late."

She stopped, ignoring the tug of his glove on her mittens. Her brows lowered as she considered what he'd said.

"Late for what?"

"Trivia night."

"What?"

He grinned at her. "Yeah, on Thursdays no one plays darts. It's trivia night."

He pulled again on her hand, and this time she let him tug her forward. He could almost hear the gears in her head spinning. This was another case where having local knowledge was going to play in his favor.

MARIAH LIKED PLANNING. She liked lists. She liked the feeling of control. She knew that it was a result of the way she'd been raised, when so often it felt like she'd had none.

She'd carefully planned this first "date" with Nelson. By coming to the Goat and Barley, they wouldn't be in Carter's Crossing. It wouldn't be a blatant declaration that they were dating. It would look like they were trying to be discreet, but from what she'd heard, news would trickle back to Carter's Crossing. Then they could make a couple of dating appearances in town. People already knew they were spending time with Nelson's horses and at his place… It was a narrative that would work.

So how had she missed trivia night? She didn't miss things. She researched and double-checked. She made backup plans. Then she made backup plans for her backup plans.

Well, she wouldn't be caught out again.

This was her job. It was important to her. Nelson couldn't mess her up.

Nelson had insisted on taking care of the second date, taking place in Carter's Crossing. With some reluctance she'd agreed. She hadn't realized he was going to derail her first date, as well.

There were a lot more people from Carter's Crossing in the bar than she'd expected on a weeknight. But she hadn't known about trivia night.

She had to absolve Nelson of sabotage. It's not like he could have asked the pub to set this up for the same evening she'd picked for their date. From the surprised looks being tossed his way, he obviously wasn't a regular for trivia night. He knew the routine well enough, though, that the two of them ended up at a table together with drinks and the paper lists that all registered teams received. He'd even given their team a name: Carter's Crew.

She mentally rolled her eyes at that.

Most of the other tables had more than two people. She resigned herself to making an embarrassing showing in this competition.

That was another miscalculation.

Nelson was smart. She should have known that. He hadn't completed his veterinary studies at the top school in the country because he was stupid.

She was surprised, though, that some of the time she was the one to carry the team.

Her education had been completed on the boat until she'd come on land to go to college. She'd done okay academically, but she'd been out of sync with her classmates when it came to pop culture and lifestyle.

It turned out that she had a good grasp of history, and her geography was totally on. She knew she was lucky such a big section of that night's quiz was based on bodies of water. It was almost as if whoever arranged the quiz had picked her brain for that section.

Sports? She was at a loss. Nelson aced that.

They both struggled with television and music. They didn't win, but they came in third. Since there were twelve teams, it was a respectable showing.

They high-fived each other and got a round of applause from the crowd as they went forward to receive their prize: a gift certificate for Moonstone.

It wasn't exactly the date Mariah had planned, but they certainly made a public splash, so she'd call it a win.

Mariah carefully tucked the Moonstone

certificate in her purse. "We could use that for our next date."

Nelson leaned over the table. "You sound confident that I'm going to ask you out again."

Mariah leaned toward him. "I'm a big girl. I can ask *you* out."

Nelson's mouth quirked up in that grin that she was getting too familiar with, but someone stopped by the table to congratulate them before he could respond.

When they were left alone again, he ran his fingers over their quiz sheets.

"You know a lot."

The compliment warmed her.

"You were homeschooled, right? Since you were always traveling on your boat."

Mariah nodded. "Till I moved to land. My dad taught us."

Nelson leaned back in his chair. "What was that like? I always had boring regular school, like everyone else I know."

Mariah traced a pattern on the table with her finger. "I don't know if I can describe it very well. I have no idea what school is like for other people, only what I've seen in movies and read in books."

"Fewer pretty people, less drama and lots of boring lectures."

Mariah looked up with a smile. "Well, we

had only the three of us, my two brothers and me, so the drama was limited to sibling fights."

"And the boring lectures?"

"There's not much point in lecturing your three kids. We already got that for chores around the boat and making sure we wore our life jackets. Dad was a good teacher. He made things interesting. And once we finished our assignments, our school day was over. It wasn't too boring.

"I always felt like I was the stupid kid, because I was the youngest, and as much as possible Dad would have us all study the same things at the same time."

"Now, that, I find hard to believe."

Mariah narrowed her eyes. "Which part?"

"I can't believe you let yourself think you were stupid. If you were keeping up with older kids, you couldn't have been."

She shrugged. "I did eventually figure that out." Maybe too late?

"Where did you have classes? Was there a special place on your boat?"

He sounded interested. Like this was something he'd been curious about.

"It varied, depending on what we were doing. There wasn't enough room on the boat for a separate classroom space. We usually sat either in the cockpit or the salon."

"That sounds cool. Did you run laps around the boat for gym? Climb the mast for recess?" Nelson had a teasing light in his eyes.

Mariah felt her expression go carefully blank. Their life on the boat wasn't cool, not at all. "We didn't really do gym. Dad always said we got enough exercise helping on the boat and swimming. And no, we didn't do recess, either."

"Was it weird to only have three students?"

"It's not weird when it's all you know. And sometimes, when we were with boats with other kids, we'd do classes together."

Mariah was ready to move on to another topic, but Nelson still had questions.

"Did you have friends on those other boats?"

Mariah looked away. "When they were around, we would play or hang out together."

"And when they weren't?"

"It was just us."

Mariah thought back over her words. She thought she'd sounded all right. Not too pathetic.

"That must have been rough sometimes. I mean, growing up, there were a lot of times I didn't want to be with my family, so it's hard to imagine not having Dave around."

Mariah squished down that envious pang she felt. She would have loved a Dave around. Or a Rachel, or a Jaycee.

She shrugged again, since it was her turn to respond. It was what it was.

“Is that why you’re not navigating around the world with your sextant now?”

She glanced up at Nelson. The words were teasing, but there was too much sympathy in his eyes. He’d figured out that having only her family around hadn’t always been enough. But he was also letting her off the hook.

She gave him a grateful smile. She’d rather he hadn’t seen through her, but at least he wasn’t picking into her psyche, either to figure her out or try to fix her.

She’d gained a lot, growing up on the boat, traveling the world. Her brothers appeared to have picked up that wanderlust. But for her, it had made her want something different.

She wasn’t looking for pity. Her childhood had been unconventional, but it had its advantages, as well. She was an adult now. She was making the life she wanted for herself. A job she enjoyed. Her own community, one that could be constant. A home that stayed still.

This job in Carter’s Crossing was a stepping-stone to all of that. It was showing her the things she wanted.

Her glance caught Nelson's, and for some reason she felt her cheeks heat up. He hadn't read her mind, and he wouldn't think of himself as one of those things she wanted.

At least, she hoped so.

CHAPTER THIRTEEN

"OH, NO."

Nelson had been secretive about this second date. Now Mariah knew why.

"Come on, you need to know how to skate. You're planning a skating party!"

She was also planning a vow renewal and didn't need to have been married fifty years to do that.

"How did you get my size anyway?"

Maybe not the best way to refuse.

Nelson was kneeling at her feet, holding out a skate. Mariah had her feet tucked safely under the bench; one she'd arranged to have installed here at the mill for the upcoming skating party.

"Your boots are in the closet at Grandmother's. I peeked."

She glared at him.

"Come on, Mariah! It'll be fun!"

That was Jaycee, already on skates and demonstrating that she was well able to handle blades on ice.

Dave was also on skates. And Rachel. Nelson's surprise date had been to bring her ice-skating. He'd told her to dress warmly, so she'd initially thought they might be going out to the farm.

Better the horses than skates.

Nelson had picked her up from Abigail's and driven her to the mill. She'd seen familiar cars. Curious as to what the others were doing, she'd hardly noticed that Nelson had grabbed a duffel bag from the back of the car.

And now she was stuck here on the bench, everyone encouraging her to try skating for the first time. In her life.

The ice had been cleared of snow, making enough space for skating, but there were no boards around the sides, no railing, nothing to hold on to. There was no way she could do this. She'd fall and break something. She couldn't afford that, this close to Valentine's Day.

Now Mariah had a few things to add to her party to-do list. Because not having something like a board fence was just stupid.

"Come on, Mariah. I won't let you fall. I promise." Nelson was looking up at her, a glint in his eye.

That phrase. *I promise.* So easily said, so easily broken.

Nelson narrowed his eyes. “First fall, you can quit. How’s that?”

With the others all egging her on, she finally pulled out her foot and allowed Nelson to take off her boot.

“Good girl!”

“I’m not a dog,” she gritted out.

“Sorry. You gotta admit, though, this is a great date. People here to see us hanging on to each other. And a kiss would definitely be appropriate.”

Mariah dropped her head, letting her hair cover her warm cheeks. The trivia night date had ended with another kiss in the parking lot. There may have been cheering from people passing by. And she may have enjoyed it, a little too much.

She flinched as Nelson gave a hard tug on her skate laces. “That’s really tight.”

He flashed a grin up at her. “You don’t want floppy ankles.”

“How do you know?” She had to push back. This was too much in Nelson’s sweet spot.

“Because you don’t want to embarrass yourself.” He was working on her second boot now.

Mariah frowned. Big deal. No one wanted to embarrass themselves.

Another few tugs, and she had skates fastened tightly to her feet.

Nelson sat beside her and pulled out his own skates. While her borrowed footwear was white, his was black.

"Why do you get the black skates?" Hers were a little scuffed, so the dark color would have been nice to cover that up.

He pulled off a boot, and stuck his foot in a skate, bending over to lace it.

"Mine are hockey skates. We don't have a lot of women hockey players here, and they're a little proprietary about their gear. Yours are figure skates—you've got a pick on the toe of the blade. That can help you stop."

Being able to stop sounded good.

In no time Nelson had both skates on, and their boots safely stashed in his duffel bag. He stood up, easy and confident. He turned and held out a hand to her.

"You sure about this? First fall?"

He caught something behind her words. His gaze was serious. "I gave you my word."

He'd also promised Zoey, she thought, and wondered where that had come from. She shook her head and reminded herself this was just fake dating. She let him grab her hand and pull her to her feet, where she balanced precariously on the two narrow blades.

"I've got you."

She considered the ice surface just beyond them. The other three were crisscrossing the ice, confidently and surely. They looked like they were having fun. She took a breath and lifted her first foot.

MARIAH WASN'T COMFORTABLE without having control, and Nelson wanted her out of her element, at least for a bit.

He'd thought that bringing her skating, something she had no experience with, would shake things up a bit. And showing some affection, while he basically supported her around the ice, would give the other three lots to talk about. Word would get around that something was going on with Nelson and Mariah.

That was what they wanted, right?

The fake dating had turned into a lot more fun than he'd expected. And Mariah was… maybe not exactly a friend, but something. He knew a lot about her. He'd shared some things with her he didn't normally talk about. It gave them a bond.

He hadn't realized how much he did know her, until he promised to keep her safe while on the ice and he caught her reaction.

She almost flinched at that phrase—*I promise.*

He was going to ask her about that, but first, he was going to skate her around the ice, keeping his promise. Then he was going to kiss her.

He was looking forward to holding her on the ice while she had to cling to him to stay upright. And he was really looking forward to kissing her.

They might argue, but something, maybe that sparring, added to their kisses. He didn't think it was his technique, Mariah's list notwithstanding. Not that he was bad, but something happened when he touched Mariah's lips with his. Something extra.

She was hesitant, shuffling on the skates through the snow to the edge of the river. He kept hold of her hand, helping her balance. He stepped ahead of her onto the ice and turned back to take both her hands.

She glared at the ice, as if she could make it behave by sheer willpower. Then she put one blade on it, and almost went down.

FORTUNATELY, NELSON WAS braced to support her. She had to grab his arms hard to stay upright. She had to trust him, even though she didn't want to.

He kept her upright.

She huffed a cloud of foggy breath into the cold.

“I don’t like this.”

“Don’t give up,” Jaycee encouraged.

She took a firm grip on Nelson’s hands and put the second blade on the ice. Nelson kept her upright as she wobbled while trying to find balance.

“People really do this for fun?” she asked.

“Look at them.” Nelson took advantage of her distraction to slowly skate backward, tugging her forward onto the ice.

She gasped but stayed up.

“What are you doing?”

“Skating.”

“Backward?”

He nodded and pulled her out farther.

“How much does it hurt when you fall?” she asked, eyes focused on her skates.

“Doesn’t matter.” Nelson picked up his pace from snail to tortoise. “You’re not falling, remember?”

She moved her gaze up to his face and stumbled. He brought her closer. “I’ve got you.”

That shouldn’t have removed the tension in her shoulders and legs. It shouldn’t have relaxed her facial muscles and pulled up the side of her mouth in a half smile.

And he shouldn't have smiled back at her.

Because the next thing she knew, she was allowing him to drag her all over the ice, with Jaycee and Rachel and Dave cheering her on as they passed by. When Nelson held her hips and pushed her forward in front of him, as if she was actually skating, it was even fun.

Until he decided to teach her how to skate. On her own.

"Push with your right foot. No, not step. Push, leaving the blade on the ice."

"I am!"

"No, you're not. If you want to learn how to do this, you need to listen to me."

"If I want to learn how to do this, I need to find someone who can explain things properly."

The others laughed, and eventually Mariah was able to take a few shuffles on her own, Nelson close beside her.

"You don't need to hover."

"I promised I wouldn't let you fall."

That phrase again. *I promised.* It distracted her, and she caught the pick of the toe of her skate on the ice. She felt her balance go, and she started to topple forward.

A pair of hands caught her waist, keeping her from hitting the ice.

She caught her breath. "Thanks." His face was right there.

It was only natural that he brought her close and kissed her.

She almost forgot that it was for show.

RACHEL HAD MADE thermoses of hot chocolate, and they enjoyed the warmth once they'd given up on skating. No one mentioned the kiss. Hadn't anyone seen it? He should have paid attention, been a little less lost in the kiss.

Dave and Jaycee got into a car together, and Rachel drove off, leaving Nelson and Mariah alone. There had been a lot of significant glances aimed their way, even if nothing had been said.

Nelson wasn't thinking of that right now. His mind wanted to linger on the kiss, on how good Mariah had felt in his hands and arms while he was guiding her over the ice.

But he also had a question to ask her. It felt important. He wasn't sure if he could convince Mariah that she should tell him, but he needed to know. For him. He needed to know why she got that look on her face when he'd promised to keep her from falling. Which, by the way, he had.

Nelson turned the car on, dialing up the seat warmers, but didn't put the car in gear. He looked over at Mariah, cheeks and nose pink from the cold. She looked like she'd had a good time after all.

"What's the deal with promises, Mariah?" He hoped to catch her off guard.

Her head snapped toward him.

"What do you mean?"

"Every time I promise something, you react."

She waved a hand. "You're imagining things."

He let the silence rest for a moment. "No, I'm not. I don't make promises lightly, and I do my best to keep them. Why do you flinch, like you're sure I'll break my word?"

She didn't respond.

"I mean, yeah, we all have to break a promise sometime, but we don't stop believing people unless there's a reason. Has someone broken a promise to you? A big one?"

Mariah looked out the car window. Her chin jutted out as she shook her head.

"My dad has never made a promise he couldn't keep."

"Never?" Nelson couldn't hold back the question. How did someone always keep a promise? Life happened, and sometimes you couldn't follow through.

Mariah shook her head again. "He wouldn't make a promise unless he knew he could keep it. All those nice soporifics people say to kids? He never did. Never promised we'd make it through a storm. He would promise to do everything he could, but he never promised we would be safe."

Nelson leaned back and considered. Was that the best way to talk to kids?

"He had a good reason for that. When he wanted to leave the family business, get out of the rat race, buy a boat and sail the world with my mom, my grandfather was furious. He said the only way Dad would be able to access his trust fund was if he promised to never marry 'that woman.' My mother.

"Dad promised. He got his money. Then he bought the boat and sailed away with Mom. But he never married her."

"That was harsh."

Mariah nodded, still not looking at him. "Still bothers my mother. My grandfather apologized, took back the deal, but my dad won't budge. He made a promise, so he won't break it. Not for anything."

Nelson considered keeping his word a good thing. But that promise? Given under duress and kept even after the need was withdrawn? That was some messed up family dynamics.

It was no wonder promises made her skittish.

"When I was a kid, on the boat, and I'd make a friend…eventually, they'd travel in one direction and we'd go somewhere else. We always promised to keep in touch. But kids can't always do that, so those promises were broken easily."

She finally turned and looked at Nelson. "So yeah, I have a thing about promises. Most of them are worthless, and the ones that aren't? They can be devastating.

"I don't make promises now. I do my best, but I won't promise because it's too difficult to know I'll keep it. The costs might be too high."

Nelson put the car in gear and pulled out of the mill parking lot. Mariah didn't speak, and he let the silence stretch.

He was sure Mariah's father had meant well by his children, but based on Mariah, he'd still managed to mess them up. Just like every parent did somehow.

Mariah snapped to attention when he stopped in front of Abigail's porch. She shook her head when he reached to undo his seat belt.

"No, don't bother. I'll be fine. Tomorrow

we'll use that gift certificate at Moonstone, right?"

Nelson hesitated but decided to let Mariah go into the house on her own. She'd given him a lot to think about. He was surprised she'd shared that much. Maybe she was, too.

He watched her go up the steps and open the door. Once she was safely inside, he drove back to the carriage house. Away from the woman who didn't believe in promises.

CHAPTER FOURTEEN

THE DAY EVERYTHING fell apart started like any other. Mariah woke up and checked the weather, like she did every morning. She hadn't been this conscious of climate conditions since she'd been living on the boat.

The weather was cooperating. The fourteenth of February was going to be clear and cold without crossing the line into brutal windchill that would keep everyone indoors.

There were no emails from vendors unable to fulfill their obligations. The morning passed with phone calls and to-do items checked off her list in almost monotonous regularity. The three events: anniversary/vow renewal, engagement and proposal, all planned for and on track.

She should have known everything couldn't go that well.

Abigail was the bearer of the first bad news. Gord had fallen and broken his hip. He was in the hospital.

Mariah was relieved that her first thought

was about Gord and his health instead of how this would mess up her event. At his age, falls could trigger a slide into poor health. He'd been out throwing salt on the sidewalk to make sure no one slipped on the ice and hit an icy patch and gone down.

Gord, meet irony.

The doctors were going to operate, and every indication was that he should make a full recovery. For his age, he was fit and healthy, and he was obstinate enough to get on his feet before he was supposed to.

He would not be on his feet before the fourteenth, however.

He would not be at the church where he and Gladys made their wedding vows fifty years ago, ready to meet her at the altar to repeat them.

After they'd covered all those caring-people issues, they had to focus on the party.

"How bad is this?" Abigail wanted to know.

Mariah considered. "This was probably the least marketable of the three events. It was definitely a feel-good story, and would make Carter's look good, but I wasn't expecting a lot of requests for fiftieth anniversary celebrations to come this way.

"But the work your committee did, finding the members of their wedding party and some of the guests, and arranging for them to come, that was impressive. It could inspire visitors. A video could have gone viral.

"Do we know when Gord will be back on his feet? Maybe we have the party a little later?"

They'd miss the publicity kick her grandfather was providing, but they'd still have material for the website and promotion. The out-of-town guests, however, might not be able to make it to a later event.

"I'll make some calls," Abigail said. "Find out when Gord is back home and mobile, and if we can rebook everyone."

Mariah thanked her. With less than a week to go before Valentine's Day, she wasn't sure they could cancel the food. Mariah pulled up her list for the anniversary party, ready to prepare a new list for cancellations.

It was closing in on dinnertime when her phone rang. Mariah frowned and pulled it up, expecting someone else was calling to tell her about Gord's fall. She'd had eleven calls to let her know already. The number on display was Jaycee's, however, so she pushed the talk button.

"Hey, Jaycee—"

The rest of her greeting was drowned out by a wail. Mariah pulled the phone away from her ear, hoping to be able to understand what Jaycee was saying if she wasn't being deafened.

It took a few minutes. Jaycee was crying. It was hard to make out words, and for a moment Mariah wondered if Jaycee had heard the bad news about Gord and was closer to him than Mariah had realized. But it wasn't Gord who was making her cry; it was Dave.

Dave had broken up with her.

"I'm on my way. What do you need?"

MARIAH HAD NO experience with breakups of this magnitude. Wine, ice cream and chocolate were the staples according to books and movies, so she arrived with those.

Jaycee answered the door with swollen eyes, a red nose and a voice so congested Mariah had a hard time making out what she was saying. But no words were needed to tell her that her friend was in pain.

Mariah peeled off her outerwear and followed Jaycee into the kitchen. "I brought rocky road, Snickers and pinot. What do you want first?"

Jaycee's response was indecipherable.

Mariah chopped the Snickers bar into pieces, swirled it in with the ice cream and poured the wine into a beer mug. She brought it into the living room, where Jaycee was curled up on the couch, an empty Kleenex box on the floor with a pile of used tissues, another half-full box on the coffee table.

Mariah put the ice cream and wine on the table in front of her and sat down beside her.

"Hug?"

Jaycee nodded. Mariah wrapped her arms around her. She felt the quivering in Jaycee's body and tightened the embrace.

"I'm so sorry. What happened?"

Jaycee's crying renewed. Eventually, she calmed enough to speak in words that Mariah could interpret.

Last night she and Dave had practiced their dance skate. She'd been frustrated that Dave still didn't remember the routine. She asked about the new clothes she'd told him to get for the party, and he hadn't gotten those yet. She'd been upset, and they'd said their good-nights on tense terms.

Today Dave had called her. He said things weren't working, and he thought they should put a halt on the wedding plans, including the engagement party.

Jaycee had asked him what exactly he meant.

They should cancel the engagement, and

make sure they wanted the same things going forward.

Jaycee said if they weren't getting married, they weren't going backward to dating.

Dave had said if that was what she wanted…

Jaycee burst into renewed crying.

Mariah had rubbed her back, handed over more tissues and offered wine. She agreed that Dave was an idiot but also was the love of Jaycee's life. Jaycee wavered between joining a convent and plotting his murder.

Mariah could only offer comfort and caution about shooting someone in daylight in front of witnesses, but her mind had started making new lists.

Lists to cancel another event.

She felt bad for Jaycee. She thought Jaycee and Dave were a good, strong and committed couple. She thought it might even be possible that they could work this out between them. Eventually.

But things weren't looking good for the engagement party, and on top of the anniversary cancellation, and even the fake proposal, Mariah was looking at failure. She pushed the selfish thought to the back of her mind, but it lingered.

When Jaycee mentioned the name of Nelson in her ramblings, Mariah went on full alert.

"Nelson? What has he got to do with this?"

Jaycee snuffled into another tissue. "I don't know. Dave just said something about him. Maybe it was just because Nelson was stood up at the altar. Maybe Nelson talked him out of this. I don't know. I just…just…

"I just don't know how he could do this if he loved me. His mother…she's going to be thrilled. She never wanted us to get married.

"You're going to New York, right, Mariah? Could I go with you? I can't stay here, not now, not with everyone looking at me…"

Mariah wrapped her arms around Jaycee again and passed her another tissue.

"If you want, of course you can come to New York with me. But not yet. Rachel's coming over. We need to use those thumb-screws on Dave first."

IT HAD BEEN a bad day.

Two family pets had to be put down, and the rescue people brought in a dog they'd found. Nelson considered himself an easy-going guy, but when he saw what had been done to the dog, he was ready to put the hurt on whoever had done that to an animal.

He was grateful that this wasn't a night for dinner with his grandmother and Mariah. Until he'd put some of the day behind him, he was in no mind-set to make polite conversation. What he needed was a long punishing run, followed by a game on TV and some whiskey.

Not a lot. He couldn't put himself out of commission if an emergency came in, but he needed something to take the misery of the day away, and if not, at least move it to enough distance that he could sleep.

He'd had his run and dropped in front of the TV with the game and a shot glass before he bothered showering. His level of caring about that was in the negative numbers. So of course, someone pounded at his door.

He considered his options. Grandmother wouldn't pound, and she'd come in if she felt it necessary. Dave was supposed to be busy with Jaycee. The door pounded again, and he grimaced. Must be Mariah. He wasn't sure what he was supposed to have done this time, but that was angry pounding if he'd ever heard it.

He opened the door. Yep, Mariah on the warpath.

"Come on in," he said to her back as she stomped her way past him.

She stood, glaring at the half-empty whiskey glass.

"Are you drunk?"

"Unfortunately, no," he said, sitting down and taking another sip. "Did we have something planned this evening? Did I miss a scheduled PDA? 'Cause I don't remember one, and I'm not in the mood."

She crossed her arms. "Did you talk to Dave?"

He dropped his head on the back of the couch and looked at her. She was upset, for sure, but he was in the clear. He'd done nothing but his job all day.

"No. I haven't talked to him at all today."

"What about yesterday?"

Nelson frowned. "He was with Jaycee yesterday. I haven't seen him since darts night."

"You're saying you didn't talk him into this."

"Into what?" Obviously, Mariah was angry with him for something he'd done, or she thought he'd done, but he was pretty sure he was off the hook this time. And he was hurt. Weren't they past this now?

"He broke up with Jaycee."

"What?" Nelson jerked upright. Impossible. He knew Dave had been upset about some of the party stuff, but Nelson also knew without a shadow of a doubt that Dave loved Jaycee.

Mariah watched him, then, apparently reassured, dropped into his chair.

"Why don't you stay?" It wasn't polite, but he needed to process this news, and talking to Mariah was not going to help.

"I'm sorry. I thought you'd been talking..."

Nelson didn't have patience right now. And he couldn't believe Mariah was still so suspicious of him. He'd promised.

But she didn't put faith in people's promises.

"No, I haven't been trying to talk Dave out of marrying Jaycee. I've been too busy putting pets to sleep and dealing with animal abuse to start with people."

Mariah's face fell.

"I'm sorry, Nelson, really. I shouldn't have jumped to conclusions like that. It was just that Dave mentioned something about you to Jaycee when he broke up with her. I'm sorry you had a crappy day, as well. I'll go, unless there's something I can do?"

Nelson shook his head. "I think I'd better go see how my buddy is doing. I know he loves Jaycee, so something serious must have gone down."

"Jaycee right now is considering putting a hit out on him, so tell him to watch his back. And I am sorry, about—"

She waved her hand in a circle, indicating the whole mess that had been today.

He shrugged. Yeah, today was just a total crap show.

DAVE DIDN'T WANT to talk.

"There's nothing to say. You were right."

Nelson drew in a sharp breath. Maybe he *was* in trouble.

"What do you mean? She figured out she was too good for you?"

Dave tried to give him a smile, but it was a poor attempt.

"No, about these big wedding events. Jaycee is so focused on this party that she's forgotten about us. If she wanted a guy who could dance on skates, she should have gone looking for someone in the Ice Capades.

"I told her the party was getting out of hand, and we should just give it up. She threw a fit. I asked if the party was more important than us, 'cause from what I could see, the party was driving us further apart."

Dave picked up what looked like the latest in a line of beers. He held one up for Nelson, who shook his head. Dave shrugged and took a long swallow.

"She said that the party was a test of how we could handle things together. But this party has never been a together thing. I didn't ask for it, and she didn't ask me to plan it. I told her I didn't want a party, and that maybe she needed to figure out what was most important to her.

"She said the party was for us, and if I wasn't going to even try… I told her I'd tried, and I was done. She could have the party, or she could have me. She said she wasn't choosing, so I told her I was.

"It's just like you said. I thought we were solid, but Jaycee has been a different person with this party stuff. And maybe she's right. If we can't handle this, then maybe we can't handle other things. Better to end it now."

Nelson had time-traveled and was reliving his last conversation with Zoey. He'd made all the same points Jaycee had. But Nelson had been told this was normal for brides, so he'd ignored everything Zoey said.

And ended up with no bride at his wedding.

He felt guilty, as if he'd been prioritizing the wrong thing again. But he wasn't the one focused on the party, not this time. He'd learned his lesson. Not just about parties, and about weddings, but about manipulating and forcing people into doing what he wanted. He'd been good at that.

Not anymore.

He left Dave alone, once he made sure Dave had no more beer and was going to head to bed. He didn't try to talk him into anything. He wondered if Dave would have been as bothered by the engagement party planning and seen it as a breaking point if Nelson hadn't talked to him about his own wedding, but he'd never know.

He stopped by his grandmother's house, after texting Mariah that he needed to talk to her. She met him in the lounge, looking defeated for the first time since he'd met her.

That bothered him, more than he'd expected.

"I tried to talk to Dave. I don't know if he and Jaycee can work this out, but he's not interested in the party, and I don't think they can figure things out in time for it anyway."

Mariah nodded, her arms wrapped around her body.

"That's what I thought."

Nelson had to try to cheer her up. "You could still have the skating party. Take pictures, use it for some publicity. And you've got the anniversary and our proposal."

Mariah shook her head, eyes on the ground.

"Gord fell and broke his hip. He'll be in the hospital on the fourteenth."

"Oh." Not the greatest response, but Nelson wasn't sure what else to say.

"It's over. I'm going to tell Grandfather to cancel the press. I'll have to talk to the committee, see if they want to try again."

"You're giving up?" Nelson was shocked. He didn't think anything could stop Mariah once she was going.

"What else can I do? I told Grandfather we had a fiftieth anniversary/vow renewal, an engagement party and a marriage proposal. All happening here at Carter's Crossing, all designed to show how romantic this place can be. Now all I have is a fake proposal. That's not going to bring people here."

Abigail came into the room in her robe. "You've heard the news, Nelson?"

"I have, and I'm sorry." Seeing Abigail raise her eyebrow, he shook his head.

"I know, I haven't been a big supporter. But you're trying to save this town, and I shouldn't have let my hang-ups get in the way."

Despite the problems, the approving look from his grandmother was a touch of warmth.

"I should go call my grandfather now, let him know."

Abigail looked at Mariah, her posture drooping, her voice tired.

"I'll do that, Mariah. You go and rest. You've been working hard. Get a good night's sleep, and things might look better in the morning."

"Nice try, Abigail, but I'll let you talk to Grandfather if you want. I can wait to hear what he has to say. And we have vendors to cancel—"

"Tomorrow," Abigail said. "I've called a committee meeting tomorrow. Don't give up just yet."

Mariah gave Abigail a hug and nodded to Nelson as she left the room. He missed the embraces they'd shared, selling their fake dating.

That was probably over now.

It hit him then. Mariah was done. She'd be leaving. There'd be no more fake dating, no more time spent working together with Toby. No arguing, no annoying her. No kisses, no proposal. No Mariah.

It wasn't the best time to realize that the dating had become more real than he'd understood. Not with his grandmother watching, and Mariah ready to leave town.

Abigail poured herself a glass of scotch from the liquor cabinet that lived on the far side of the room. She raised an eyebrow, and Nelson nodded.

It had been a spectacularly bad day.

Nelson wanted to make it better. He couldn't change what had happened at work, but what about the rest of this disaster? For most of his life, he'd gone after what he wanted with a single-minded focus. Captain of the school hockey team. Valedictorian. USC. The best equine practice in the US. His drive and ambition had always been something people admired. He'd thought it was good.

Until his wedding. When he'd discovered just how much he would do to get what he wanted. How much he could hurt people he cared for, in order to get to his goal. He'd tried to justify it, to say it wasn't just for him, but he'd had to come to terms with how selfish he'd been.

He'd reined himself in after the debacle with Zoey. Part of that was guilt, part of it a need to punish himself. He couldn't go around spreading hurt like that.

When he started a veterinary practice in Carter's Crossing, it had been something that was just his. That success had been his, but it hadn't come at a cost to anyone else. He could focus all his drive into his practice without it spilling over on anyone else.

He was so bad at darts that there was no fear of going overboard there. He'd played rec hockey and baseball, but that was a team activity. And he'd always made sure to keep it on a fun level, not serious competition.

But since the wedding, since he'd decided he had to make some drastic changes and not to take things over, he'd never had anything he wanted as much as Mariah, here, fake dating him. He didn't want that to end.

Why did he feel that way?

The answer hit him hard and fast. Because he'd never be able to convince her to make it real otherwise. He needed more time with her.

His mind went right to finding a solution—a way to keep her here, at least through the fall when her year was up. That meant salvaging at least some of the Valentine's Day events. He could think of ways to do that. But those ways meant pushing himself into people's lives, playing God. Things he'd sworn not to do again.

He mentally struggled. He could do it, he was sure. If he went to Dave, he could convince him that Jaycee was right, that the engagement party was a test, and that things would be better after that. Dave trusted him. He could tell him all the ways that he, Nelson, had been different from Jaycee. Nelson knew, now, that he'd been driven by ambition. He saw the wedding as part of his career plan, and for that, he'd overlooked Zoey, and how she felt.

Which meant he hadn't felt for her what he should.

But he didn't want to manipulate his best friend just to get what he, Nelson, wanted. He didn't want to be that guy. Not anymore. He couldn't do that to Dave.

But he wondered, as he thought it through, what *was* Jaycee's reason for her fixation on the perfect engagement party? This party wasn't going to help Jaycee's career. She'd never been the kind of person who had to have the biggest and best of anything. This was costing her the man she loved. There had to be a reason.

If he could find that reason, then maybe they could still make this work. Without taking over or bending others to what he wanted. Could he? Could he put the brakes on once he started?

Nelson dropped his tumbler on the coffee table, untouched. "I'm heading out, Grandmother. Got some things to do."

She gave him a slight smile. "You do that, then. I think it's too late to call Gerry, so I'll wait till morning. Unless I hear from you."

His grandmother saw too much, but right now he had a mission.

Five minutes later he pulled up in front of Dave's house.

He'd changed his mind about asking Jaycee what the thing was, whatever was driving her to go crazy about this party. He knew what it wasn't, but he also realized, it wasn't his issue, and not his relationship. Dave needed to know why she was doing it. Not have Nelson tell him.

Dave had given up the beer to physically work out his frustration, Nelson deduced as his friend finally answered the door. He was sweaty, wearing ratty shorts and a faded T-shirt. His eyes were blurry and had a tendency to wander. He looked angry at being disturbed, a frown crossing his face. Nelson had taken a note from Mariah's book, and given the door a hard pounding, and refused to give up.

"Whatcha doin' back here?"

Nelson shoved his way in. Dave lurched back.

"Dude. Not cool."

"I need to tell you something."

Dave focused his gaze on Nelson. "Now?"

"Now. I should have told you before."

Dave stumbled into his kitchen and sat on

a stool, a beer in front of him. Nelson thought he'd run out. Apparently not.

"Say it 'n' get out."

Nelson's fingers itched to put away the empty bottles and wipe the counter, but he restrained himself.

"I should have told you why I pushed Zoey so hard on the wedding."

Dave frowned as he looked at him, but he was interested. Nelson had kept most of the details of that disaster to himself.

"Why?"

"For my career."

Dave looked shocked. Bleary shocked. "Really? You used your wedding for that?"

Nelson nodded, feeling the shame that he should have felt three years ago.

"I know. I was selfish and stupid. But Zoey's dad was a partner in the practice, and so many of the guests were people that I needed to impress. I wanted to be partner someday, and I was already working toward that."

"That why you wanted to marry Zoey?"

"No. I loved her..." Had some part of him seen Zoey as a step on his career path? Just how self-centered had he been?

"I don't know. But Jaycee—"

"Not what Jaycee is doin'." Dave set down his beer bottle.

"I know," Nelson said. "The party isn't going to help her job, and it's not helping her with you. She's never been a diva. So why is this so important to her?"

Dave shrugged. "I dunno."

Nelson leaned toward him. "Then you should find out."

Dave stared at him. "Does it matter?"

"I don't know. But it might make a difference. And you don't want to throw away what you two have for something stupid, do you?"

Dave's gaze shifted to his beer bottle, but he didn't look like he saw it. Nelson waited, letting him think it through. He picked up a couple of empties and dropped them in the recycling box. Dave didn't notice.

He sat down beside his friend again.

Dave's lips tightened. "Yeah, I wanna know what's more important than what we have. It better be worth it."

Nelson relaxed. He didn't know what Jaycee's reason was, and he didn't know if finding out would make a difference, but this was something they needed to work out. It was good for Dave.

It might make a difference to Mariah. If the engagement was back on, then maybe the party would be. But Nelson was stopping now. Instead of pushing through to get what he wanted, he was just pushing enough to help his friends.

"Now," Dave said. "I wanna know now."

Nelson narrowed his eyes. "I don't think you're up to driving. This isn't something you want to do over the phone. And you might want to be sober."

"Not waiting anymore." Dave covered his mouth as he burped. "I need t'know. Drive me?"

Nelson saw the pain on his friend's face. Might as well find out while he was partially numb, if this wasn't going to work.

"You might want to put more clothes on."

JAYCEE MET THEM at the door with red eyes and nose, and flannel pj's that covered her from head to toe.

She shot Nelson a dirty glance. "What do you want, Dave?"

He pointed a finger, that just missed her nose. "I wanna know why."

Nelson thought Dave had sobered up on the cold ride over. Now he wasn't sure. He kept an eye on him.

"Why what?" She wiped a tissue across her nose.

"Why does this party have t'be perfect?

Why do I have t'dance? Why can't you think about anything else but the stupid party?"

"It's not a stupid party!" Jaycee yelled back. "Why can't you see that?"

"I dunno! But I can't! Tell me, what is so important about it? We coulda just had a dinner, like Mom said."

Jaycee shrieked. Nelson covered his ears, wondering if her neighbors' dogs would hear that and cringe.

"Yes, your mother would have loved a dinner party with all her friends, where she could make nasty little digs all the way through the meal about how unworthy I was and how much better Nelson's sister would have been. That's why the party. I wanted to prove to your mother that I'm not trash. I'm just as good as the Carters."

Nelson knew he shouldn't be here for this, but he didn't dare interrupt.

"This party was going to be the best engagement party Carter's Crossing ever had, and then all her snide remarks about it would stop. All her friends were going to love my party. It was going to be so perfect..."

Jaycee started crying again. Dave, not that drunk, and not that stupid, quickly folded her in his arms.

"Oh, baby. No. Shhh, shhh. It's okay. I'm sorry about Mom. I'll talk to her."

"I wanted to handle her by myself. I didn't want to make you choose sides." Jaycee sniffled.

"I'm on your side, babe. Always. I'll tell Mom to back off or she's not invited to the wedding."

Jaycee raised tear-drenched eyes to Dave and hiccupped.

"Really?"

"Of course. I didn't know she was doing that. I'm sorry I didn't notice. But the truth is, you're too good for me, and I know it."

Jaycee drew in a shuddering breath. "I'm sorry I was so awful. I just wanted everything to be so perfect… You don't have to dance. We don't have to have a party. Just you. If you don't mind if your mom—"

"I'm not marrying my mom. I'm marrying you. And we're making our own family. If she doesn't treat you with respect, then she's not invited to be part of it."

Jaycee's chin trembled. "I love you, Dave."

"I love you, too, Jaycee. I'm so sorry—"

"My job is over?" Nelson needed to extricate himself.

The two turned to him, having forgotten all about him.

"Thanks for the ride," Dave said. "But I think I can take it from here."

"You're letting him stay, Jaycee?"

She gave Dave a wobbly smile. "Yeah, I think we have some things to talk about."

"Enjoy your talk," Nelson said, winking.

"Go away, Nelson," Dave said, eyes fixed on Jaycee.

CHAPTER FIFTEEN

NELSON RETURNED TO his grandmother's house. He'd noticed the lights still on, and thought she'd want to be updated. That is, if her network hadn't already spread the news.

She met him at the door. "Well?"

Nelson stepped in, tugging his scarf loose. "Dave and Jaycee are back together. I don't know if the party is happening, but they talked, and figured out Jaycee was doing all this because of Dave's mother."

Abigail grimaced. "I can see that. I suppose Jaycee was trying to impress her. She's going to have a difficult time unless Dave is willing to support her."

Nelson gave a tired smile. "He told Jaycee that his mother isn't welcome if she doesn't treat Jaycee right, so that should help."

"Excellent." Abigail turned to go.

"I had a thought, Grandmother."

Abigail turned back and invited Nelson to sit down in the lounge with a wave of her hand.

"What kind of thought?"

"About Gord and Gladys. I know he's in the hospital, but can't they still have their vow renewal? Unless he has complications, he should be almost ready to send home by the fourteenth."

Abigail shot him a look. "That's an interesting point, Nelson. I had assumed he'd have a long recovery."

"Everyone is an individual, and their recovery will be, as well, but it might be worth looking into. If Gord is in good enough shape, could the anniversary party be moved to the hospital? It would take some work to make the place look right, but since you've arranged for everyone to be here, and I'm sure the food has been ordered..."

Abigail rested a hand on Nelson's. "That is a very good suggestion, Nelson, and I'm surprised I didn't think of it myself. I must be getting old. I'll look into it. I appreciate that you're helping out with this."

Nelson shot her a glance.

"Someone told me it was time for me to move on."

"Someone is rather clever."

"Yes, she is." Nelson leaned over and pressed a kiss to his grandmother's cheek.

"Good night, Grandmother." He stood.

"You've made it a good night, Nelson. Thank you."

MARIAH WOKE TO a few precious seconds of oblivion before everything came crashing into her head.

Gord had broken his hip. And Jaycee and Dave had broken up.

She pulled the covers up over her head. For just a few moments she wanted to entertain the possibility of staying in bed, forgetting her responsibilities and letting the whole mess go by without her. Perhaps a twenty-four-hour flu?

She couldn't do that. People were counting on her. But she wished they weren't.

It began to get uncomfortably warm under the covers, so she threw them back. It was time to face her day.

She unplugged her phone from the charger on her bedside table. She pushed herself to a sitting position and pressed it on.

At least, at this point, there wasn't any more bad news that could be waiting for her. Could there?

She had a text from Jaycee. Mariah drew in a breath. She'd left Jaycee with Rachel. She wondered if she was feeling any better. Or they might be committed to seriously hurting Dave. The text had come in at 2:00 a.m., so it could be interesting…

We're back together. We've got a couple of suggestions for the party.

Huh? When Mariah left last night, the convent idea was still being discussed. This was an abrupt one-eighty. Mariah wasn't sure how she felt about the suggestions part, but if the party was back on…

The party was back on! Mariah could feel her body energize as that realization sank in.

Okay, she wasn't done, not yet. She had an engagement party, and she still had the fake proposal to put on. She'd need to let her grandfather know about the anniversary/vow renewal, but that was totally a random problem. What were the chances of someone breaking their hip?

Well, probably good at Gord's age. That was something she'd need to factor in in the future.

Right now maybe there was even something she could do about that.

Abigail had been right. A new day, sleep, and things could look totally different.

Mariah didn't waste much time getting

dressed. She had her laptop and notebook with her when she descended the stairs to the main floor and made her way to the kitchen.

Abigail was on her phone. The coffee maker was burbling, so Mariah helped herself to a cup.

"Let me know what you find out. Thank you, Mavis."

Abigail clicked off her phone. "Good morning, Mariah. You look better today."

Mariah couldn't hold back a grin.

"I got a text from Jaycee. The engagement party is back on."

"That *is* wonderful." Abigail tapped her phone. "I may have some good news for you, as well."

Mariah sat down. "Hit me. I could use it."

"We might be able to have the vow renewal at the hospital."

Mariah blinked. "Really?"

"Nelson told me Gord might be close to coming home by the fourteenth. Gladys confirmed that he should be home on the sixteenth, so she's checking with the doctor to see if he can handle a party. We're hoping it will be allowed as long as he stays in bed."

Whoa. Could they do that?

"Do they have space there?"

"They do have a room. Mavis is looking

into whether it's available now. It's not going to be as pretty as it would have been at the church."

Mariah opened her notebook and turned to a fresh page.

"If it's available, I'll take a look at it as soon as possible and I can come up with ideas."

Abigail nodded. "Also, Gord and Gladys met when he was a patient. She was his nurse."

Mariah's mouth dropped open. "You're kidding. Oh, we can definitely work with that."

"I thought that might cheer you up."

Mariah took a long breath. "I cannot tell you how relieved I am. Last night I felt like it was all over. I…well, I didn't think we had a chance. I should thank Nelson for thinking of that option for Gord and Gladys."

"You have more than that to thank him for. He went to talk to Dave last night. I don't know what he said to Dave, but apparently, he and Jaycee had reconciled by the time Nelson left them. He didn't know what they were going to do about the party, but they were talking. Dave's mother is, I'm sorry to say, a snob, and she had been making Jaycee feel like she wasn't good enough for Dave. As a result, Jaycee had fixated on the party to prove herself."

Grateful didn't cover how Mariah felt. Nelson had gotten involved. On his own, despite his own history, his own dislike of big events, he had come up with an option for Gord and Gladys and brought Jaycee and Dave back together.

Nelson had changed from the angry man she'd first sat down with at the dining table. And that gave her mixed feelings.

Some of those feelings were warm ones. Gratitude, and maybe pride? Had he changed because of her? Had she convinced him that he was wrong?

But other feelings were problematic. *Had* he done this for her? They'd spent a lot of time together. She'd come to enjoy that time, not just because it helped them set up their proposal. She'd happily spend time with Nelson now just because she enjoyed his company.

In spite of their arguing, or possibly because of it, they had fun together. Maybe too much.

Mariah had her dreams. She was going to work for her grandfather, get her own place and make a home for herself. One with roots she could set down. She could make friends, friends who wouldn't sail away, unsure if she'd ever see them again.

She should have grown beyond that little-girl feeling of abandonment, but she hadn't. Not when making a circle of permanent friends and family was driving her dream.

There was more room for advancement and variety in the city. There were so many people, enough for her to find some who would like her. She wanted to work for her grandfather partly because she understood the advantage of connections and relationships.

And that meant leaving Carter's Crossing this fall. Once the groundwork was laid for the Center for Romance, there wouldn't be a job for her in Carter's Crossing. Her grandfather wouldn't pay for her to work here, and Abigail and her committee could keep the work going without her.

There wasn't enough work for her to stay.

She was making friends here, and she hoped to keep in touch with them. But she wanted her own community, and while she was leaving, these people were all staying here. Forgetting that would lead to more of the same disappointment she'd become so familiar with as a kid.

People didn't have to live on a boat to leave.

"WHAT DID YOU want me to see?"

Nelson's voice came from within the barn. "Just a sec. We're coming."

Mariah stomped her feet. The air was brisk and cold, and her toes were prickling. If she'd been spending another winter here, she'd need warmer boots.

She shook her head. Not happening.

She'd done her best to ignore Nelson. She'd had two days to rearrange the anniversary party, and to deal with Dave and Jaycee's suggestions. She'd kept herself busier than necessary. But when Nelson asked her to come to the farm, to see something with Toby, well, she had to say yes. She had a soft spot for Toby.

Part of her had been only too happy to have an excuse.

She heard a jingling sound, one that she now knew came from a bit of horse harness. Toby had been doing amazingly well the past couple of weeks, and she had stood holding his halter while Nelson tried stuff on him. Bridles, saddles...they all had metal bits that jingled like that.

Toby had not responded well to the saddles, so maybe Nelson had finally found one he was comfortable with.

The jingle was joined by the clop of hooves, and another strange swooshing noise, and they came around the corner.

Toby was wearing a bridle, and a harness

over most of his body. Behind him was…it was a sleigh. An old-fashioned sleigh. Like something out of a Christmas card or Norman Rockwell painting.

Nelson wasn't in the sleigh, but was walking beside it, holding the long reins that extended from the bit in Toby's mouth, to his neck where they passed through the harness and on to Nelson's hands.

"It's a one-horse open sleigh, isn't it?" Mariah had never seen one in real life. But this was the stuff of romance.

Nelson nodded, a big grin crossing his face. "He didn't like the saddles, so I thought, let's try a harness. The Fletchers had this old sleigh, so once Toby was good with me driving him from behind, I hitched him up. He seems to like this."

Mariah crossed to Toby and stroked his neck. "Good boy. You look so handsome."

"Why, thank you."

Mariah rolled her eyes. "I was talking to Toby. I called *him* a good boy. I don't think you qualify."

Nelson pressed a hand to his heart. "You wound me. You wanted to have sleigh rides, and here, when I present one to you, nothing but insults."

Mariah ignored his teasing.

"Do you think Toby could give sleigh rides?"

He shrugged. "Not now. He's just getting used to the sleigh. I'd want to be sure that he's completely comfortable with that for a first step. Then we'd have to introduce him to crowds. He may never be able to handle that."

Mariah saw the concern in Nelson's eyes. Toby was in good hands. Nelson would never push him into something he couldn't handle. Nelson might not be a good boy, but he was definitely a good man.

She wasn't supposed to be thinking of things like that!

"Are you taking him out in the sleigh now?"

Nelson shook his head. "I'm going to drive him up and down the driveway for a bit, see how he does. But he wanted you to see how handsome he was."

Mariah rubbed Toby's forehead, and he responded by snuffling in her chest. He'd come a long way in just a few weeks. It made Mariah feel like she'd accomplished something, something as important as reviving Carter's Crossing, to know she'd had a key role in his rehabilitation.

"He's a handsome and good boy."

"I'm only going to be about fifteen minutes more. Want to go for dinner after? You could visit Sparky inside—he's feeling neglected lately."

Mariah's cheeks flushed. It wasn't just Sparky who'd been neglected lately.

"I don't know… I've got a lot to do—"

Nelson narrowed his eyes.

"Is something going on, Mariah? I know you have a lot of work to prep for Sunday, but we're supposed to be so madly in love that I'm planning a proposal. Right now it's looking more like we're having a fight. Unless you've changed your mind—"

Mariah busied herself with straightening Toby's forelock. She couldn't tell Nelson she'd avoided him because she was catching some real feelings.

"No, you're right. We should—"

"Can you say that again?"

Mariah turned her gaze to Nelson, brows furrowed. "I said, we should—"

"No, the 'You're right' part. I love hearing that."

Mariah turned her attention back to the horse to hide her laugh. "Toby, this guy may be good with you, but honestly, the ego on him."

"Not fair. How can I have a big ego when I so rarely hear anything like 'You're right, Nelson'?"

"And yet, you do."

Nelson laughed. "Go on in and stay warm, Mariah. We'll be back soon."

THEY WENT TO MOONSTONE, and Jaycee gave them the same table as their first dinner together. Jaycee was glowing these days and gave both of them credit for her rekindled romance with Dave. Now that she wasn't worried about impressing his mother, or not as much, she was looking forward to her party.

"What were the changes that she and Dave had for you?"

Mariah laughed. "The skate dance is out."

"I know that was Dave's idea. He hated it."

"I think he was purposely messing it up to try to get out of it."

Nelson shook his head. "No, he was trying, I swear. He wanted to make Jaycee happy."

Mariah swallowed. "I'm just glad they worked that out."

"Because your event is back in play?" His voice was suddenly serious.

"Well, I can't say I'm not relieved, but I'm mostly glad they're happy again. Parties come and go, but couples with a chance of making it are rare."

Nelson nodded.

"And the vow renewal is good to go?"

"Totally. We've been able to take over the cafeteria in the hospital. I know Abigail pulled some strings for that. We're providing food in the lounge for anyone who would normally use the cafeteria while we have it out of commission. Gord will be in a hospital bed, but since Gladys was a nurse when they met, the committee was able to recreate an old nursing uniform for her.

"When I first met the committee, I seriously underestimated them. They work hard and get stuff done."

Nelson grimaced. "I'm pretty sure they're not above using blackmail."

Mariah's eyes danced. "Have they blackmailed you?"

"Laugh now. You won't find it so funny when it's your turn to 'help them out.'"

Her eyes widened. "But I already am!"

"That's what you think."

She shrugged. "I can handle them. But that reminds me, we should finalize the proposal plans."

Nelson eyed her warily. "Have you made changes to that?"

He was supposed to have veto rights.

Mariah rolled her eyes. "Honestly, what are you so afraid of? We're just creating a romantic setting, and adding music, and a little firework display."

"There's no such thing as a *little* firework display."

"That is patently untrue. Besides, Abigail told me you like fireworks."

Nelson sighed.

"I liked fireworks when I was a kid. And I go to the Fourth of July display in Carter's Crossing, because everyone does. It's not like I travel the country to catch any firework display going."

"But at least this is something you might do. And something we can pull off here. I mean, if Toby was ready, and we could have him pull us in that sleigh? That would be great, but he's not, so we need something to make it special."

A picture flashed in Nelson's mind. Toby, pulling the sleigh. Mariah snuggled in with him, her coat red and cheeks pink. Nelson could almost imagine proposing to her in that setting.

Whoa. He was fake proposing. They were fake dating and fake falling in love.

But somehow, when he looked across the table at her, it didn't feel fake. He'd asked her to have dinner with him because he wanted to, not because it was part of their carefully orchestrated romance.

But maybe that was just him. Did Mariah even like him?

They argued. They didn't agree on many things.

But Nelson enjoyed what they did. He enjoyed bantering with her more than a regular conversation with anyone else. He liked knowing that he'd never maneuver her into doing what he wanted against her wishes.

No, he was in more danger of being manipulated by her. And he liked it.

Did she enjoy it, too? He thought so. Her eyes were bright, her cheeks slightly pink, and she had leaned forward, as if she was invested in their conversation. That look she used to give him, wary and suspect, was gone. He'd told her about his biggest failure, and she hadn't censured him.

She hadn't approved. But she'd been sympathetic.

She'd told him about her family, and her upbringing. He didn't know if many people knew how lonely she'd felt growing up. He suspected her parents and brothers didn't know.

Maybe she'd told him simply because they'd spent so much time together. Maybe it wasn't because she felt close to him and trusted him.

Like he trusted her. Something that was almost miraculous, considering.

The most telling thing? The kisses. The ones that were supposed to convince everyone else that something was going on between the two of them. They were convincing him.

Could someone fake those kisses? Nelson, if he was honest, couldn't. There was something there.

He needed to find out. He needed to kiss her, not for show, but for them, and see how she responded.

They were fake dating, and had a fake proposal in three days, but Nelson wanted to move their fake dating to real.

SMILING AT NELSON across thc tablc, Mariah relaxed. Everything was working out.

Not perfectly, not as originally planned, but this was her job. She had to take the bumps and potholes on the road and handle them to make things work. With three days to go, everything was on track.

She couldn't fix everything. If a couple decided not to get married, she wouldn't try to force it. Her job was to provide the wedding they wanted, and if at the end, they wanted to not have one, that was what she needed to provide for them.

But things were going well here in Carter's Crossing. Even if one of her vow renewal people got sick, they were at the hospital, so barring an act of God, that one was good. Dave and Jaycee had worked out their problem. Dave's mother had been stunned by her son's anger over her treatment of Jaycee and was on her best behavior.

And she and Nelson were good. Good at the fake dating.

She thought, after all this time together, they were friends. After their rocky beginning, she was surprised by that, but it was true. They argued, but it no longer had any anger in it. They enjoyed it.

She thought he liked having someone stand up to him. And she liked that he didn't patronize her. He was arrogant at times, but when she knocked him down about it, he laughed.

So yes, they were friends. It made the fake dating easier. And the fake kissing.

Technically, the kissing wasn't fake…after all, their lips were really touching. It was just scripted. Still, she enjoyed it.

For some reason, that made her cheeks warm. Which was silly.

She shook her head to dispel those uncomfortable thoughts. Instead, she focused on Nelson across the table.

That didn't help. He was smiling at her, but it was a warm smile, intimate, unnervingly realistic for a man about to fake propose.

He was a better actor than she'd thought.

When they got up to go, he insisted on paying. When she tried to argue, quietly so that Jaycee wouldn't hear, he whispered back that he didn't allow his dates to pay all the time.

That silenced her.

Then he held her coat for her. Again, yes, it was selling the dating image, but it felt…real.

They drove back to Abigail's in silence. It wasn't an uncomfortable silence, but it wasn't comfortable, either. It was…it was like the silence was saying something, but she didn't know the language.

She didn't like not knowing.

When he pulled up at the front door, she reached for her seat belt. Before she could grab the door, Nelson asked her to wait.

She turned to him, slightly puzzled. If he'd wanted to talk, they'd just not talked for several minutes. And right now she was feeling on edge, thinking too much about kissing, and it would be better if she just got out of the car…

Instead, he reached over and cradled her face in his hands.

She was about to ask him what he was doing when he pressed his lips to hers and answered the unspoken question.

She responded without thinking. Her arms slid up to his shoulders, gripping them tightly, and she kissed him back.

She didn't know how long it was until the kiss ended, but in the dim light from the veranda, she could see that his lips were slightly swollen, his breathing ragged.

She didn't need a mirror to know she looked the same. And something inside told her this wasn't good.

She called on every reserve of self-control she had.

"Good night, Nelson."

She opened the door before he could get out of the car, but he followed her to the bottom of the steps and waited while she opened the front door of the house.

"Good night, Mariah."

She slid through the door, glad not to find Abigail waiting for her. She could tell Abigail they were kissing to sell their romance, but she didn't want Abigail to know just how well they were selling it.

Then, like a hammer to the head, it hit her.

That hadn't been a show for the town. No one had been there to see it. The only one who could have was Abigail, and she knew it wasn't real.

Mariah pressed her fingers to her lips.

What was going on?

CHAPTER SIXTEEN

FORTUNATELY, MARIAH HAD lots to do the next day. She'd lain awake far too long, remembering the kiss and wondering about it.

She'd finally convinced herself it was just practice. Mostly. That was the only logical conclusion. Taking more meaning from it led to places she didn't want to go. It had still taken her too long to fall asleep.

She'd used extra concealer under her eyes and approached her day, list at hand, dressed in jeans for a day of decorating. She refused to think about Nelson. She shoved those thoughts down whenever they popped up. It gave her mental muscles a workout.

There were plenty of hands available to help with this, the first day of setup, even though it was a Friday. The committee, or Abigail in this case, had hired the local construction crew to help. The crew was led by a young woman named Andrea. Mariah had met her and admired her. It couldn't be easy to lead a team of men, especially in such a traditionally male field. But she did it, without any obvious difficulties.

Mariah could take notes.

The priority was the mill. The engagement party was the biggest event and would require the most work. Mariah had cornered the market on fairy lights, and they needed them everywhere: on the trees, suspended over the ice, on the side of the mill and around the parking lot. Having ladders and laborers at hand made things go faster than she'd expected. There was still setup for Saturday, but the hard labor was done.

Mariah then drove to the hospital to assist in the work to transform the cafeteria. Most of the committee was already there.

The committee got things done. However, they were mostly elderly women, so there were some obvious things they couldn't do. They couldn't do the heavy lifting, or reach up high, and they had a provoking habit of being sidetracked by chatter, but the largest pieces were moved out, thanks again to Andrea and her crew.

Mariah knew, but was supposed to pretend she didn't, that things were going on at the gazebo in the town square, as well. More fairy lights were involved there, but she was spending the evening with Jaycee and Rachel working on party decorations for the engagement party while Nelson supposedly supervised at the gazebo. Thanks to Abigail's personality, no one really expected Nelson to do much.

Frustratingly, Abigail refused to send her any pictures, so that Mariah would be surprised. Mariah didn't want to be surprised by an event she was responsible for.

Still, it meant she didn't have to see Nelson. And that was all for the best. She didn't need any more practice kissing. The kissing part was great, but unsettling. She didn't need any distractions.

NELSON HAD AN idea but needed time. He asked Abigail if he could skip some of the event planning on Saturday.

He didn't like the look she gave him, but she agreed to tell the crew working on "his" proposal location that he was needed at the farm. That was exactly where he headed.

Toby would now come to him, even when Mariah wasn't around, to get treats, but it was obvious that Toby was disappointed when Mariah wasn't there.

Nelson scratched the horse under his forelock. "Me, too, buddy. But let's give her a surprise. A nice one."

He tied Toby in cross ties in the barn, and

spent some time grooming him, tidying up his mane and tail and smoothing out the thick winter coat. Then he put on the freshly polished harness. Toby didn't react when the leather gently settled on his body, which gave Nelson a warm feeling. Thanks to Mariah, Toby was going to be okay.

He led Toby to the sleigh and hitched him up. Toby tossed his head a couple of times but didn't jerk away. Nelson gripped the reins and encouraged Toby to move forward. After a look back at Nelson, he walked forward, down the driveway again.

After fifteen minutes of completely uneventful pacing up and down the drive, Nelson pulled him to a halt. Then, moving slowly and keeping up a constant low-pitched conversation with the horse, he slid into the sleigh.

Toby didn't move.

"Okay, Toby. Let's do this for Mariah."

Nelson flicked the reins, encouraging him to move forward. After a short pause, Toby did as requested.

The sleigh was heavier this time, and Toby's head jerked up.

"I know, boy. This is a little different. You're pulling me, as well. But do this nicely, and we can put Mariah in the sleigh, and we both know that's what you'd really like."

With a shake of his head, Toby took another step. And another. And then they were walking smoothly down the drive.

Nelson grinned. They'd done it. This time when they came by the barn, he didn't stop Toby, but let him continue along the old laneway that headed down through the trees.

Toby, having accepted the idea of the sleigh, continued a steady walk. After a quarter of a mile Nelson turned him into the field, and, pivoting the sleigh, they came back the way they'd come. This time he coaxed Toby into a trot, and the trip back to the barn was quicker.

Nelson drew Toby to a halt. He climbed out of the sleigh and came forward to rub Toby's neck.

"What do you think, Toby? Ready for a show tomorrow?"

THE WHOLE TOWN, it appeared, had come on Saturday to help Mariah and her Romance Committee make Valentine's Day a success. Most of the time she was able to stay on the sidelines, supervising her crew of volunteers. With the big items done yesterday, things were being ticked off her list with impressive speed. And anytime something needed to be picked up, Mariah was gently encouraged to stay put while someone else did the run.

Mariah knew she was being kept away from the gazebo in the town park, but she pretended not to notice. In the meantime, the two venues she was overseeing were transforming.

Thanks to her volunteers' enthusiasm, everything on Saturday's list and a good portion of Sunday's were done by the time pizza was served to the volunteers in the empty mill. Space heaters, some of which would remain there tomorrow, some of which would be placed closer to the skating ice, kept the interior warm. Abigail, or the committee, had provided the pizzas and drinks to thank the volunteers.

Watching Abigail, Mariah could sense her satisfaction with how things were going. The town was pulling together, supporting this new business she was trying to launch. This was the kind of community Carter's Crossing was, and why she wanted to save it.

Mariah wanted this to be a success, too. It was no longer just for her own future. She'd grown attached to the people here. She wanted success for them.

Her future was in New York City. And

success here meant that she'd have a good foundation on which to base her work for her grandfather. But she was learning more than how to plan and organize different events.

She wanted a community like this for herself. It had been her dream as long as she could remember. But now she knew it was also a dream she could realize.

If she could make friends here, she could do the same in New York. It would take time and effort, but she was slowly learning to trust people. People in this town might not be able to keep every promise, but their intentions were good, and they stayed. Mariah could live with that.

She was too aware of Nelson's return to the mill. He'd been away most of the day, busy at the gazebo, she assumed. She knew the basics of what was happening: the gazebo decorated, the live music, the flowers and the fireworks. Abigail insisted they needed to add some surprises for Mariah, since it was her "surprise" proposal, and Mariah was on edge, wondering just what those surprises might be.

Surprises were rarely good when planning events.

But Nelson was here now. Something inside relaxed when she felt him beside her.

He placed a hand on the small of her back,

and her whole body warmed. She turned to look at him to say hello and felt her cheeks flushing.

She saw several knowing looks being cast her way.

It made her nervous.

It shouldn't. After all, they'd only had a few weeks to sell this romance story, and it had worked. People thought they looked like a couple. A serious couple. It wouldn't shock them when Nelson fake proposed.

The problem was that it didn't feel like work. It didn't feel fake. It felt…real.

Mariah kept a smile on her face, but inside a shiver of ice was dispelling the warmth of Nelson's touch. And that cleared her mind.

This wasn't real. She'd set this up with Nelson as fake. But somehow, something inside her, that lonely girl, had grabbed on like it was real.

This was bad. This feeling wasn't real. And if it was, it wasn't going to last. It would turn out the same as it had been on the boat, people drifting away. Promises left unfulfilled. She wasn't putting roots down in Carter's Crossing; this was temporary.

When she'd arrived here in the fall, she'd considered this a pit stop on the road to her final goal. She couldn't allow herself to linger in another place that wasn't going to be home.

SUNDAY MARIAH WOKE UP with an unusual feeling on event day.

She didn't have more to do than hours in which to do it. In fact, last night Abigail had taken her list and removed most of the items, transferring them to other people on the committee.

Even more surprisingly, Mariah had let her.

Mariah wasn't good at that, loosening the reins and letting someone else take the lead. That meant trusting someone else to do the work. But no one could describe Abigail as anything but competent and intelligent. As well, she'd agreed to let Abigail take most of the to-do items from her list because people in Carter's Crossing needed to handle this all on their own.

The sooner Carter's Crossing became Cupid's Crossing, the sooner Mariah would be able to transfer responsibilities over to the residents of this town, the sooner she'd be able to end her fake engagement and go to New York, and then the sooner she could start her next life working for her grandfather and finding what would be *her* place in the world.

She didn't have to stay a full year if she got the job finished.

Last night, to keep herself focused, she'd started a new list of rentals in New York. The place she'd end up staying.

She shook her head. Enough navel gazing. Time to work.

Mariah stopped by the mill. The fairy lights weren't visible in the daylight, but she'd done this often enough to be able to picture how they'd look when darkness settled.

The mill was…well, still the mill. They wouldn't take photos of the building until it was renovated. But once she followed the path down to the river behind the building, she saw her vision of an old-fashioned skating party come to life. She checked and double-checked, and everything was under control.

Leaving the mill taken care of, she stopped by the hospital and found the same smooth operation underway.

The cafeteria had been transformed to replicate a hospital from fifty years ago. They'd been careful to bring in items thatt would have been available at the time. The menu was based on the simple one Gord and Gladys had had at their wedding. Out-of-town guests had already arrived and been safely settled. Costumes, attire from the decade of Gord and

Gladys's dating and marriage were already tried on, altered and were waiting in a side room to be donned as guests arrived.

It was confirmation that Mariah was good at her job. She'd worked really hard, wanting everything to go off smoothly, both to impress her grandfather, and the press he was bringing with him, and also to give these people she'd come to know and like the events they deserved.

It also meant that now the only thing she hadn't checked out was the proposal site, since she wasn't supposed to know it was happening. She could feel the urge to surreptitiously drive by the park, just to be sure everything was going as planned there, when she got a message, saving herself from an unpopular decision.

Nelson wanted to see her at the farm. Mariah let Abigail know where to reach her, in case of problems, and asked her to let her know when her grandfather arrived. Then she got in her car and drove away from the park and toward the farm.

She noticed several people watching to make sure she drove off in the right direction: away from the town green.

She really liked this town.

NELSON WAS NERVOUS. This was undoubtedly the craziest thing he'd done in a long time, possibly ever.

He remembered his proposal to Zoey. He'd booked reservations at the best restaurant in town and asked her to marry him between the main course and dessert. He'd talked to her father beforehand. It was all organized, by the book, and he'd been as certain that she'd say yes as anyone could be.

This was…crazy. He'd never met any of Mariah's family. He had no idea how she'd answer. He was sure there was something, something special between them. It was stronger than any connection he'd felt in his life. He was sure she felt it, too.

She wasn't indifferent, but whether she'd be willing to take a chance…he had no idea.

He just knew he couldn't do the staged, elaborate proposal they'd planned as a performance piece, not before he did something real. Because for him, the time they were spending together wasn't fake. Not anymore.

He wasn't an event planner. And he didn't want to try to manipulate Mariah into the response he wanted by staging an elaborate setup. Especially when he might not get that response.

He needed to know how she felt, and he wanted her to know what he was offering.

He was all in.

Toby was hitched up to the sleigh. Nelson had stashed a couple of warm blankets inside. He had the family ring that Abigail had provided for the staged event this evening in his pocket.

That was all he had. That and the way he felt.

He felt an awkward lurch in his chest when her car pulled into the driveway. Something inside him warmed when he saw her heading his way. She was smiling, but it might just have been at the sight of Toby and the sleigh.

"He looks so good!" Her gaze was on the horse.

Okay, the smile was for Toby. He remembered what he was doing, and the tension ratcheted up. He took a breath, determined to make the most of his moment.

"Want a ride?"

Her eyes widened and sparkled. "Really? He's ready?"

Nelson nodded. He stood by the sleigh and watched her greet Toby.

She accepted his hand as he helped her in. They didn't touch skin, both bundled in winter clothing, but Nelson felt a responsive tingle. His breath was shallow, his palms clammy, and he had a horrible suspicion his stomach was ready to hurl the contents of his breakfast. This was nothing like last time.

He drew in another deep breath and settled into the sleigh beside Mariah.

He gently slapped the reins, and Toby started at a walk. He didn't bolt, and his ears were forward. He looked proud of himself, and Mariah told Toby what a good boy he was.

She turned her shining expression to him. "Thank you for this, Nelson. Your grandmother took over most of the jobs I had left, and I was getting nervous without anything to do."

Nelson cleared the lump in his throat. "I thought you'd like to see how Toby was doing and enjoy a one-horse open sleigh ride, just like the song."

"It's incredible. I've never done this before." Her eyes were sparkling, her smile wide. She was beautiful.

He felt it like a jolt of lightning. It scared him. He took a breath.

"I wanted to talk to you, so, um, it seemed like a good idea."

Mariah's gaze skittered over his face, then returned to Toby.

"Okay."

Was her voice breathless? What had she seen on his face?

Nelson told himself to quit stalling.

"Mariah, I know we got started on the wrong foot, back when you came to town."

Mariah bit her lip. "Yeah, but we're past that now, right?"

He was.

"I've had more fun fake dating you than I expected."

He saw her forehead crease. He pushed on, the words awkward on his tongue.

"A lot more. I know we disagree on some things…"

"You mean we argue."

"I don't know if it's really arguing. More like bickering."

Mariah looked at him, the corners of her lips clenched from holding back a grin. "Are we arguing about how we argue?"

Nelson felt his own mouth quirk up. "I guess so. But I like that you don't back down."

"Really?" Her voice was skeptical.

"Well, most of the time. I know you'll tell me how you feel, and you won't let me talk you into doing something you don't want to."

"Well, duh. No one is going to do that to me."

"I know. It's good. And even though we disa—argue, we have fun."

"We do. And we've done a good job. People believe we're really dating."

This wasn't as difficult when it had been Zoey. He knew why. He was risking more this time.

"Right. I think people believe it because we aren't acting. We get along."

Okay, just shoot him. *We get along.* He'd expressed his feelings better back in high school.

"Where are you going with this, Nelson?" She looked confused.

How could he be messing this up so badly?

Nothing ventured…

"Will you marry me, Mariah?"

Now Mariah looked worried. That hadn't come out as smoothly as he'd wanted. None of this had.

"Are you practicing, Nelson? Is that what this is about? Because I thought you'd have a better speech. But it's okay, we can work on it."

Nelson pulled Toby to a halt.

"No. I'm not practicing. I did work out a speech for later, just like you wanted. This isn't a practice."

"But what… I don't understand."

Nelson found he couldn't meet her gaze. With heated cheeks, he said, "It's a proposal. A real one."

There was a long, awkward silence. Nelson couldn't think of a way to break it. He could jump in and say it was a joke, but he wasn't sure he could sell that.

He needed to know.

She was going to turn him down as soon as she understood he was serious. He could see that now. But he wanted it said. He didn't want to have to second-guess, worry that he hadn't been clear.

He needed to *know*.

He waited for her to let him down nicely. Mariah wouldn't be cruel, not after the time they'd spent together. But while she didn't give him the answer he wanted, she spoke seriously.

"Nelson, how can you possibly do that? You tried this before and it didn't work out."

A vise had wrapped around his ribs. But at least she was talking about it.

He turned to her, hoping his face showed that he meant what he was saying.

"This is different."

Mariah rolled her eyes.

"Don't do that. It's exactly because I've been in this place before that I know that this is different. It's real. It's real in a way it wasn't with Zoey. I don't hold back with you. And I like it. I can be myself, but better."

Mariah looked away. He couldn't blame her. This was a mess. He was a mess.

"Nelson, you can't know, not for sure. You can't keep a promise like this. Things change. People change, and how they feel changes. I'm sorry, but I just…can't believe you. I mean, even my dad…that promise of his hurt my mom so much…"

She swallowed.

Nelson knew that this would hit him later, but right now he was still numb.

"Mariah, I know there aren't a lot of things people can promise and keep their word every time. Either those are little things, things that don't matter, or they're big things. And yeah, I can't promise that I won't be hit by lightning, or that we'll always get along. I mean, in real life, things aren't easy.

"But people make promises, and they try, and sometimes, sometimes that turns into something stellar. I think we could be that. I love you, and I want to spend my life with you, whether we bicker or argue or disagree every day. I'd rather have that every day, than wait for some perfect thing that will never happen."

He paused, drawing in a shaky breath. Mariah was still staring determinedly to the side. She shook her head.

He thought he saw tears in her eyes. He was sorry to have put them there, but he wasn't sorry he'd tried.

He would be later. Later he'd realize how awkward he had just made things. His feeling, that there was something between them, something that needed to be out there before the fake proposal, was wrong. But he was still sure he'd done the right thing.

He sighed and nudged Toby to start the turn back to the barn. He'd thought he was right before, with Zoey. He'd forced what he wanted to make it happen.

This time he hadn't pushed and shoved, but again, he was on his own.

This time, he knew, it wasn't professional embarrassment that was going to be the hardest part. But he shoved that thought aside.

He had to return Mariah to her car, and then meet her in the gazebo tonight. To make a romantic, scripted, totally phony proposal.

It was all wrong. He should just give up on romance.

No matter what Mariah and his grandmother might do, this was not the place where romance lived.

MARIAH DESPERATELY WISHED for the ability to teleport. If she could just get away from Nelson, away from the farm, out of this lovely sleigh, with Toby proudly pulling them through the snow…then she could get somewhere safe before she started crying.

She could feel the tears in her clogged throat, the burning in her eyes, the clenched muscles in her stomach.

What was wrong with Nelson? They had a perfectly good time together. This wasn't an actual romance. She wasn't really feeling things; she'd just been searching for that sense of belonging she'd always wanted.

He wanted to make it real. Really real. Commit to each other real. That terrified her.

She knew people did that. Made the promise, took the leap. Jaycee and Dave, Judy and Harvey…Gordon and Gladys. No, forget Gord and Gladys. They had succeeded, but there was too much risk.

Mariah didn't want promises. She wanted things she could control. That way she couldn't be disappointed, not again.

Losing friends as a kid? Nothing compared to losing someone you loved—

No, not loved. She didn't truly believe in that.

Or did she? Her parents were still in love,

she knew. But her dad had put his promise ahead of her mother, and she'd seen how much that hurt her mom. If you promised, you couldn't break it. And how could you promise a feeling? Feelings changed. And if you promised, and didn't break that promise, what did you do when those feelings changed?

It was just…messy. Painful. Better avoided.

Maybe she was missing out. She could be missing something good, but it also meant she was missing the chance of something monumentally bad.

Her phone rang, and she pulled it out in relief. She didn't want to stay here in silence—heavy, disappointed silence—while they returned to the barn and she had to speak to Nelson again.

"Hi, Abigail! What's wrong?" Abigail would only call if there was a problem. She wanted a problem. Something that meant she had to go and solve things and not think about this last half hour.

"Oh, right. He's here now. I'll be there as soon as I can. Thank you."

She'd completely forgotten her grandfather was coming. How could Nelson do something like this now? Now, when so much was at stake? She couldn't afford to be distracted.

"My grandfather is here. I should go see him."

She saw Nelson nod from the corner of her eye. She didn't dare look at him.

She scrambled out of the sleigh with more haste than dignity when they got back to the barn. She fled to her car, quickly starting it up.

Nelson had exited the sleigh, as well. He had hold of Toby's bridle and was leading him to the barn.

For a moment she wanted to call out to him. She wanted to go back to that easy relationship they'd had. To forget the parties she had planned, the fake proposal, and just go in and help him settle Toby. To have nothing more to do than argue about what they should have for dinner and what they should watch on TV after.

No. She had her plans. Plans she was in control of. They were safe. They were sure. That was what she wanted.

CHAPTER SEVENTEEN

MARIAH NEEDED THE whole drive back to town to get her mind focused on her job again. Truthfully, she probably could have driven back and forth a couple more times, but once was going to have to do.

Her grandfather and Abigail had arrived at the skating party. Mariah had some last-minute details she wanted to check, but when she arrived, Abigail had everything under control. Including her grandfather, it appeared.

Jaycee and Dave were there, buzzing with excitement and obviously in love. The creek was strung with fairy lights, ready to bathe the skating area with romantic light when the daylight faded. The high school students had arrived to oversee parking. Music was playing over speakers near the ice. The bonfire was lit, with her approval, so there would be glowing embers for toasting marshmallows later. The makeshift bar was preparing hot chocolate.

There were skates available to borrow for those who didn't have any. Benches carefully arranged around the creek, and Porta-Potties tactfully set back. And a fence around the section of ice set aside for beginners.

For those who got cold, the mill interior was warmed with heaters and more seating.

And now, people. People skating, talking, drinking hot chocolate and selecting sticks to use for s'mores. Exactly as she'd imagined.

"Abigail, everything looks beautiful."

"Thank you, Mariah, but it's thanks to your careful planning." Abigail smiled warmly at her.

"Looks good, sweetheart," her grandfather said, but his attention was focused on the woman he'd been talking to, rather than the party set up around him.

Mariah couldn't blame him. She wasn't entirely focused on the party, either.

"Everything here is under control. I should go check on the vow renewal now."

Abigail glanced at Mariah. "Why don't we all go? The press will be here soon, so we might as well make sure it looks effortless when they arrive."

If Abigail hadn't been running a mill, she'd have been an awesome event planner.

Mariah found herself in the back seat, with

her grandfather and Abigail up front. Mariah felt very much a third wheel.

She hardly noticed. Her mind kept playing back her conversation with Nelson. What was he— How could he— And why did this upset her so much?

Why did she feel like she'd made a mistake? The decision she'd made was a no-brainer. She had her plans. She was creating a romantic destination. She wasn't here for romance for herself.

As always in Carter's Crossing, it didn't take long to get anyplace. The three of them were soon walking down the hallway to the hospital cafeteria, now repurposed as a hospital room from five decades earlier.

Mariah had seen everything yesterday, but it still surprised her. She could almost believe it was fifty years ago. The women on the committee had found furniture and clothing from that period.

Gord was in the hospital bed, looking alert and pleased. Mariah had learned over the past few months that that was not his normal expression. Gladys was wearing a nurses' uniform from fifty years ago and appeared happy to be bossing Gord. Members of the committee were bustling around, in costume, making sure the food was just so. They had even recreated the wedding cake from Gord and Gladys's wedding.

It was perfect. She could see that her grandfather was impressed. With the limited resources and budget they had, they'd made an incredible setting.

Then the guests started to arrive.

Except for Gord and Gladys's children, the guests were all older. It was touching to watch the reunions among friends who hadn't seen each other for years. There was a problem with the coffee maker, and Mariah kept herself busy for a few minutes, getting everything set.

Gladys came over to get a cup for Gord.

"Thank you so much, Mariah. This is…perfect." Her eyes were glistening with tears of joy.

"I'm so pleased you like it." This was the real reward for her work.

Gladys surprised her with a hug.

"It's not just the food, and the room…but all these people, some I haven't seen for so many years…it just means so much."

This was the part of her job Mariah loved. Making people happy, making the big moments of their lives memorable. Doing the work so that they could simply experience it.

"I'm happy to do it, Gladys. You and Gord

and your friends enjoying yourselves is all the thanks I need."

Gladys looked over at Gord and shook her head. "Even Gord is loving this, despite the hip. If there's anything you ever need..."

Mariah hadn't planned it, but the words shot out. "Can I ask you a question?"

"Of course." Gladys held the cup in her hands but turned to Mariah.

"How did you know?"

Gladys's brow furrowed.

"Know?"

"That you and Gord were real. That it would last, this long."

Gladys's eyes widened. "Ah, that." She narrowed her gaze and looked over at Gord.

"Part of it, we were crazy about each other. Head over heels. The way that man could kiss..."

Mariah stole a glance at Gord. Nope, not the guy she would have pegged for a great kisser. Now, Nelson... She shook her head to rid herself of distractions.

"But also, we were determined. And realistic." Gladys's expression was serious.

"Some days he annoyed the snot out of me. Still does. But with compromise, commitment, love and sometimes just plain old mule-headed determination, we got through the tough days. And it was all worth it."

Mariah watched Gord catch Gladys's eye. She saw the smile on his normally grumpy face.

She could easily imagine that there were days Gladys wanted to give up on him. But they'd made it work.

She didn't know what the secret was that made some couples last and some not. But she understood determination. She was good at making things happen, and not giving up. She thought Nelson was, too.

Nelson certainly made her crazy. They could argue or bicker or whatever he wanted to call it. But they never crossed the line into deliberate meanness. She could picture them still arguing when they were the same age as Gladys and Gord.

And yes, he could certainly kiss.

Her stomach muscles tightened, and she had a hard time breathing in enough air. Maybe Nelson was right. Maybe this didn't just seem real. Maybe it was.

Could she make a promise? She didn't want to ever break her word.

Maybe she just had to make a promise she knew she could keep.

NELSON THOUGHT HE might be an idiot.

No, he was sure of it.

Why else would he be showing up at the

town gazebo, ready to pretend propose to the woman who had turned down his real proposal?

He closed his eyes. Tried to forget the afternoon.

He'd promised Mariah that he would do this. He'd salvaged the anniversary party for Gord and Gladys. He'd talked to Dave to get the engagement party back on track. This was it, the last of Mariah's three events.

He should be doing this for Grandmother. This was the final event to get Cupid's Crossing launched. He knew she'd invested money and time and brain power to make this happen. But as much as he loved his grandmother, he wouldn't be here, offering his heart on a platter only to be crushed again, for her.

Oh, this time Mariah would say yes. But it wouldn't be real. And after tonight he was going to have to pretend for who knows how long that they were in love and getting married, when he was the only one in love, and a breakup was already programmed into Mariah's calendar.

He could have canceled. Had a fake bout of colic for Sparky or one of the other horses. Claimed a flu bug. Anything to avoid this painful farce.

But he wasn't breaking a promise to Mariah. She might not value it, but he would give her this last gift.

The gazebo looked beautiful. It was covered with white and red fairy lights, lending it a soft glow. The seats inside had cushions that he'd never seen before, red and white, of course. There were roses, deep red and white, in a tall vase thing, braving the freezing weather.

There was music, too, a string quartet by the sounds of it, playing out of sight. He wondered how they kept their hands and instruments warm, but knew Mariah would have planned for that, and told his grandmother how to take care of it.

It was beautiful, romantic and fake. He hated it.

He patted his pocket, checking that the ring was there. It was the only element that would be a true surprise for Mariah. He'd hoped she'd like it. She'd pretend she did, in any case. Just like she'd pretend to say yes.

Making himself take the first step, Nelson slowly walked toward the gazebo. There was no point in showing up if he wasn't going to go through with it.

He heard footsteps behind him, just before he reached the steps. He turned, and saw Mariah, rushing toward him.

She was early. She was also wearing that red coat. Her dark hair shone beneath the white cap, and her cheeks were flushed above the scarf wrapped around her neck. She looked beautiful, all red and white, with shiny black hair and boots.

It was for the cameras, though. Not for him.

He forced a smile.

She looked at him, then at the ground between them. "I wasn't sure you'd come."

He swallowed over a lump in his throat. "I promised."

She flinched. He looked away. It wasn't his intention to hurt her.

"Can you take this?" She passed him a piece of leather, which he noted was a leash. Attached to Tiny. He'd been so absorbed in her that he'd totally missed the Great Dane at her side.

Before he could ask why she had Tiny, she'd turned to go, with a quick comment over her shoulder. "I'll be right back."

He stared down the path where she'd disappeared. What was going on? She'd promised to let him know the details of this proposal. Since it was being recorded, it was all programmed, the timing of everything set. He had his script and was here to follow it.

Tiny had not been part of it.

He and Mariah were supposed to meet at the gazebo, dance, then he'd go down on one knee. Tiny wasn't going to help with that. If Tiny didn't trip anyone during the dancing, he'd mess things up for the camera by licking Nelson's face when he kneeled.

Maybe that wasn't why Tiny was here. He looked at the dog. Had Mavis called Mariah because Tiny had eaten something?

Tiny was sitting on his haunches, tongue hanging out. Patiently waiting for the next fun thing. No digestive complaints.

Nelson looked again. Tiny was wearing a sweater. A red sweater, with white blobs on it. Seriously, it was a homemade sweater, done by someone who wasn't very good at knitting. Probably Mavis. Didn't bother Tiny, though.

Nelson had no idea how long he was supposed to wait, so he tugged on Tiny's leash and climbed the steps to the gazebo.

There were heaters under the seats, keeping the space warm, and the roses from freezing and drooping. Nelson sat, and Tiny sat beside him, chin on Nelson's thigh. He was drooling, but Nelson couldn't see that it much mattered.

He heard hoofbeats. That caught his attention. Had Mariah found a horse-drawn sleigh to add? He looked away, blinking his eyes rapidly. A short time ago they'd been in his horse-drawn sleigh. Not a memory he wanted to revisit.

With his emotions back under control, he turned to where the hoofbeats were louder and couldn't stop his jaw from dropping.

Mariah was leading Sparky up the path. Sparky, wearing a big red bow.

Nelson found himself on his feet. He headed down the steps, toward his horse, dragging Tiny behind him.

Tiny was a dead weight. Apparently, he wasn't fond of horses.

Nelson stopped, ten feet between him and Tiny, Mariah and Sparky.

"Why do you have Sparky? And why do I have Tiny?"

Mariah looked down, then off to the side. She took a deep breath and tugged on Sparky's lead. She crossed the ten feet separating them, Sparky clopping behind her, glad to see Nelson. Nelson had to brace himself, since Tiny was trying to back away. He tugged the leash.

Mariah dropped on her knee in front of him. He reached out to catch her, not having seen her slip. But she pushed his hand away.

"Theodore Nelson Carter the third, will you marry me?"

Nelson looked around, trying to understand the change in plans. He didn't see anything to clear up the confusion.

He reached for Mariah's hand again. She was staring up at him, eyes shining with what looked like tears.

He tried to tug her up, but she tugged back. Then Tiny gave his own tug, and Nelson fell on his butt, losing the leash.

Tiny took advantage and ran back to the gazebo, sticking his head under a seat.

Mariah was biting back a grin. Nelson, flat on his back, felt pain running down to his frozen posterior, but it was nothing compared to what he was feeling inside.

"What are you doing, Mariah? We're supposed to be in the gazebo. I'm the one who 'planned' this. I was the one going down on one knee, remember?"

Mariah crawled over to him, and held herself up over his chest, staring at him intently. There was an expression on her face—he didn't dare try to label it. It was too tempting to read things into it, and he'd already fooled himself enough.

He closed his eyes. He couldn't look at her this closely if he was going to get through this.

"Nelson, this isn't the proposal for Carter's Crossing. The one for the pictures. This is for me."

"I don't understand."

"Nelson. Look at me."

He drew a long breath and opened his eyes.

"Nelson, I, Mariah fraidy-cat Van Delton, have fallen in love with you and want to marry you. I'm hoping you haven't fallen out of love with me since this afternoon."

He felt Sparky nudging his foot. It grounded him. This wasn't some weird dream or imagination. Tiny and Sparky? Not part of anything he would make up.

"What happened? This afternoon—"

Mariah put a white mitten over his mouth. "This afternoon I was scared. You know I have a problem with promises.

"Then, at Gord and Gladys's party. I asked Gladys how she knew. How they could last. And she said it was not just feelings but sometimes hard work and determination."

Her eyes blinked back tears.

"I can do that. I can work hard, and I'm stubborn. You are, too. So I promise you, Nelson, that I'll work my hardest to love you for the rest of my life, if you'll promise that, too."

She took her hand from his mouth and paused, watching him. Nelson looked up at the face of the woman kneeling over him. The woman he loved. And this time he saw the same thing in her face.

She also looked ready to cry. He reached a hand to her cheek, drawing her down for a kiss. She collapsed on top of him, returning his kiss with fervor.

He didn't know how long they stayed there, making promises with their hands and lips, but he finally couldn't ignore the cold creeping up from the frozen ground below him.

He pulled away, smiling at the dazed expression on her face.

"Yes." He felt light, despite the cold seeping into his bones. "Yes, I'll promise to work with everything I have to love you for the rest of my life. Are we being recorded, by the way?"

Mariah took a moment to focus. "I don't know. Maybe. The press is here."

"Then I have proof that *you* proposed to *me*."

A smile crossed her face. "Really? You're going there?"

He traced her nose with a shaky finger. "If we don't get up, I'm going to have frostbite."

Mariah shoved herself up and off him. "You know, you proposed first."

Nelson pushed himself to a crouch and then stood up, pulling Mariah up with him.

"You turned me down." This time it didn't hurt the same.

"It still counts."

"Nuh-uh."

"It absolutely does."

He cut her off with a kiss. Best way to win an argument.

Sparky interrupted that one, almost knocking Nelson over with a hard shove of his head. Nelson pulled back with reluctance, and curiosity.

"What's with Sparky and Tiny?"

Right now he just wanted to be alone with Mariah, but they had two large animals to take care of. It wasn't what he'd expect from Mariah's meticulous planning.

Mariah turned to Sparky, surprised, as if she'd completely forgotten the horse was there.

"I didn't have a lot of time, and I wanted to make this proposal something for us. Something real. And well, we met with Tiny, and we spent all that time with the horses. But I couldn't bring Toby, or any of the others, so..."

Nelson laughed, a happy, full sound.

"I love you, Mariah. But you are a little bit nuts."

Mariah wrapped her arms around him. "Well, obviously. I just messed up a beautiful proposal…"

Nelson tugged her toward the gazebo. "We can still have a dance. And I have a ring in my pocket."

Her eyes lit up. She tugged him to the gazebo steps, Sparky clopping behind.

"Okay, Nelson. Sweep me off my feet."

It was a challenge. One he planned to meet every day for the rest of their lives.

"I'M CONFUSED," GERRY SAID. He and Abigail were with the photographer, watching her shoot pictures of Nelson and Mariah dancing. "This part I get." He nodded toward the gazebo. "But what's with the dog and the horse? And whatever they were doing on the way to the gazebo?"

Abigail smiled. "I think that was 'the real thing.'"

His brows drew down, putting a frown on his forehead.

"What does that mean?"

"I think there might have been a real proposal in there."

Now his eyebrows flew up. "What? I thought this was a publicity event. Fake."

"It started out like that, I know, but I think they actually like each other."

He shot her a sharp glance. "Does this mean you've poached my granddaughter?"

Abigail threw out her hands. "This was all Nelson, not me."

Gerry had a skeptical expression on his face. "I have more respect for your abilities than that, Abigail."

She turned her head to the couple in the gazebo again. From this distance, she could hear their voices. She suspected a lot of arguing would be involved in that relationship, but Nelson needed someone strong enough to stand up to him.

"Is your grandson going to move to New York?"

Abigail shrugged. Gerry had enough to deal with now.

"Mariah is only supposed to be here another seven months."

Abigail nodded. "That's the plan."

"Have you got another plan, Abigail?"

She turned to Gerry and raised her eyebrows.

"Me?"

He scoffed. "Of course you have a plan. Give me the news, I can handle it."

"If Mariah wants to stay, the committee could cover her salary. If she's not going to end up in New York City, for whatever reason, it wouldn't be reasonable for you to cover those expenses. We would reimburse you."

Gerry leaned back. "So you *are* poaching my granddaughter. But if she stays here, what will you do?"

Abigail pursed her lips. "I needed to know that Carter's Crossing will survive. That people can work here, raise their families here, and if their children wish, they have the opportunity to stay here. I have a lot of faith in Mariah. If she can implement her plan, the way she has begun, then I'd be happy to step aside and let her run everything."

"Then what are you going to do—knit?"

A corner of her mouth tugged up. "No, not knitting. I'm not sure what I'll do."

"There's not that much else you can do here."

"You might be surprised. Who said I'd be staying here?"

Gerry was staring at her now, expression serious. "You'd consider leaving Carter's Crossing?" There was doubt in his voice.

"If I know it's thriving, then yes, I've done

my job. I've already started the process to change the name officially to Cupid's Crossing, to support the romance initiative."

She shrugged. "Then I could do something else. I deserve some fun."

"You're serious."

Abigail didn't respond.

"If Abigail Carter can leave Carter's Crossing behind, maybe there's hope for me yet. Maybe I can step back, have some fun, as well."

Abigail gave him her serene smile. He narrowed his eyes, suspicious.

"I guess we'll see."

* * * * *

COMING NEXT MONTH FROM

HARLEQUIN

HEARTWARMING

Available March 9, 2021

#367 SECOND CHANCE COWBOY

Heroes of Shelter Creek • by Claire McEwen

Veterinarian Emily Fielding needs help with her practice, but she refuses to hire Wes Marlow, who left town and broke her heart years ago. Can Wes win back her love if he convinces her he's home to stay?

#368 THE DOCTOR AND THE MATCHMAKER

Veterans' Road • by Cheryl Harper

Naval surgeon Wade McNally has a plan: date the perfect woman and build a perfect family. But charmingly unpredictable Brisa Montero catches his eye, and she's always been great at ruining plans...

#369 THE SOLDIER'S UNEXPECTED FAMILY

by Tanya Agler

When Aidan Murphy shows up to take guardianship of his nephew, he doesn't expect to find that Natalie Harrison has already accepted the position! And neither of them has any intention of quitting the job.

#370 A WYOMING HERO

Eclipse Ridge Ranch • by Mary Anne Wilson

For Quinn Lake, following tech CEO Seth Reagan to a ranch was purely business, but a case of mistaken identity gives her a reason to stay—and after learning to love again, Quinn can't imagine leaving.